CW00433824

"As ever, Val Penny grips us from the first line. *Hunter's Secret* dives right into the story, which is both intriguing and unsettling, and brings back the familiar characters which make us smile and frown, groan and cheer."

Simon Hall – *Cambridge University Lecturer and bestselling author of The TV Detective series*

"A bold, gripping and thought-provoking rollercoaster that delves deep into Hunter's psyche."

Katherine Johnson – *bestselling author of The Suspects*

"Val Penny is a rising star in the crime fiction genre. In this story of secrets and lies, the author delivers another gripping book in her Edinburgh Crime Mystery series."

Erin Kelly – *bestselling author of He Said/She Said*

"Really enjoyable romp through the seedier byways of Edinburgh, with a strong cast of police and villains. Two murders thirty years apart: a story of bigotry, deceit and intolerance, with the all-too-believable persecution of a defenceless group. A great summer read!"

Michael Jecks – *bestselling author of The Knights Templar Mysteries*

"An enthralling and refreshing read. it's always like meeting up with old friends when I read a Hunter novel."

Kate Bendelow – *CSI best-selling author of The Real CSI*

Hunter's Secret

The Edinburgh Crime Mysteries #5

Val Penny

Also available:

Hunter's Chase
Hunter's Revenge
Hunter's Force
Hunter's Blood

www.darkstroke.com

Discover us online:
www.darkstroke.com

Join us on instagram:
www.instagram.com/darkstrokebooks/

Include **#darkstroke** in a photo of yourself
holding this book on Instagram and
something nice will happen.

To Lizzie and Phil, Vicky and Thomas
with all my love

About the Author

Val Penny is an American author living in SW Scotland. She has two adult daughters of whom she is justly proud and lives with her husband and two cats. She has a Law degree from Edinburgh University and her MSc from Napier University. She has had many jobs including hairdresser, waitress, lawyer, banker, azalea farmer and lecturer. However, she has not yet achieved either of her childhood dreams of being a ballerina or owning a candy store. Until those dreams come true, she has turned her hand to writing poetry, short stories and novels.

Her crime novels, *Hunter's Chase Hunter's Revenge, Hunter's Force* and *Hunter's Blood* form the bestselling series *The Edinburgh Crime Mysteries*. They are set in Edinburgh, Scotland, published by darkstroke. This, the fifth novel in the series, is also published by darkstroke. Her first non-fiction book *Let's Get Published* is available now.

Acknowledgements

I would like to thank everyone who read the manuscript for this book and offered suggestions for improvements – in particular, Elizabeth Ducie, Michael Jecks and Katherine Johnson. There are also many others to thank for their hard work and support – my editor Laurence Patterson, Simon Hall, Stuart Gibbon and Erin Kelly. I am also grateful to all at darkstroke books, including Steph Patterson. I remain eternally grateful to my long-suffering and supportive husband, Dave and our beloved girls, Lizzie, Vicky and Becca. Thank you also to my readers. I am thrilled you enjoy the novels.

I am most grateful to those who afforded me medical and technical advice. Any mistakes, it goes without saying, are entirely my own.

Hunter's Secret

The Edinburgh Crime Mysteries #5

Prologue

You never forget. Certainly, Hunter never did. The sight, the stench, the dirt, the blood and the panic. You just never forget your first corpse.

December 12, 1983

The brothers paused to talk and jumped off their bicycles, although the evening was too cold to stop for long and it was too dark to see much, and Fraser wanted to push his advantage.

"You willing to admit defeat, bro?" Fraser asked.

"Defeat? I don't know the meaning of the word!" His brother jeered.

"It means I win again. I'm just faster than you. Faster and smarter and better looking. That's all. Admit it."

"Says the thirteen-year-old squirt. Yeh, right. You do know that I just let you win to make you feel good."

"Ha, ha, ha, and I don't think. You want me to believe that? Honestly, Christian. Even my name is better."

"Fraser Ross Spencer Wilson? Just as well you weren't born with a lisp. Anyway, I've decided to change my name," his brother said.

"What? How's that going to work? It won't matter what you call yourself, to Mum and Dad you'll always be Christian. Everybody you know calls you Christian. You were born on Christmas day to a church minister. So tough luck to you."

"Thanks so much and I don't think. I'll be sixteen in two weeks and I'm changing it and using my middle name, Hunter. I'm doing it, whether they like it or not."

"They won't. Not one bit. And they won't ever use Hunter, you'll always be Christian to them."

"I suppose I know that, but I'm going to use Hunter anyway, so you can start now, or I won't let you win again."

"Good luck with that. With both of those." Fraser grinned as he threw his leg back over his bicycle.

"Anything's better than Christian," Hunter said.

"I agree, but Mum and Dad won't. That's all I'm saying."

Hunter looked at his brother. They were so similar in so many ways but so different. His brother's grey eyes danced with mischief and his interests varied with the season. In Hunter's opinion, Fraser's confidence was misplaced because his own footballing ability and his darts prowess were better than Fraser's. He knew his parents thought of him as more serious than his younger brother. He was older, so they had always asked him to look out for Fraser. He knew this had given him a greater sense of responsibility and that he was observant.

"So, are you ready for more defeat?" Fraser asked.

"I'll not be giving you a second win today!" Hunter began to mount his bike. As he did this, his gaze swept the area and he noticed a plaque. "Hey, Fraser! Look. Old councillor Billy Hope only opened this part of the Water of Leith Pathway this year!"

"Who cares? He's an old crook by all accounts."

"I think it's interesting. They say this walkway will go all the way from Balerno to Leith when it's finished."

"Well that's not going to be any time soon and it's too cold to stand and chat about it. Let's get home. Come on, I'll race you, Christian. And you'll lose."

"Not this time, and it's Hunter. I won't answer to anything else."

"Aye you will! No way Mum or Dad'll use anything but your given name. We both know that. To prove it, I'm going to beat your hide getting home. Let's go!"

"No way, you're not, ya bam!"

Both boys stood on the pedals of their bikes and, with their heads down, rode as fast as they could along the pathway. Hunter led his brother. Their breath froze and hung on the air as they pedalled faster and faster. Hunter was dismayed as

Fraser overtook him in the charge towards home along the route which goes through the heart of Edinburgh.

"Hey! Eat my dust!" Fraser shouted over his shoulder. He laughed.

They passed the neglected Warriston Cemetery, with its fallen, overgrown gravestones, and raced near the Leith-Canonmills bike path. It's a former railway line with old platforms, stone railway bridges, and tunnels. Hunter thought it looked cool, then he noticed that Fraser was not looking where he was going. With his head down to streamline his body Hunter was sure there was no way Fraser could see well in the falling gloom. All of a sudden, his brother's bike shuddered to a halt and he saw him lurch forward and topple over the handlebars. There was no time for Hunter to stop. He followed on his brother's heels and hit the hard, wet ground immediately after Fraser.

"Shit! What the hell was that?" Fraser said rubbing his arm.

"Why did you brake? Just to be a jerk? You're such a liability."

"Naw, don't be an arse. My bike flicked over that old branch. And the ground is all wet. It's soaking. I just didn't see the branch and now my arm's bloody sore. Do you think I've broken it?"

"Naw, don't be a baby. Your arm is fine. Shit!"

"You think it's not broken? How can you know? You haven't even looked at it."

"I think that's not a branch, Fraser. Look!" Hunter shone the light from his bike onto the offending item. It's a fucking leg! And look at all that blood. His head too. He's taken a real beating. Oh fuck, no! You're sitting in it! You're covered in his blood."

"Bloody hell! Oh God! There's a knife."

"Do you think he's dead?"

"I'm not bloody touching him. You do it."

Hunter screwed up his face. "Aaw, come on, you've already got his blood on you. I don't want to touch him."

"You've got his blood on you too."

"Not as much as you."

5

"You better check him, Christian."

"Hunter."

"Hunter, whatever your name is. You know you'll feel guilty if you don't check whether he's still alive and you know very well that I won't."

"Shit. This is gross." Hunter bent over and gingerly felt the wrist of the man on the ground. "He's still ever so slightly warm but there's no pulse that I can feel. Fuck, this is horrible. Now I've got his blood on my hand. Even though I can't feel a pulse, if he's still even a bit warm, maybe it can't have happened so long ago."

"How come you know so much?"

"First aid badge at Boys' Brigade."

"They teach you how to work out the time of death of a corpse, do they?"

"Don't be an arse, Fraser. It's only common sense. It's freezing outside and he's still got some heat in him, so he can't have been dead for long."

"Whoever did this, might still be around. They might get us. Let's get out of here, quick, and get home. Tell the folks. They'll know what to do."

"Aye. Should one of us stay with him?" Hunter asked.

"Why? He's not bloody going anywhere and I'm not staying alone with him. And if it was a fight, maybe the other man is still around. I don't want to hang around, do you? Come on."

***

There were several policemen around the spot where they'd found the corpse when Fraser and Hunter returned to the scene with their parents. The tall blond detective was clearly in charge. He stood officiously with his feet wide apart and his hands on his hips.

"Yes, I can see the blood, thank you. So where is the fucking corpse, Inglis? Or was it not a corpse? Do you think the lads that phoned it in were having a laugh?"

"Certainly not, officer." Hunter's and Fraser's father walked

6

forward. His dog collar betrayed his profession. "Allow me to introduce myself, Reverend Andrew Wilson." He shook the big detective's hand. "My sons say they saw a man dead on the path, so that is what they saw. My older son checked for signs of life. He has passed his first aid certificate with St. John's Ambulance through the Boys' Brigade and my boys are not given to having a laugh about death."

"Then where's the body? A corpse didn't just get up and walk away, did it?"

"DI Myerscough? I've found a bloody knife over here and the grass is all flattened."

"That knife was nearer the body when we saw it," Hunter said.

"Well, lad, it now looks like the body was dragged away in this direction."

"OK, Charlie. Bag up the knife and get the area cordoned off," the big blond detective said. "One of your lads will need to stand guard. I'll get the crime scene investigators over tomorrow morning when it's light. DC Inglis, arrange a briefing for tomorrow morning at eight am, I want the team together before we put out a press bulletin."

"Just what my team needs two weeks before Christmas," Charlie growled.

"I'm sure the victim is very sorry for the inconvenience," DI Peter Myerscough said sarcastically. "Rev Wilson, I'll need to arrange to interview your sons, sooner rather than later and they will have to spend time with a police sketch artist to produce a picture of the man they saw."

"Shall we say tomorrow morning? The boys are young and have had a shock. I want them to get some sleep now," Reverend Wilson said.

"That's fine. Speak to Detective Constable Inglis and give him your names and address, lads. And yours, sir. A responsible adult will need to be with the boys when they are questioned."

"I'll be there." Hunter's father nodded and after informing DC Arthur Inglis of their names and address, he turned to lead his wife and sons home.

Chapter One

Thirty years later

DC Tim Myerscough and DC Bear Zewedu began warming up. They always took time to do this before they started jogging along the banks of the Braid Burn and through the Hermitage of Braid. The big men had known each other since their childhood days at Merchiston Castle School and had seen each other through thick and thin. Today they were going to do some rugby training as their club was closed for the holidays, but they liked to keep fit off season anyway.

They had chosen to do their training on the Hermitage of Braid Circular. They would need to run around the path several times to get their training completed as the trail is about two miles long and goes along by the rippling water of the Braid Burn. The men enjoyed the sound of the river as they exercised.

"Are you going to take the plunge and ask Mel to marry you? Christmas is a good time of year to do it." Tim said to his friend as he pulled his shoulders from side to side. "You've been together for years now."

"Oh, for goodness sake. And make a decent woman of her, you mean? That ship sailed long ago!"

"Do you want me to tell her you said that, big man?"

Bear laughed and they began to star jump.

"There's no need to rock the boat, my friend. Come on, I'll race you!" Bear said and sped ahead of Tim.

They were both determined to stay fit over their winter break from rugby and enjoyed training together when they had time off from Police Scotland.

"We're lucky in Edinburgh because we have quite a few off-road running options within the city limits, don't we?" Tim said.

He and Bear stopped to do a series of burpees.

"Yeh, that's true but my favourite, by far, is the Braid Hills circuit and the paths that link it to Hermitage of Braid. The hills, the trees, the rocks and the river. It gives us good training for our rugby matches in beautiful surroundings." Bear smiled. "If you're so keen to marry me off to Mel, why don't you lead the way and tie the knot with Gillian?"

"Oh, no, no, no. Not right now. I've got enough on my plate. Dad gets out of jail today and I have to pick him up and get him settled."

"Has your Dad even met Gillian?"

"No, not yet. I kept meaning to get around to it, but it never seemed to be a good time. To be honest, Bear, I'm not sure how they'll get on."

"Christmas is just the time to throw folks together! I think you're mad. You knew they'd be living in the same house when he got out." Bear grinned. He started running on the spot, lifting his knees high and Tim followed suit.

"They won't be together for long. I'm planning to go back to Whistler for a couple of weeks in February and go skiing with Gillian. I thought Dad would be settled by then and we'll go early in the month." Tim paused. "Race you to the visitor centre, bro."

The two big men sped along the path. At six feet four inches tall, Tim was only two inches taller than Bear, but they were equally broad shouldered. They raced along the path. When Tim reached the visitor centre, located in Hermitage House, he bent forward and held his knees briefly until Bear caught up. Tim thought the 18th-century property a fine building.

"You cheated. You didn't give a ready steady go!" Bear charged off shouting the last word back at Tim.

"Bastard!" Tim shouted as he chased after his friend. But Bear had only run about two hundred yards when he stopped abruptly. Tim ran into the back of him.

"What's up? I thought this was a race, not a game of tig."

"Look over there by the side of the river. That guy's in bad shape," Bear said.

"Shit! Lot of blood. And it's so fucking cold. He won't survive long lying there in this temperature." Tim tried to steady himself. "Give me a hand to balance me, Bear. I'd better check him. I don't carry my phone when I run. Can you call an ambulance?" Tim held on to his friend's arm and felt the fallen man's neck.

"Shit. My phone's dead," Bear said.

"Like this poor bugger," Tim said.

"Where's the closest phone going to be?" Bear asked.

"Look at the state of us. Huge, sweating and now I've got his blood all over me. Nobody is going to let us into their home. Let's go over to Jamie Thomson and Frankie Hope. They live in West Mains Road. We'll be able to use a phone there."

"Should I wait with him?" Bear nodded towards the corpse.

"Well, he's not going to get any worse and he's not going anywhere. Only crazy people like us are out here in the cold, two weeks before Christmas."

"Someone else is out. He didn't do this to himself," Bear said.

"He should be safe enough. Come on!" Tim started to run in the direction of West Mains Road.

***

Tim leant on the doorbell and Frankie came to the door. He looked up at the two detectives and wondered if anybody had ever told them they looked like negatives of each other. Considering the size of them, he thought probably not. He decided to spare the detectives his thoughts.

"What are you doing here? What has my idiot cousin done now?" he asked.

"We need to use a phone, Frankie." Tim pushed past the bewildered man.

"A please, thank you or excuse me would have been nice."

Bear stood on the doorstep to explain the problem to

Frankie. He said that they had gone for a run and held up his phone to show Frankie that he had run out of charge.

"Tim doesn't take his phone with him when we run, and we found a stiff. We need to use a phone to report it."

"Aye sure. At least you're not all splashed with blood," Frankie said and waved Bear into the house.

Jamie was sitting on the floor of the living room doing a little puzzle with Frankie's twin daughters. "Hey Blondie, where's your manners? Don't you shove my cousin about, or I'll pull your dad's protection in the big house."

"He gets out today. So that's a bit late, anyway. He'll be on the tag, so I can keep an eye on him. Can we use a phone?"

"You have to come half the way across the city to use a bloody phone? I thought you were mega rich."

"We were running through the Hermitage and I didn't have a phone and Bear's was dead. We found a corpse and need to call it in."

"Why didn't you say? Here you go." Jamie pulled his phone out of his pocket and handed it to Tim.

"Thanks, Jamie. Sorry Frankie. Just need to get this reported quickly."

"Whatever."

***

Tim and Bear ran back to the Hermitage only to find DI Hunter Wilson and DC Rachel Anderson staring at the pool of blood beside the river.

"So where's this corpse, Myerscough?"

"Right there, boss. Look!" Tim pointed. He frowned and glanced at Bear. "Where is he?"

"There were two of you and neither of you stayed put?" Hunter growled.

"Well, be serious, boss. We didn't think he was going anywhere," Bear said.

Jamie and Frankie wandered up, pushing the girls in their buggy.

"What the hell are you doing here?" Hunter asked the lads.

"This is a crime scene. Not an outdoor event for you to come and gawp at."

"Just coming to see how it's going. Seein' as how we did our bit to help our fine boys in blue."

"Shut it, Jamie," Hunter said. "Where is your body, young Myerscough?"

"We thought we'd come out for a bit of fresh air for the girls," Frankie said.

"And we thought we'd have a look see about this dead body that's caused all the excitement," Jamie said. "Where is it, Blondie?"

"It's gone. Where the hell has he gone, Bear?"

"How would I know? There's a lot of blood, but he's definitely gone." Bear stared at the bloody riverbanks in disbelief.

"I think I'd realised that all by myself. Fuck! I'll need statements from you both," Hunter said.

"Can I get mine to you tomorrow, boss. My dad is to be released from HMP Edinburgh over in Saughton today and I have to pick him up and make sure he stays put until they fit the tag."

"First thing tomorrow, without fail, young Myerscough."

"No problem, boss."

"You got an excuse, DC Zewedu?"

"Idleness, boss?"

"No, Bear. That will not do it. But tomorrow morning is fine for you too. I have a meeting to get to, this evening."

"Ooh, a bit of romancing with Meera, boss?" Bear grinned.

"Or a darts match. Which is it, boss?" Tim asked.

"None of your bloody business, that's which it is. And it's Doctor Sharma to you, Bear. Unless you want me to change my mind and demand those reports today you two get out of here."

The big men nodded and raced each other back through the Hermitage towards Tim's car that was parked in Morningside. Tim certainly did not want to keep his father waiting.

"Patience is not amongst Dad's virtues. Need a lift home before I go to collect the old man, Bear?"

"That would be great. Thanks. Good luck with your dad."

"Don't you mean good luck to the rest of us who will have to put up with him?" Tim laughed.

"Maybe. I still think you're crazy not to have introduced him to Gillian before now. You know what he's like with good looking women. So, best with that too."

Chapter Two

Tim saw his father standing ramrod straight with his hands on his hips. He noticed that, even today, he wore a bespoke navy-blue suit and his new black leather shoes glistened in the winter sunshine. He saw him scouring the street with that familiar impatient stare until he caught sight of Tim's car. He pulled up outside HMP Edinburgh and watched his father climb into the large, spacious BMW.

"You're late."

"Good to see you too, Dad." Tim switched off the engine and turned around to hug his father. "You're looking very dapper. Were you expecting someone else?"

"And you are filthy, son. That looks like blood.

"Anyway, although the governor put out that my release date was tomorrow, I was concerned that some of the press might be here to crowd me with unwanted attention. I didn't want them to find me looking less than my best."

"A bit late for that now. Come on, let's get you home."

"They gave me the balance of my spends and my discharge grant, so let me take you out for breakfast, son. I've got £196 burning a hole in my pocket." Sir Peter Myerscough smiled at his son.

"That's some breakfast. But the HDC officer could come any time. I don't want you not to be there. We're going home."

"HDC?" Sir Peter clicked on his seat belt.

"Oh, for fucks sake Dad! You were Justice Minister. It stands for home detention curfew. In other words, you're going to be on the tag for six months and some poor sod will have to listen to your chat while they fit it." Tim swung into the line of traffic. "We're going home."

"What bit your bottom today? You really are a bad-tempered grouch."

"Well, if you must know, Bear and I found a corpse while we were training in the Hermitage. That's where the blood came from. We didn't have any signal and by the time we went to phone it in, and the boss got there, the body was gone. Missing. Vanished."

"Didn't one of you stay with it? Where did it go?"

"No and I don't know. But that's why I'm out of sorts. There was a lot of blood."

"Now I'll tell you something. Many years ago, when I was just a humble detective inspector," Sir Peter began.

"Dad, you were never humble and I'm not really in the mood for one of your stories. Could we please just get you back to the house, preferably in silence?"

Tim felt anger emanating from his father all the way from Saughton to Morningside. As he swung the car into the driveway of the house, Kenneth and Alice stood on the doorstep to welcome them.

"Sir Peter, it's good to have you home," Kenneth said.

Alice smiled. "We have missed you so, Sir Peter, but the children have done their best," she said.

Tim could not help but bristle as he and his sister Ailsa were described as 'the children'. At thirty-one and twenty-nine years old respectively, he did feel they were rather long in the tooth for that description. Still, he knew Alice meant no harm.

"Please could you rustle us up some breakfast, Alice?" Tim asked.

"Yes, a full Scottish breakfast would hit the spot," Sir Peter said.

"With Stornoway black pudding. And I've made a few fruit scones, for after, Sir Peter. You won't have had any home cooking for a while."

"Indeed, I have not, Alice. I will look forward to that very much."

"Come up to the dining room, Dad. We'll have some coffee until breakfast is ready."

"Let's do that, and I can tell you about that case I was mentioning."

Chapter Three

Jamie and Frankie were supervising the twins' lunch of fish pie. The opinions as to whether it was 'good' or 'poo' were split directly down gender lines. The boys wondering how Donna managed to get Kylie-Ann and Dannii-Ann to eat this with such gusto. It was obvious to the boys this was not their favourite meal.

"Saved by the bell," Jamie said. His phone rang. An unknown number showed up on the screen.

"Who has yer pop mugged for a phone this time?" Frankie asked. He took the bib Jamie handed him and wiped the twins' faces efficiently, one with each hand. He listened quietly as Jamie told his pop about their morning walk to the Liberton edge of the Hermitage.

"And there was this huge puddle of blood, Pop," Jamie said.

"And the pong of poo, Uncle Ian," Frankie shouted.

"Poo!" Kylie-Ann giggled.

"Poo, poo, poo," Dannii-Ann repeated.

"But the body was gone. I mean there's no way it got up and just walked away. Not after all that blood, honestly, pop. It was making the river all red. Disgusting."

"I know about dead bodies, lad. I don't need you to tell me. And tell Frankie no' to teach those wee lassies bad language," Ian Thomson said.

He sat in his cell in HMP Edinburgh chatting to the family. He had managed to win a phone with credit in a card game. Both gambling and mobile phones were against prison regulations, but Ian tried not to let rules interfere with his way of life, inside or outside of the jail. That was probably why he had spent so much of his time behind bars.

"It reminds me of a corpse that went missing years ago. I don't know if they ever found it. I was just a lad."

"Oh aye? When was that? Pop? Pop? Fuck he's gone. And he says no' to say bad words in front of the girls."

Frankie just shook his head. He knew Jamie was quite unaware that he had just cursed. He lifted the girls down from their chairs. It was far too cold for them to play outside, so he pointed them in the direction of their toys, and they waddled happily hand in hand towards the colourful box. They began to take out their tea set, but Frankie did not think fish pie would feature on their imaginary menu.

"What was yer pop saying?"

"He was talking about a disappearing body when he was a lad, but then he got cut off. I suppose the phone didn't have too much on it."

"Suppose." Frankie looked at Jamie. "Would you be ok to look after the showroom tomorrow morning?"

"Yes. Why?"

"Now that Donna is finished at college, she and I want to go shopping for Christmas presents while the girls are at nursery. We should be back by lunchtime."

"Not a problem, cuz. Got some fun ideas for the girls?"

"Oh yes. And I've got something really exciting for Donna. Want to see it?"

"Not in front of the children," Jamie said. He grinned at his cousin.

"Shut up, Jamie," Frankie said as he fumbled in his pocket. He brought out a small, blue, plastic ring box and showed Jamie the ring inside. "It's real garnet with proper zircon. And it's real nine carat gold. None of your rubbish."

"Wow! That's bloody marvellous, Frankie. Are you sure? I know Donna's a lovely girl and all that, but marriage, it's a big commitment."

"Aye. But I'll never find another girl like Donna."

"You said that about Annie, cuz."

"I was right then and I'm right now. The girls love her too. We'll no' get married until yer pop can be with us, of course."

"And yer Mam?"

"Can rot in hell. But you'll be my best man?"

"Aye, I'd be honoured. I wonder who the bridesmaid'll be?

I hope she's pretty. Oh, that's my phone again. It's the jail. It'll be Pop."

"Don't tell him, Jamie. It's still a secret."

Chapter Four

Hunter stood in his office staring out of the window. It was far too dark to see anything but his own reflection. But he stood, sipped his coffee, and stared at the glass. There was a gentle tap on the door, and she walked in.

"Thank you for coming," Hunter said. "It means so much to me to have this time with you."

"I know. Nobody wants to look like a fool in public. Especially in front of the family."

"All true." Hunter smiled. "Would you like a coffee? I do excellent coffee."

Hunter poured the coffee and brought it over. He moved the chair next to her and sat down beside her at the front of his desk. Their heads were close together. His arm draped over the back of her chair and they whispered quietly together.

Hunter was quite unaware that Bear popped his head around the door to speak to him but left without doing so. Hunter did not hear him come or go.

He concentrated closely on his companion and all she had to say. He watched her flick her long, black hair behind her ear, felt her warm breath and revelled in her enthusiasm for their task.

He knew that she enjoyed his struggle to comply with her instructions. He smiled at her, stood up and stretched. Hunter went to get them more coffee and noticed the door of his office was open. He was quite sure he had closed it tight.

***

Bear was puzzled by what he had seen. What on earth was going on? What was the boss doing? Who was that woman? Where was Meera?

Bear decided not to hang around. He would not phone Tim, he would be too busy with his dad and getting him settled in. Bear decided his day had been long enough and went home to Mel.

"Hey beautiful," he said.

"What do you want?"

"Nothing. That's very hurtful, Mel."

"Well if you don't want anything what have you done wrong?" She pulled him close to her and smiled up into his eyes. Her dark curls bobbed around her pretty face. "I know that guilty expression. What's up big man?"

"You will not believe what I saw." Bear wandered into the kitchen and grabbed two beers from the fridge. He opened them and handed one bottle to Mel.

"You mean apart from a disappearing corpse?"

"Oh yes, much stranger than that. I went to talk to the boss about the body, or lack of it, I went to his office and found him hunched over his desk."

"And you call that news? Honestly Bear, next you'll be telling me that he had a coffee too."

"Yes, he did. But it was who he was with that was mind-blowing."

"Okay, I'll bite. Who was it?"

"Nobody I have ever seen. An elegant woman and they were far to close."

"Maybe they were studying evidence? Was she pretty?"

"I don't know, I only saw the back of her head. But if that was studying evidence, I only want to study evidence with you." He lifted her up and kissed her long and hard on the mouth. "What's for dinner?"

"Chilli. It'll keep."

"Good." He carried her through to the bedroom.

Chapter Five

Hunter could hear that the team had gathered in the incident room. It sounded like Tim and Bear were the centre of attention as everybody wanted to hear about the disappearing corpse. Hunter watched Colin finish his apple and throw the core into the bin just as he and DCI Mackay walked into the room. He saw Bear trying to gobble half a bacon roll in one bite. It was large mouthful, even for Bear. Hunter could not help smiling at the big man's discomfort.

He sat down and listened while Mackay called the team to order.

"Could we have a little quiet, people?" The volume did not decrease. "Shut the fuck up. We need to get started. It's two weeks to Christmas, I have a missing corpse, a pool of frozen blood, and MIT breathing down my neck. I expect Superintendent Miller to send his team over later today. I must have some kind of a report to show them.

"Perhaps we can start with you, Zewedu. You and Myerscough found the body, didn't you?"

"Yes, sir. Yes, we did. We were out doing a bit of off-season rugby training: stretching, jogging, burpees and so on in the Hermitage. We started at the Morningside end and planned to go all the way to the Liberton end and back again. It makes a good loop."

"And a good story, Zewedu. But I don't have time to listen to your fairy tales. Could we keep it relevant?"

"Of course, sir. Sorry. Tim and I were racing along the path when I noticed a man lying at the edge of the river. He had lost a huge amount of blood. Tim leant over to check for a pulse, but the fellow was dead. Nobody could lose that amount of blood and survive."

"Where did you get your medical degree, Bear?" Colin asked.

"Okay, no need to get sarcastic. But there really was a hell of a lot of blood."

"And you phoned emergency services?" Hunter asked.

"No boss. I don't take my phone when I'm training, and Bear was out of charge."

"Fanbloodytastic," Mackay said.

"We raced across to Jamie Thomson and Frankie Hope's place to use their phone."

"All the way to West Mains Road? Why didn't you ring on any doorbell on the way?" Hunter asked incredulously.

"Look at us!" Tim pointed up and down himself. "We're huge, and at that point we were also sweaty, dressed in blood stained track suits and with no i.d. Honestly, boss, would you let us in to your home?"

"No, but I know you," Hunter said with a smile.

"Why did you both have to go and find a phone?" Mackay asked. "Why didn't one of you stay with the body?"

"We didn't think he was going anywhere, sir," Bear said.

"Elementary error," Mackay growled.

"I think we realise that now, sir," Tim said.

"Can you describe the body, Tim?" Hunter asked.

"I'll try but we weren't with him for long, boss. I'd put him at about five feet five inches tall."

"Maybe slightly less. He had on built up, worn boots. Small feet too," Bear said.

"Small boned. I noticed his narrow wrists and slim neck when I felt for a pulse. His hands were tiny compared to mine."

"You have hands like shovels, Tim. Everybody has tiny hands compared to you," Mel said.

"Very funny. He was smartly dressed, but not formally, but he had a paisley patterned tie around his neck."

"Are you sure? Who the hell wears a paisley patterned tie nowadays?" Mackay asked.

"I don't know, I'm just telling you what I remember, sir. He was well dressed as if he were going to out, or to work or

22

something like that."

"And he just went to the great hereafter, poor sod." Hunter shook his head sadly.

"My dad got home yesterday and while we were waiting for the woman to come and fit his tag, I was telling him about how the corpse disappeared, and he mentioned a similar case he was in charge of many years ago. It was never solved, but he said you were involved in it, boss. You must have been incredibly young."

Chapter Six

I will never forget that first corpse. The blood, still warm and sticky on my hand as I felt for a pulse and prayed I would find one. Of course, I didn't. I remember the dead eyes staring up to the clear cold skies. Oh God, it was scary.

My heart raced, my breathing was quick and shallow. My breath floated away on the freezing air but suddenly I was sweating under my jacket. Hot. Suffocating.

Then I looked at Fraser. He was covered in the dead man's blood. His blue bike was coated in that dark, red, mucilaginous liquid. Blood feels sticky and has a metallic smell when it is spilt in that quantity. I didn't know that. I was terrified and I could tell Fraser was scared too. His smart remarks stopped. He was panting. Sweat covered his face. He tried to wipe it away and smeared the blood from the dead man all over his forehead. Then he threw up.

I wanted to comfort him, but that would have meant touching him, and the blood, again. I looked at the dead man. He wasn't any taller than Fraser. His hair looked quite long, and he was fashionably dressed but covered in blood.

I couldn't see where the blood was coming from. I couldn't see an injury, but it must have been bad. Could he have done it to himself, slipping on the icy ground? Had someone attacked him? They might still be watching us. We had to get away. They might come back for us. I'd better get Fraser home. We should ride home as fast as we can and tell Mum and Dad. They can phone someone. Dad will know what to do. He's seen everything. People tell him anything. Fraser doesn't want to touch his bike, but we must get home quickly and get help.

Chapter Seven

"Hunter? DI Wilson?" Mackay said.

"Sorry, sir. I was thinking about what DC Myerscough said. Yes, I do recall a murder where the corpse disappeared. Many years ago, though. I was just a boy. I can't see there could be any connection. What did Sir Peter say, young Myerscough?"

Tim looked up. "Yesterday was a difficult day. Dad was released from Saughton."

"HMP Edinburgh," Mackay said.

"Yes, sir. He had to come straight home to wait for the HDC official to come and put his tag on. It had to get tested all over the house and Dad became really irritable."

"Patience has never been your father's long suit, bro," Bear said.

"You're right, so it was quite good to have something to distract him with. I told him about the body that Bear and I found and he told me about a similar case that he was involved in when he was a DI. He said that a couple of young lads claimed they had found a body but that by the time he arrived with his team, the body had disappeared and was never recovered although there was a huge pool of blood."

"Yes, there was," Hunter said.

"He mentioned that he thought he remembered the lads being you and your brother. Is that right, boss?"

"Yes. We were riding our bikes along the pathway by the Water of Leith when my brother, Fraser, took a dive over his handlebars and into the bloody puddle. It must have been around this time of year. The ground was frozen solid so not much of the blood had seeped into the earth."

"How long ago was it, boss?" Tim asked.

"I was only fifteen and Fraser was thirteen, so it was thirty years ago exactly. I know these two incidents seem similar, but I can't see there can be any connection when the time span separating them is so wide."

"Well, I can see an immediate connection, and that's you," Mackay said. "If I remember rightly, our desk sergeant here, Charlie Middleton, was a young PC about that time and there was a useless, rather rude DC Inglis. I don't remember his first name."

"Arthur Inglis. He's a DCI now."

"How on earth did he get promoted to that?"

"Longevity, pure and simple. I think they kept promoting him to get him out of harm's way. His brother is a prison officer if I remember rightly."

"Both on the side of the angels?" Hunter asked.

"Yes, but a decidedly unangellic pair. Anyway, have we got the initial CSI report back from yesterday?"

"No, it's too early to expect that, sir," Hunter said. "But if you think it's worthwhile, I could get the casefile from that earlier murder brought out, sir."

"Yes, do that, Hunter. Maybe take it to Sir Peter, because he will have a professional memory that might be useful now."

"Sir, perhaps the major incident team would be best to speak to him."

"You go anyway, Hunter. Can you set that up with your father, Myerscough?"

"Of course, sir. I know he would love to help, but could the meeting be at our house? It's just in case it over-runs while he's on the tag."

"Yes, that's sensible. In the meantime, let's arrange door to door enquiries at both ends of the Hermitage walk and we'll need to see what is revealed by CCTV," Mackay said.

"There is no CCTV in the Hermitage, sir," Tim said.

"No, but there will be on access roads leading to it. Set it up, will you, Sergeant Reid?"

"Yes, sir." Colin Reid smiled at DC Nadia Chan. "You up for a day in front of the small screen together, Nadia?"

"Only if you bring popcorn."

"Tim, will you get that old case file? You and Bear can see

if there are any similarities with what you saw?" Hunter said. "And write up your reports from yesterday. Perhaps get a sketch artist in to put together a picture of the deceased. I remember Fraser and I doing that as kids, we felt so important."

"Good idea, boss. We're on it," Tim said.

"Angus, you and Rachael arrange with uniforms to do the door to door visits," Hunter said to DC Angus McKenzie. "And keep your fingers crossed that Miller sends DS Jane Renwick from MIT."

Chapter Eight

Jamie wandered into the showroom at Thomson's Top Cars only to find that head mechanic Mark was already busy in the garage.

"Morning Mark. You're early. Want a coffee?"

"Yeh, go on. I want to get all the repairs done and back to the owners before Christmas. You're closing us down from Christmas Eve through til January 6th, right?"

"Yes. It'll be good. Almost a fortnight off."

"Aye. Fab." Mark took the mug of coffee that Jamie held out for him. "No sign of Gerry yesterday. Little shite. He's no working out so well, Jamie. Can we look for someone new after the holidays? Shug and I cannae do everything we're two selves."

"I know what you mean. Gerry's late a lot and that must have been his third day off in a month. Hell, he's only just doing more hours than my pop, and he's in the big house!" Jamie laughed. "I'll no' look to take in anything but emergencies before the holidays."

"Thanks Jamie. No biscuit with the coffee, then?"

"Don't push your luck, you cheeky bam."

The phone in the showroom rang and Jamie went to answer it. "Thomson's Top Cars," he said.

"Is that Thomson's Top Cars?" The woman sounded worried.

"I just said so. Who's this?"

"Gerry's auntie Pam. Is he there?"

"No and he wasn't in yesterday. He's rootin' fer a bootin' if he doesnae get his act in gear. You can tell him that from me."

"What? What do you mean he wasnae in yesterday? Where the hell was, he then? He left for work in good time and he

28

didn't come home last night."

"Look Missus, I'm no' just being horrible, but Gerry hardly ever arrives here in good time and I'm no' his keeper. If he turns up, I'll get him to give you a shout. Right?"

"Aye, okay, son. Sorry. I'm just awfully worried."

"Try no' to worry. Have a cuppa tea. That'll help. I'll get him to phone you." Jamie put the phone down and went to the office to get himself another cup of coffee.

He wondered what Frankie and Donna would get the twins for Christmas. He thought it would be fun if he got one of the girls a wee pram and the other a buggy to push their dollies in. He sort of hoped Frankie and Donna wouldn't take all morning to do their shopping. It was boring rattling about here on his own. He picked up a packet of chocolate digestives and took them through to Mark. It gave him an excuse for a chat.

"Thought I'd spoil you and bring the biscuits through. That was Gerry's auntie on the phone. She says she thought he was in work yesterday."

"Well she's wrong. Did you tell her he's no exactly dependable?"

"I told her that, but she really did sound worried."

"Worried enough to pass us another biscuit?"

"Aye, okay." Jamie laid the packet of biscuits on a shelf in the garage. "I'll leave them there and we'll see what Gerry has to say for himself when he turns up."

"If he turns up," Mark said.

***

"It's really fun going around the shops with you for the girls," Donna said. "Are we going to get the wee things for their stocking as well as their presents from us?"

"Yeh, and from Santa. He gets them most of the good stuff."

He smiled at her and Donna laughed.

"Let's do our shopping and then I'll take you for lunch at La Lanterna. It's a wee family Italian place in Hanover Street. They do wonderful home-made lasagne and ravioli too,

Donna. Do you fancy that?"

"Oh, Frankie, that would be lovely. It's been ages since we were out just the two of us. Do you think Jamie will be alright about us being away from the showroom for that long?"

"He'll just have to be, won't he?" Frankie sounded much braver than he felt.

"Good! Where are we going for the girls' toys?"

They wandered arm in arm around the centre of Edinburgh going from shop to shop picking up little things to put into the girls' stockings and selecting large gifts for which Santa would get the credit: a rocking horse for Kylie, and a toddler trampoline for Dannii. He's a fine man, that Santa Claus.

Chapter Nine

Tim and Bear stood beside the kettle watching it boil. It was their turn to make the teas and coffees. Bear lifted the mugs out of the cupboard and put a tea bag in Nadia's and a chamomile tea bag into Rachael's. He saw Tim spoon coffee into mugs for himself, Bear and Angus.

"Colin, are you on the hard stuff?"

"Yes, I've got a glass of water here, thanks, Tim."

"It's always the same when Colin and I have movie date. He brings his own drink and there's never any popcorn." Nadia smiled.

"Well, before we have our date, we have to work out which cameras will be useful. You got the plans?"

"Right here," Nadia said.

"Does Maggie know about your movie dates with Nadia?" Bear asked as he handed Nadia her tea.

"She does, and my dear wife is delighted not to be included," Colin said.

"The boss is living in hope that Jane will be assigned to this case from MIT. It would be nice to have her back, even just for a while, wouldn't it?" Tim handed Rachael the mug of chamomile tea.

"It always works for me. When my better half is based in Edinburgh, she takes her turn cooking dinner," she grinned. "Now, Angus, who is going to lead the negotiations with uniform, you or me?"

"I would always bow to your longer experience, Rache."

"Let's work out how many we need while we finish these drinks."

Bear followed Tim to desks so they could type up statements of all they could remember about the corpse they found. He concentrated on the details he could bring to mind.

He recalled looking at his phone before it died, so the time he knew quite accurately, 9.51am. The weather and the frozen ground were imprinted on his memory and then there was the blood. The large puddle of dark, red viscous blood seeping from the belly of the corpse across the banks and into the river. Bear retched at the memory.

"You all right, big man?"

Bear didn't speak but nodded at Tim. His eyes watered and he took a long slurp of his coffee to try to calm himself.

Then the corpse. Shorter and slighter than average, about thirty-five. He couldn't tell if the hair was dyed or stained by the blood, but it was styled up in a man bun and the guy was smartly dressed. Not formal, but smart. Brushed cotton navy chinos, a blue waterproof jacket, a brown V-necked jumper and a shirt that was probably once white but now stained red with the paisley patterned tie hanging loosely around his neck. And shoes, well, boots, worn black boots soaked by the river water, Bear remembered them as quite small. Of course, his knew his own feet were huge and so his idea of a normal shoe size was probably influenced by that.

"Want to swap to check them through?" Bear asked Tim.

"Good idea."

Bear stood up and drained his coffee cup to get a refill. He picked up Tim's mug too as he walked past.

By the time Bear returned with the fresh coffees, Tim had emailed his report over and Bear sat down to read it through. He found it interesting to see what they had both mentioned and what was different.

Bear read Tim's report. He had not been carrying a phone, but he was wearing his Breitling watch, so had put the time of their find at 09.52. Bear deduced his own mobile was out by a minute. Tim had mentioned the weather and ground conditions too, but he also detailed Bear holding him as he grabbed a tree to balance himself and stretch over to try to find a pulse. He expressed his disappointment that he found none. Bear thought Tim was being a bit soft about that.

He skipped through the description of the clothes. That bit was much the same as he had written. Tim put the age of the victim at early thirties. Bear thought he was slightly older, but that was not a significant detail. Then Bear paused. He re-read the paragraph in which Tim detailed the injuries. Like Bear, he had mentioned the copious amounts of blood, but Tim had added something else. Tim had stated that the jacket was open at the front. Bear thought for a moment and remembered that this was correct. Tim's report included that the sweater and shirt were sheered, probably by a knife wound because that's where most of the blood was coming from. But when he felt for a pulse on the neck of the corpse, Tim noticed marks around the neck and a wound in the skull. It looked to him as if the man had been hit from behind probably before he was stabbed or perhaps he hit his head as he fell. His report posed the question, as to whether the attack was carried out by one perpetrator or two.

Bear had not bent down to examine the corpse, so he had not seen this, and Tim had not mentioned it at the site. Bear gazed at the computer screen and recalled the scene. He just remembered the blood.

He looked over at Tim and they nodded to each other before sending their emails to Hunter.

"Shall we go and find the reports of that cold case your dad worked on, Tim?"

"Yes, we should do that. But it was such a long time ago, I doubt they even had DNA testing back then."

Chapter Ten

"Yes, of course, DI Wilson. I would be pleased to meet with you and discuss that old murder case, if it will help, but I'm afraid the gathering will have to be at my house, though. You appreciate that my movements are somewhat constrained at present," Sir Peter said.

Hunter knew that Sir Peter could quite easily come down to the station during the day as long as he returned home before his curfew started. However, he also knew that to return to the building where he had once served as Chief Constable, but now as a convicted criminal, would probably not be very comfortable. As Hunter was under strict instructions from DCI Mackay to 'play nicely' he agreed to meet at Sir Peter's home that afternoon. He explained that a representative from MIT would accompany him, as would Tim and Bear because they had found the body.

"Of course, of course. I shall have Alice prepare afternoon tea for all of us. I can't tell you how much I missed her home baking while I was away," Sir Peter said.

Hunter was mildly amused by this idea that Sir Peter had 'been away' as if he had taken a social trip rather than being incarcerated on drugs offences. Again, he let that slide and wondered how much more of the older man's pomposity he could bear in silence.

"We'll see you about 3pm, Sir Peter."

As he put down the phone there was a knock on his door. Hunter looked up and grinned broadly. He stood up from his desk and walked towards DS Jane Renwick.

"Jane, dear. How good to see you. I am so happy to have your assistance from MIT."

Jane smiled. "Thank you, DI Wilson. And this is my

colleague DCI Arthur Inglis. I'm sure his experience will also be of great benefit." She looked straight into Hunter's eyes and winked. She stuck out her tongue but as Inglis stood behind her, he saw none of that.

"Sir," Hunter said. "It's been a while." He offered Inglis his hand.

"It has, Hunter. It's certainly been a long time, you were just a boy, and I was still a DC when we first met, if I remember correctly."

The men shook hands. Hunter held Inglis' stare.

"Let's see what you've got. So far, all that I've heard is that two of your guys managed to find a corpse and lose it, all in under an hour."

"I don't think it would be quite like that, sir," Jane said.

"Don't try to defend these amateurs, DS Renwick. You are a member of MIT, the Major Incident Team, now. Please bring us up to speed with what your team has done so far, Hunter, then I believe we have a meeting with the inestimable Sir Peter Myerscough. He's another fucking joke. Acted like he was the only man to ever lose a family member."

Inglis strode over to Hunter's coffee machine, took a mug from the side of it and poured himself a generous serving.

"Help yourself, sir." Hunter raised his eyebrows and glanced at Jane. He could tell Inglis hadn't changed.

The three detectives sat around Hunter's desk. Hunter explained how the investigation had been divided up to date.

"Yes, just keep us posted on what comes from the house to house enquiries and the CCTV checks. I don't expect to get anything useful. The Hermitage is really too isolated for that. Let's see the reports from the imbeciles who found the corpse. Oh fuck, one is a Myerscough! Why am I not surprised?" Inglis's stream of consciousness was interrupted by a knock at Hunter's door.

"Good afternoon, boss. Hello Jane. Good to see you." Tim walked over to kiss Jane lightly on the cheek. He and Bear had been best men at her union with Rachael Anderson, and they had all remained close friends.

"DC Myerscough, I don't think you know DCI Arthur

Inglis from MIT? He worked with your father some years ago."

"My condolences, sir." Tim smiled.

"Accepted. Your father is a congenital idiot and I understand that you are just as foolish. You and this DC with an unpronounceable name managed to lose a dead man in an empty park. That takes some doing."

Tim flushed red with anger. Hunter knew the signs; Tim had a long fuse, but family was the fuel that always lit his temper. Hunter watched the big man as his huge hands hit the desk with a thump, but Tim spoke to Inglis in barely a whisper. Hunter stared at an unimportant sheet of paper on his desk and decided to let Tim have his say.

"We may only just have met, but I know my father was right when he described you as an arrogant, rude bully, sir," Tim said. "There is nothing you can say about my father or my service that I have not had muttered behind my back a dozen times before and sometimes said straight to my face. But my father is no idiot. He is a former Chief Constable and former Justice Secretary of the Scottish Parliament. Both offices to which you will never aspire. Yes, he has committed crimes, but he has served his time. He is not a bad man. He just did bad things and has paid his price in full.

"I graduated from St. Andrews University with a first-class honours degree, I attended the wedding of our future king and I can buy and sell you, any day of the week. I am certainly not an idiot. So, sir, if you ever speak about me, any member of my family or any of our colleagues in that overbearing, derogatory or pompous way again, I will file a complaint against you, and I will have your badge. I will not tolerate bullying in any shape or form. You will be so sorry you were ever born, sir. Do I make myself perfectly clear, sir?"

"Hunter, are you going to let this young DC speak to a senior officer like that and threaten me in this way?"

Hunter looked up from his desk. "I'm sorry, sir. I was looking at this dispatch. Did you hear DC Myerscough threaten DCI Inglis, Jane?"

"I have been suffering from an ear infection lately, boss. I

36

regret my hearing is severely affected by it and I heard nothing of the sort."

"Ha fucking ha. Like that is it?" Inglis glared at Jane.

Tim turned to Hunter. His calm demeanour and composure returned.

"Boss, I came in to mention a couple of things that Bear and I noted from the old investigation. But they can wait until you are free. How would you like us to travel up to Morningside?"

"You take Jane and Bear in your car, young Myerscough. I will drive DCI Inglis to your father's home."

"Of course, boss. I would respectfully suggest that anybody who feels unable to treat my father courteously in his own home, may wish to absent themselves from the meeting."

Chapter Eleven

Frankie and Donna had thoroughly enjoyed lunch together at the busy little family-run restaurant. Afterwards, they jumped into a taxi from La Lanterna in Hanover Street to go back to Thomson's Top Cars.

"One day I'm going to pass my driving test and we won't have to pay for a taxi."

"Maybe, Frankie, but we wouldn't be able to have those tasty beers with our meal either."

"You could, if I was driving."

"Are you going to tell Jamie that we stopped for lunch?"

"No way! That'd be right daft."

"I wonder what Jamie will have to say when we get back."

"Nothing good. But he will like that putting machine we got him when he opens it on Christmas morning and those tiny teddies to go into the girls' stockings are right fun. They'll love them, won't they?"

"I hope so. They are such great kids," Donna said. She squeezed his arm and smiled.

Their taxi pulled up slowly and Frankie paid the fare. Jamie was striding up and down the forecourt.

"Where the helluve you been? You've just took the mick, Frankie. It's no' fair. I've no' even had my lunch and wee Gerry's no' come in either. His auntie phoned. Said she thought he was in yesterday, got right worried when I said he wasn't.

"Luckily, Mark and Shug are getting on with what needs done and there's an old guy sniffing about the black limo. That would be a good sale for us. He says it's for his funeral business, as if I'm a man who cares what it's for. If he's got the dosh, he can have it."

"Of course, Jamie. You go and get your lunch. You going to KFC?"

"Frankie, I always go to fucking KFC, don't I? Aye, I'm going to KFC. Then I'm going Christmas shopping myself and that will take me the rest of the day. Youse two can stay on till closing time and lock up."

Jamie turned his back and jumped into the car to drive up the road towards the KFC. He was grinning like a Cheshire cat. He did plan to get a bucket of chicken and chips from KFC but had less than no intention of going boring old Christmas shopping when he could go home and watch some of the FIFA world cup from Morocco on the tele. Football? Shopping? No contest.

"Well that's us told," Donna said. "Shall I make us all a coffee?"

"Good idea pet. Mark and Shug never say no to one. I wonder what happened to Gerry again today. He's really no' worked out so well."

Just at that point Frankie saw a tall, slim grey-haired man limp into the showroom. He was leaning heavily on a walking stick. Frankie thought he looked odd because his grey clothes and hair made him look like a ghost. The man waved his stick and called Frankie over.

"I am looking for a new limousine for my business. The cold weather makes for a busy season for us funeral directors. Old folks die of the cold. Incredibly sad, but good business," said the man.

"If you say so. We only have one limo at the moment. That black one. But if you're looking for something different, I could order it for you. It wouldn't be with you till after the holidays, of course."

"Of course, of course. But this one would do me if it drives smoothly and the price is right. I was speaking to a young gentleman earlier. He offered me a substantial discount."

Frankie burst out laughing. "That would be Jamie, but you are wrong on two counts. Jamie is no gentleman and he's never offered anybody a discount in his life. So, if you don't like the price, there's no point in going for a test drive."

The man smiled at Frankie. He opened the car door and sat in the driver's seat. Frankie stood and watched him as he checked the inside of the vehicle then he got up and limped all the way around the limo before leaving the showroom in silence.

Frankie closed the door of the limousine and went to join Donna at the reception desk, and they drank their coffee together.

Chapter Twelve

When I was a kid, I was often teased about my dad being a 'God botherer'. My mum's job only being to run the church Brownies and Girl Guides and bake scones for coffee mornings. Mind you, she made great scones and all my friends liked coming to my house to eat her home baking.

Sometimes the teasing would get me down. But the night Fraser and I found that corpse, I was glad of my dad's convictions and my mum's gentle support and care.

We were panicking and breathless and covered in a dead man's blood when we got back to the manse. I hammered on the door and Fraser was bent over, his hands on his knees, vomiting into the flower bed. We had slammed our filthy bikes up against the garden fence.

Mum and Dad went into their automatic care roles. Dad helped us in off the street and Mum screamed at the sight of her sons covered in blood. As soon as they realised that neither of us was hurt, they listened to our account of what we had seen. Then we began to shiver.

Dad immediately called the police and mum told us both to strip off. She wanted to make us clean and warm. She got us each to stand in the bath, one after the other, and hosed us down with the rubber hose that fitted onto the taps. She usually only used it to wash her hair, but this job was much bigger.

Normally, Fraser and I would have been embarrassed standing naked in front of mum as teenagers. But that night, all we could think about was the dead man's body and the blood. When we were clean and dry and in our warm pyjamas, we went downstairs, and mum gave us each a cup of cocoa. I remember beginning to calm down and then Dad said the

41

police wanted us to go back to the site of the corpse because there was a problem. We had to go to help.

I was filled with terror. I saw Fraser turn white. I knew neither of us wanted to leave the house.

It was awful, getting dressed into clean clothes when I knew I would never be able to wear the other ones again. I was shivering, not because it was cold, although it was cold, but the shock had finally hit me. I looked at Fraser. We didn't want to go, but dad was a man respectful of authority and if the police wanted to see us, we would go. Mum insisted on coming too. She said she was not going to let us out of her sight ever again. At the time it sounded like a good idea.

Then, when we arrived at the scene a tall, blond, intimidating police detective was obviously in charge. He was there with police officers and people in white overalls dancing to his tune like drones around the queen bee. He was shouting and swearing. And as soon as he saw Fraser and me, he accused us of lying. As if anybody would lie about something so horrendous as that. But there was no body. The corpse was gone. Had we really seen it or was it a sick joke?

Oh, we really saw it and I see it in my dreams regularly to this day.

When you look into the eyes of a corpse, because many people do die with their eyes open, it is like looking into the eyes of the lost. I didn't know that before I saw the dead man. I stared at him and the pool of blood he was swimming in. It made me feel sick. I couldn't see him breathing. I had to feel for a pulse. Someone had to check if he was alive and Fraser wasn't going to do that, he made that perfectly clear, so it had to be me.

I didn't blame him for that. To be honest, I didn't want to do it either, but I am the older brother, so I felt I had to do it. I mean, a dead man couldn't hurt me, could he? But when I looked at him again, I was scared. His eyes were wide open as if with alarm and stared blankly looking into nothingness.

Chapter Thirteen

Kenneth opened the door to Hunter and Inglis.

"We have a meeting with Sir Peter," Hunter said.

"I have been made aware of that," Kenneth said. "The young master suggested that one of your colleagues may not be welcome. I'm sorry about that DI Wilson."

"I beg your pardon, my man," Inglis spluttered.

"Accepted."

Hunter smiled.

"I assure you, and Sir Peter that both DCI Inglis and I are here to ask for assistance. We have no intention of upsetting anybody."

Inglis harrumphed and glanced at the ground.

"On that basis, you may both enter. You will be meeting in the dining room. Sir Peter thought it would be sensible with such a large group to sit around the big table. Coffee and refreshments are on the sideboard. Please help yourselves. DI Wilson, would you like me to introduce you, or do you know the way?"

"No problem, Kenneth. I'll lead the way. I know you always have plenty to do."

As they walked in, Hunter saw Kenneth grab Inglis by the arm and he heard Kenneth growl.

"You cause any problems, any disagreements, any issues, Sir Peter will ring the bell and I, personally, will ruin your fine suit. And believe me, that will be the least of your worries, DCI Inglis."

Hunter saw the astonishment on Inglis's face and signalled to Kenneth that his intervention would not be necessary.

When they walked in, Inglis was still brushing down his suit. Hunter noticed that Sir Peter was sitting at one end of the table and Tim at the other. Bear was sitting near Tim and Hunter was grateful when he indicated the chair next to him was his. Hunter nodded to Jane who sat opposite him between Sir Peter and Inglis. There they were, battle lines drawn, Hunter and Bear on one side, MIT on the other and the Myercoughs at either end. He had no doubt that this was not by chance.

Hunter watched as Tim offered a drink to Jane first. There was nothing in Tim's body language that betrayed his earlier clash with Inglis, but Hunter noticed little things that told him Tim was out to make a point.

"When Alice heard you were coming, Jane, she made a pot of chamomile tea." Tim handed her a bespoke china mug bearing Sir Peter's coat of arms.

"How kind of her to remember. More importantly, she has made banana bread and her famous lemon drizzle cake. I can smell it." Jane grinned.

Everybody else accepted coffee and slices of the cake.

"Now that we are all fed and watered, let's begin, shall we?" Sir Peter took over as chair. "Can we consider the historic case first, because that was never solved, was it?"

"No, it was not. We were both on the investigating team and you were the senior officer in charge, but the case was never solved," Inglis said.

Hunter noticed Tim shift in his chair.

"Did you manage to find the case files about it, Tim?" Hunter asked.

"Yes, boss. That's why I came to see you earlier. I know the CSIs have been all over the site where Bear and I found the body yesterday and we're waiting on their report and the forensics."

"We are, but I've asked them to expedite it. Especially as it's so close to Christmas."

"But when Dad and I were talking about the earlier case, the one where you and your brother found the body, he reminded me of something."

"What would that be? Because the body was never found." Inglis asked. He turned to Sir Peter.

"Well, it's something we all forget about. But forensic serology and DNA testing only came into their own in 1986 and this historic crime went all the way back to 1983. However, we do still have the murder weapon, the knife that we took a thumb print from. Of course, the print wasn't on record, but the knife also has traces of the victim's blood on it. We could test that now to find out more about our victim."

"It's even possible that the print is on file now too," Bear said.

"Good idea. You and Tim take charge of that, Bear," Hunter said.

"We also have the clothing you and your brother were wearing, boss. That's all pretty bloody."

"I remember all too vividly, Tim. The chances are that the blood is the victim's not the perpetrator's, but we should get it examined and see what it tells us."

"What else do you remember about that day, DI Wilson?" Sir Peter asked.

"Goodness, I was only a lad. And my brother was even younger. We were cycling home along the Water of Leith. I can't remember where we'd been, but I do remember Fraser falling off his bike because the leg was stuck out across the path. I felt the wrist for a pulse, and it was still slightly warm when I touched it. His eyes were a bit cloudy too. Open. Staring up to the sky. It freaked me out. And there was such a lot of blood. I still have nightmares about it."

"I'm not surprised. You were so young," Sir Peter said. "Now what did we find out about the perpetrator? Hand me that file, will you Tim?

"The body had been dragged away from the scene. There was a small scrap of material from his clothes caught on the railings. Was that kept?" Sir Peter looked up.

"Yes, I think this must be it here, Dad." Tim rummaged through the box of evidence.

"I'm not sure that should have been taken out of the station," Inglis said.

"It's a thirty-year-old cold case, sir. Even Charlie Middleton couldn't find it in his heart to forbid me from bringing the box to this meeting."

Inglis shrugged. "I'm amazed Charlie hasn't retired by now.

He was a PC back then and only made it to sergeant, that tells me all I need to know."

"Tim, does the scrap have any blood on it?" Jane asked

"No, but a brightly coloured tie was found near the scene. It was spattered with blood." Tim pulled it out of the box. He coughed and closed his eyes because the evidence bag was very dusty.

"We never actually knew if that was connected to this murder. We thought it probably was, but we couldn't be sure because it was found several yards away from the scene," Sir Peter said. "What else is in there, Tim?"

"The knife. I saw from the file that there were various smudged fingerprints on that, but only one thumb print that was identifiable could be taken. But there was blood on the handle of the knife, as well as the blade. I suppose it is worth getting that tested now, because it might be the murderer's?"

"It's thirty years ago. He's probably dead by now," Inglis said.

"Why do you say that? My dad isn't dead, and neither are you or Charlie."

"I suppose. Anything else from the file? Of course, these cases may not be connected at all."

"They might not, but my gut tells me that we shouldn't ignore the possibility," Hunter said.

"Am I right in remembering the man you described was below average height?" Sir Peter asked Hunter.

"I suppose that must be true. I was only a kid, so my judgement on that wasn't great and I was traumatised by the whole thing. But I seem to remember thinking he was probably about the same height as my brother and he was only thirteen."

"How old was the victim, Hunter?" Inglis asked.

"I have no idea. I wasn't used to judging adults' ages then. I was a kid, he was a grown-up. I don't recall any wrinkles and his hand, when I checked for a pulse, was small and smooth. His hair was sort of mousey brown. I didn't see any grey, but I wasn't looking for it and it was dark. He was probably in his twenties or thirties. I can't be sure."

The discussion continued with various points coming to light and being batted about. Hunter noticed Jane was quiet. He heard a knock on the door and Kenneth entered. He brought in a fresh pot of coffee and a hot pot of Jane's tea. He removed the cold pots and Alice followed him in bearing two large plates of sandwiches. She placed a plate at either end of the table and left the cakes there too.

Sir Peter suggested they take a break and enjoy the food on offer. Half an hour was agreed and Inglis went outside to smoke. Hunter thought Inglis looked stressed. Murder did that to people. He was not sure that Inglis's abrasive personality would get the correct results and MIT was considered key to solving major crimes quickly.

Jane walked up to Hunter. "May I have a word, boss?"

"I'm not your boss now, Jane. Haven't been for a long time."

"I've had an idea that I don't want to share with everybody yet."

"Shouldn't you be telling the DCI?" Hunter smiled. "Go on then. What are your thoughts?"

"Simply that if there is a connection between these two cases, I can't see them being the only two. It doesn't make sense that there would only be two connected murders thirty years apart."

"That occurred to me too. We must find out if there is anything to connect them first. Of course, there may not be, although there are coincidences and I don't like coincidences."

Inglis walked back into the room and picked up some sandwiches and a slice of cake. "Shall we recommence our discussions? Perhaps DCs Myerscough and Zewedu could tell us about the more recent find that they made?"

"Good idea, Inglis." Sir Peter said. "Bear, you got to the body first, I think."

"Yes, I did Sir Peter. Tim and I had paused to do some exercises and then raced on through the Hermitage of Braid Circular." For Inglis benefit, he clarified. "It's a path that runs by the Braid Burn and is good for all skill levels. The trail is most often used for hiking, walking, running, and nature trips but Tim and I often use it for our rugby training.

"It was still quite early, but the sun was up, so it was light enough. As we ran along the path, I was just ahead of Tim. I stopped short when I noticed the body by the river, and then Tim ran into the back of me. He's solid muscle. It was like being hit by a tank."

Tim grinned at his friend. "Well, thanks a lot! You're pretty solid too, so for me it was like running into the back of a tractor."

Bear laughed and reached for another slice of cake. He waved it at Tim in acknowledgement.

"I suppose the ground was hard too because of the frosty weather, recently," Hunter said.

"Yes, boss, it was. The blood from the corpse was all around it. Some of it bled into the river, but a lot of it was just lying on the surface, because it couldn't seep into the frozen earth." Tim said.

"And you went down to the river to check on the body, son," Sir Peter said, quietly.

"I did, dad. It seemed unlikely that there would be a pulse, but I had to check. Of course, there was nothing. The corpse was cold, and the eyes were shut. I noticed his hands were quite small and it didn't look like he did manual work. Also, he was not that tall, I don't think."

"Tim, compared to you and Bear, nobody is very tall." Jane smiled at him.

"The rest of our observations are in our reports. Does everybody have copies?"

"Yes, thanks," Hunter said.

"Did you notice a weapon near the body?" Inglis asked.

"No, sir."

"Did you see where the blood was coming from?"

"Mostly from the middle of the body, but it looked like the victim had also been hit on the head and I noticed bruises on the neck when I felt for a pulse. There was no blood coming from the neck, face or arms."

"Why did you both leave the body?" Inglis asked. "That's a rookie error."

"There was nobody about. We never imagined it would disappear, sir," Tim said defensively.

"Why on earth did you run all the way to West Mains Road to phone it in?" Hunter asked.

"Neither of us had any i.d. on us. We are both big men and we didn't want to frighten anybody by ringing their doorbells smeared in blood at that time in the morning."

"We know the fellows who live in West Mains and knew they'd let us in to use a phone," Bear added. "It may not seem logical now, but it made sense to us then."

"Let's see if we can draw any comparisons between the historic case and this one," Hunter suggested. "Both men seemed quite young. Twenties to thirties from what the reports say. Below average height and not manual workers. Tim, was your man clean shaven?"

"Yes. Hair quite long. Tied up in a man bun, but no facial hair."

"Mine too, as I recall."

"Both killed violently and just before Christmas," Tim said.

"Smartly dressed from what I can see. But most obviously both corpses were removed from the scene by person or persons unknown and never found," Jane said. "That is the most obvious connection."

"What if these two cases are just a coincidence?" Inglis asked.

"I don't believe in coincidences, sir," Hunter said. "I think it is much more likely that there is either no connection at all between these two cases, and that is my personal belief right now. But the other possibility is that these are only two corpses of many. These are the ones we have seen and know about. If there is a connection, there may be many more bodies missing that have never been discovered."

"Let's pray it's your first thought that is correct, otherwise we could have a serial killer at loose and hiding in the community," Sir Peter said.

"Shall I arrange to have the evidence from the historic case tested and see what it can tell us now, boss."

"Yes, do that, Tim."

"The old case never really got very far because the print we had was not on file and nobody was reported missing that matched the description you gave us, Hunter," Sir Peter said. "But do let me know if I can assist in any way, won't you?"

"Of course. I think we can call that a day. We should have some results in from forensics tomorrow. Briefing in the morning at eight, then, but I have a meeting due to start soon. I'll give you a lift back to the station, DCI Inglis" Hunter said. He stood up and walked over to Sir Peter. "Thank you for hosting us here."

"Boss, if you have a meeting, DCI Inglis can come back with me." Tim turned to the senior officer, "But I have to put Bear in the front passenger seat, even in my car, the big man gets cramped in the back."

"Yes, that will be fine," Inglis said.

"Darts match, boss?" Jane asked.

"No."

"Then you must be taking Meera out. Have a good evening."

"It is neither of these things, but an important meeting that is nothing to do with any of you," Hunter said angrily.

"Keep your hair on, boss," Bear said.

Hunter left swiftly, before the others. He did not want them seeing which direction he was taking. He had arranged the meeting in a discreet coffee shop away from his usual haunts. This meeting was a secret and he wanted it to remain that way.

Tim led the way to his BMW.

"How on earth does the force in Edinburgh afford this kind of vehicle? It must have cost well over seventy grand," Inglis exclaimed.

"It's not the force's car. It's mine," Tim said softly.

"Ah yes. Good your father didn't lose everything, when he went down. He always had good taste in women, whisky and cars."

"That may be, but the car is not my father's, it's mine, sir."

"Tim is a trust fund kid. He only works with us for the public good, sir," Bear said. "Don't think about it too hard, just enjoy the ride."

Chapter Fourteen

Frankie and Donna picked up the girls from nursery on their way home from the city. The little ones were extremely excited because they had been told about their Christmas party and Santa was coming to that.

They skipped up the steps and into the house to tell Jamie their news. The twins joined hands to play ring-a-ring-a roses and fell down giggling at the end of the rhyme. Frankie tickled them, one with each hand and then the girls got up and danced around singing the song again.

"This isn't at all annoying," Jamie said as Frankie started tickling the girls again.

Frankie looked at his cousin and frowned. He patted the girls on the bottom and shooed them upstairs to get their nappies changed while Donna made their tea.

He crept back downstairs with them and into the dining area. He ignored it when Kylie-Ann stuck out her tongue at Jamie as they walked by.

"What's for tea today?" he asked Donna softly.

"Macaroni with bacon bits and peas, then banana for pudding. I thought I'd make enough, and we would have that too."

"Good idea."

The girls waved their spoons in delight when Donna put bowls down in front of them. They tucked in heartily wearing almost as much as they ate, but Frankie was happy to see his girls enjoying their food. He turned to Donna.

"When I was upstairs changing Dannii-Ann, I got a message from Harry."

"Oh good, when will your brother get home for his Christmas leave?"

"He's not getting leave this Christmas. His regiment is

staying in Afghanistan because they are involved in training the local forces how to fight the Taliban. He's right bummed about it and so am I. All I really need is Jamie in a mood too."

Donna handed each of the girls half a banana and gave them some milk before she released them from their chairs.

"Shall we go for a walk with the girls before bath time?" she asked.

"No, I really cannae be bothered getting all their warm clothes on again to go out. I'll do a puzzle with them in their bedroom if you run their bath. I want to keep them out of Jamie's hair."

"Okay, Frankie, we can do that. Come on girls. Upstairs to play a puzzle with your daddy before bath time."

"Frankie, did I hear you saying Harry willnae get home for Christmas?" Jamie asked.

"Aye."

"I'm right sorry, cuz. And I'm sorry I barked at the girls. I asked Linda over for Christmas too, but she says she's going to her Mam's. She didnae invite me, though. I'm right disappointed. That's why I was in a bad mood."

"No bother, Jamie, we'll be together, as usual. Just don't take it out on the twins, eh? Did you get your shopping done?"

"No, I came home to watch the footie."

"Thought as much," Frankie said with a smile. "That man came back about the Limo. He said you were a right gentleman and offered him a good discount."

"Lying bastard. I'm no gentleman." Jamie grinned.

"That's what I said, and I said you'd never offered anyone a discount in your puff, unless he was paying cash. He sat in the car for a bit then went away."

"He'll be back. He wants that car," Jamie said. "I think I'll go for a walk later, do a bit of business to cheer myself up."

"No Jamie, don't. Don't go on the rob this close to Christmas. Stay in and have a beer with me and Donna."

"I need some excitement, cuz."

"Suit yourself. But you're an arse, Jamie, and you're going to get caught again. If you get locked up over the holidays, don't come crying to me." Frankie turned his back on his cousin and bounded up the stairs to play with his girls. That was always fun.

Chapter Fifteen

She was already there when Hunter walked in and smiled and waved to him, and he made his way over to the table. The woman had chosen one near the window. She noticed him hover before he sat down.

"Would you rather we sat further into the room?"

"No, no, I'm sure this will be fine. This little place is so off the beaten track that nobody will see us."

Hunter got up and ordered two large coffees at the counter. He asked for two glasses of tap water too. These meetings always made him so nervous. He was grateful when the waiter said he would bring them over. Hunter turned back and walked to the table.

"I like our clandestine meetings," she said. "It's so exciting. Where did you tell people you were going today?"

"I didn't say. It's none of their business."

She laughed lightly. "I told them I was meeting my sugar daddy."

"I hope they didn't believe you."

"Probably not. But it gives them something to think about. Next time I'll probably tell them I'm going to meet my pimp."

She could see how nervous he was and was happy that he smiled at her, despite his nerves. She had a wicked sense of humour and liked to use it to make him laugh.

"Have you told Meera?"

"Good God, no!"

"Then let's get down to business."

Their heads were close together as she explained things to him. They smiled and whispered as they chatted.

***

Tim got caught up in the early rush-hour traffic, so he cut off the main route back to the station to try to get around that. He pulled up at the traffic lights and glanced across to the shops.

"If I didn't know better, Bear," he whispered, "I'd think that was the boss in that café, with a pretty woman who definitely isn't Meera."

Bear looked over. "It is. I told Mel there was something strange going on. Do you think the boss in cheating on Meera?"

"He'd be a bloody fool if he is, that man is punching way above his weight with Meera."

"I agree, and he's certainly not a fool, but that woman he's with is a stunner. Did you see her?"

"Driving, watching the road, not passing strangers, Bear."

Chapter Sixteen

The briefing started bang on time. Inglis was furious to see Bear eating a bacon roll with second one held firmly in his left hand. He noticed Tim Myerscough was drinking coffee while flipping through some papers and Colin Reid finished an apple and aimed the core adeptly towards a wastepaper basket.

A group of female detectives seemed to be having a tea party in the corner and he was incandescent when he saw that Jane Renwick was part of that.

"DS Renwick, could you come over and join me here, please?"

"Of course, sir. See you later, Mel, Nadia. Maybe we could go up to the Golf Tavern for a drink after our shift?"

"That would be really nice," Mel said. Her dark curls bounced up and down as she nodded.

DCI Mackay called the team to order and formally introduced DCI Arthur Inglis and DS Jane Renwick from MIT. There was a giggle when he mentioned Jane so formally and Mackay slapped his folder on the desk.

"Could we please get started without further interruption, people. DCI Inglis is in the chair."

"Now as you all know, MIT will oversee this murder investigation, but your team's leg work and local knowledge will, no doubt, be of some assistance. We are all Police Scotland and must work together."

Mackay nodded but Inglis noticed Hunter stared at the floor. Hunter did not meet his gaze as he glanced around the room for agreement with this statement. He continued.

"Do we have anything back from forensics? I know DI Wilson instructed that it should be expedited."

"Nothing yet. We should have some results tomorrow,"

Hunter said. "Did you give them the evidence from the historic case too, Tim?"

"Yes, boss. But it will definitely be at least tomorrow before we get anything back on that."

"What else do we have?" Inglis asked.

"Nadia and I have been checking for any CCTV cameras that might help," Colin said. "There is very little, because the murder site is so isolated and there are no cameras near there."

Nadia looked up. "The only thing we noticed was someone coming from the Liberton end pushing a shopping trolley. It was a bit strange because it was empty. There was a white van parked near that entrance to the Hermitage."

"That's odd," Hunter said.

"Yes, boss. We couldn't tell which shop the trolley came from, but the nearest outlet we could think of was Sainsbury's in Cameron Toll," Nadia said.

"What we did then, was to go back through the CCTV from there and saw what looked like the same person putting a trolley into the back of a van. We followed the van up Liberton Brae, but we lost him after he turned into Orchardhead Road and the CCTV coverage stops," Colin said.

"But we think he's in the Liberton area, Colin?" Hunter asked.

"Who knows, boss. After we lost him, he could have gone anywhere."

"Registration number?"

"No, boss. Covered in mud, front and back."

"Surprise, surprise. Any joy on the door to door enquiries, Rachael?"

"No, Boss. Both ends of the walk are quite isolated. At the Liberton end we sent uniforms up Kirk Brae and Liberton Brae and down Mayfield Road but there was no joy. The information centre is closed for the holidays, so there was nobody there. The uniforms also visited the riding school but nobody who was there noticed anything. There are still a couple of stable hands to talk to, but they have gone home now for Christmas."

"Get their addresses, Rachael. You and Angus go and

interview them as soon as possible. What about the Morningside end, Angus?"

The tall islander shook his head and said, "No joy there either, boss. The uniforms went up and down Braid Road, to the little coffee shop and set up a hub at the entrance to the park, but nothing."

"We are pinning our hopes on two young stable boys being interested by a shopping trolley," Mackay said.

"Not very hopeful, is it, sir?" Hunter asked.

"But we'll get our forensics tomorrow," Inglis added. "I think Jane, rather than Rachael should take charge of the stable hands' interviews and co-ordinate the results. MIT have special skill sets."

"Of course, I'll give you the addresses as soon as I get them, Sergeant Renwick." Rachael beamed at Jane.

Inglis was surprised at the swift co-operation given to Jane by Rachael Anderson. What was going on between those two? Hadn't he seen Jane just wink at Rachael?

Chapter Seventeen

Jamie stood up suddenly after dinner and smiled at Frankie. He helped clear the table but left Frankie and Donna to wash the dishes while he jogged upstairs and changed into what he called his work clothes.

He always wore the same thing when he went to work at night: black trousers, a black jacket with a hood that he could hide behind, if necessary, and new black shoes. He made a point of wearing his shoes one size too small so that, if his footprints were found in a place where they ought not to have been, the police would not be looking for him, because the prints would be the wrong size. Jamie was delighted with his cleverness in this regard.

Jamie was stopped on the doorstep as he left. Frankie grabbed his arm.

"What the fuck, Jamie? Please don't do this. It's a really bad idea," Frankie said. "You know if you go out on the rob and get caught, you'll end up in the big house with your pop. Don't be an arse."

"I need to get out, Frankie."

"I know. You're bummed about not having Linda here at Christmas. Well, think how I feel about Harry not getting home. My bro is stuck out in Afghanistan, in danger, at least Linda is just going to her Mam's."

"But I thought Linda and I were tight, an item, like you and Donna. Getting put off by her is just pants. That's why I need to get out. I thought I'd dress properly just in case I see an opportunity. I might only go for a walk and see the Christmas lights in the big houses."

"Aye, right, sure an' you will. Jamie Thomson, the well-known Christmas lights fancier. You suit yourself, but if you get caught on the rob, don't call me." Frankie closed the door on Jamie and went through to watch *Corrie* on television with Donna.

***

Jamie walked up West Mains Road to the corner and turned left into Mayfield Road. Some of the big houses only had Christmas trees in the windows but others had lights on trees and bushes in their gardens too. Those weren't good for him. It made him too obvious when he got caught in the light. Some of the houses looked like they had been made into flats and had several trees lighting up different windows. Did some people have more than one Christmas tree? Jamie wondered about that. Maybe they did. He'd only ever had one Christmas tree in any place he'd lived.

He crossed the street and walked quietly down Wilton Road. More nice houses. Big houses. Little children playing. He didn't want to take presents from little children, that would be right nasty.

Then he noticed a house opposite him. It was a big house but with no lights showing at all. Completely in darkness. It looked deserted. Jamie swaggered across the road acting as if he belonged and opened the gate. It creaked. It seemed very loud, but he thought that might just be because the street was so quiet.

He stood, waiting to see if the noise of the gate attracted any attention. There was none. There was a big flash car and an old white van in the driveway. Odd combination. He moved silently up the path. These bloody shoes were far too tight and pinching his toes. Then he peered in through the window only to find a face staring back at him with an emotionless, disinterested stare.

The face started when it saw him. Jamie jumped and then he stopped still. His plans did not include being seen. This thin face with long blond hair was one he almost recognised. But he couldn't put a name to the face. She wore a bright pink crushed velvet outfit. Then Jamie recognised the face. He was shocked. His heart flipped and it was obvious to him that the face recognised him too. Jamie couldn't tell who was more surprised.

He watched as her expression changed to betray the fact that she knew him too. They stood staring at each other. He saw recognition flit across the face. The tall man from the showroom, who had been interested in the limousine, looked quite different now. Jamie heard him scream suddenly and saw him run back from the window.

Jamie stumbled backwards then turned on his heels and ran. What was it all about? Shit! She, he had seen him. Bugger it! Nobody was meant to see Jamie, and nobody was meant to notice him and absolutely, definitely nobody was meant to recognise him, in his work clothes like this. Shit, shit, shit.

Jamie pulled the gate open. Fuck, it really made a loud screeching noise. The man reached his front door. Jamie heard him call after him, but he ran. He ran away down Wilton Road into Mayfield Road. People at the bus-stop noticed him as he ran past. Piss. He turned into his own street and wiggled his door keys out of his pocket as he approached the house. Rushed in the door and looked into see Frankie and Donna.

"I was never out. I was with you all night."

He ran up the stairs, changed into causal clothes and tumbled back downstairs and threw himself into a large comfy chair.

"Shall I get us all a beer?" Jamie asked breathlessly.

Chapter Eighteen

Inglis made sure the morning briefing started promptly at eight o'clock. He noticed that Mel looked particularly bleary eyed. She must not be a morning person. He frowned at Bear who was still eating his second bacon roll but at least Jane Renwick looked smart, he thought she always did. She had been a good addition to MIT, but he couldn't help thinking that no matter how good the team, unless they found this body, getting a conviction would be an uphill struggle. A murder conviction without a body was always difficult to achieve.

He smiled and listened quietly while Mackay called the team to order and handed the meeting over to him.

"Thanks, DCI Mackay. DC Myerscough, have you got any results back from forensics?"

"Oh yes, sir. And I think you will find it surprising."

"Well, don't keep us in suspense, young Myerscough," Hunter said.

"The man Bear and I found is a woman."

"What?" Hunter exclaimed.

"Two DCs both see a corpse and cannot tell that it is the body of a woman! Unbelievable." Inglis glowered at Tim. "This is why we need MIT, DS Renwick, to tell the men from the women."

"To be fair, sir, the corpse looked like a male. And the blood work revealed that the victim had been taking transgender hormone therapy, female to male, but of course, although this allows the person to develop secondary characteristics associated with being male, it doesn't change the individual's DNA."

"It's disgusting, that's what it is," Inglis growled.

"I'm just glad I wasn't born with gender dysphoria, I'd be

the ugliest woman in the world," Bear said.

"You're not that gorgeous as a man," Tim joked.

"I can't tell you how glad I am that you feel that way."

"Oh, don't get me on to queers and gays either. That is quite bad enough, but this is fundamentally against nature," Inglis said.

He noticed Rachael glance at Jane and shrug. He wondered what that was all about.

"What difference does it make to you, sir?" Tim asked. "I mean, if you're not affected by the issues of gender dysphoria, why would you want other people to suffer unnecessarily?"

"It's unnatural, it's disgusting. That's why it should matter to all of us," Inglis said. He was getting quite red in the face trying to look around the room for support and Tim was beginning to enjoy himself.

"Unnatural? Good Lord! Flying might be considered unnatural, but I enjoy going on holiday," Tim said.

"Computers are hardly the most natural things in the world, but I'm grateful to Alan Turing that I don't have to do calculations or write each report out by hand," Hunter commented.

Inglis growled and Tim continued his report.

"You see, sir, while the transgender hormone therapy cannot undo the effects of a person's first puberty, it can help with developing secondary sex characteristics associated with a different gender and that can relieve some or all of the distress and discomfort associated with gender dysphoria, and so can help the person to "pass" or be seen as the gender they identify with. Why would you want anybody to suffer if they don't have to?" Tim asked.

"And the murder is no less wicked because of this," Hunter said.

"Nor any less important," Tim added.

"I suppose that, at least, is true," Inglis said grudgingly.

"But that's not the only surprise," Tim said.

"What else have you got for us, young Myerscough?" Hunter asked.

"Forensics found a trail of blood and what looked to them

like the tracks of a shopping trolley heading towards the fields. The ground was quite hard, but they think there must have been some weight in the trolley. The blood dripped mostly between the tracks as if the victim's blood was dribbling from his body."

"Good! So where did it lead us?" Hunter asked.

"Not far, it stopped about a quarter of the way into the field. Forensics could not tell if that was because the body was drained or because the assailant had stopped to put the body in something. The report says it certainly looked as if the trolley had stopped there because of the pressure marks."

"The latter would seem more likely. The body isn't going to suddenly be drained, young Myerscough."

"True, boss. But there is another thing, the DNA taken from the dried blood spatters of your victim all those years ago, show they were also female, boss. I doubt the person would have had full re-assignment surgery so long ago, but as you and your brother both thought the person was male, they probably identified as such and may have had some treatment."

"Fuck! So, there might well be a connection."

"Yes, boss. And if that is so, I doubt these two victims that we know about are the only ones," Jane said.

Chapter Nineteen

Tim suggested to Bear that they go to the Golf Tavern for a beer. As it was in Morningside, it was mutually inconvenient from their homes and, as it was the other side of the city from their station, they were less likely to be recognised. Mel, Jane and Rachael decided to join the boys, but Nadia and Colin had to get back to their families and Angus was playing five-a-side football.

Tim went up to the bar to get the first round.

"Crisps and nuts too please," Mel called over.

Tim came back carrying four pints and a large white wine for Jane.

"So, what about your twenty-first century leader, DCI Inglis, Jane?" Tim pulled the bags of crisps and nuts out of his pockets and threw a packet of pork scratchings to Bear.

"His views are so bloody primitive, he's an embarrassment. Can you imagine what he'd be like if he knew Rache and I were an item? I'd never hear the end of it."

"It's people like that who cause suicides amongst the LGBTQ community," Rachael said.

"Aye, but what we have here isn't suicide. By all accounts what Tim and Bear saw was the result of a vicious attack and murder," Mel said.

"Inglis doesn't have a very high opinion of local police teams, does he?" Rachael said.

"Inglis doesn't have a high opinion of much apart from himself, as far as I've heard. He was abominably rude about me and my dad."

"I hate to say it, Tim, but your dad might have deserved some of the grief. But you don't," Bear said.

"Of course, Tim doesn't deserve Inglis's vitriol, Bear, but

neither does anyone else he was aiming his venom at today," Rachael agreed.

"Jane, were you saying that if these two deaths are connected, there must surely be other victims?"

"Yes, I can't see there only being two murders thirty years apart."

"I agree with Jane. The two attacks we know about can't be the only ones," Mel said.

"Why don't we show him just how wrong he is? But how on earth would we find out about other victims?"

"I think our investigations must start with another drink. My round." Jane stood up and walked to the bar.

Chapter Twenty

When you see something traumatic at a young age, it never really leaves you.

I have been to dozens of murder scenes and witnessed many post-mortems as an adult. I would be hard pushed to tell you the names of the victims, although I could tell you how they were killed, when, where and by whom. I remember the assailants and for how long I got them put away, but not much more of the details.

However, that first death still haunts me. I felt the body, looked for a pulse and saw my brother covered in the man's blood. Even now, when Fraser and I talk at Christmas time, we often comment that this year is better than that year, the year we found the corpse.

It is good to have someone to share it with, to talk about it. Apart from Fraser, nobody knows how I feel. It is my secret, my nightmare and my guess is, it gives him nightmares too.

I wake up, suddenly, startled, covered in sticky sweat that feels like the blood. I try to rub it off on the sheets. I need to shower it away in a long cool shower while I regain some feeling of calm. Meera will wake, come through, ask me what the matter is. She is so gentle, kind and understanding. But this is too ridiculous. How can I tell her that I am haunted by the secret of a dead body I saw thirty years ago when, as a pathologist, corpses are her business, her stock in trade?

I don't tell her. I just say it was a bad dream, or I am uncomfortably hot under the covers or I am sorry I woke her. These are all true. I do not lie to her; I just don't share my secret or tell her the whole truth.

And now there is more I cannot tell her. Another secret I will not share with her, at least not yet.

Chapter Twenty-One

Frankie and Donna stared at Jamie. He was panting and gasping for breath. Frankie had told Donna what he was doing and neither of them liked it.

"Just a thought, cuz, but if you were never out and always here, where were you and what were you doing?" Frankie asked.

"On my bed, wanking. Thinking about Linda and how we won't be together at Christmas."

"Lovely. I suppose you got caught and want us to lie for you?"

"Nah, not at all. In fact, I didn't do anything. Well, not much."

"Could you stop talking gibberish and tell us what happened? You flew in here as if the pigs were after you."

"Everybody knows pigs can't fly." Jamie grinned. "I don't think you'll believe what I'm going to tell you anyway. No way will you believe what I saw."

"Probably not. But try us."

"Remember the man who was interested in the limo, Frankie?"

"Aye."

"I was standing in his garden."

"How do you know where he lives?" Donna asked.

"What the fuck were you doin' in his garden, cuz?"

"I don't know where he lives. Well, I do now, but that doesnae matter."

"It clearly does matter from the way you came fleeing in here," Donna said.

"I was havin' a wee scout about and went down Wilton Road. Nice hames down there."

"Aye, but get on with it, Jamie," Frankie said.

"Well they're all lit up wi' fairy lights an' the like and that's not good for business."

"For bein' on the rob, you mean, cuz."

"Stop interrupting, Frankie. Then I see this one big house all in darkness. I thinks, 'I'll go an' take a wee look over there. So, I crosses the road and pushes open the gate. It squeaks really loud. I mean horribly loud, but nothing moves. Nobody seems to notice. So, I creep up the path an' peer in the window to see if there's owt worth taking. And what do you think I see?"

"The man from the showroom," Donna said in a bored tone of voice.

"Aye, but he's wearing a long blond wig and a bright pink top and he's right at the window staring back at me. Now isn't that weird?"

"Nah, it's not really. Think about it, it's Christmas. He's maybe going to a fancy-dress party and standing at the window waiting for a taxi," Donna said.

"I never thought of that, of course," Jamie said.

"I would guess that the poor man thought it was weird that the 'gentleman' from the car showroom was all dressed in black and peering in his living room window, when he hadn't given us an address. Did you think of that, Jamie?" Frankie asked. "You are a right chump. You know that? You've probably lost us that sale."

Chapter Twenty-Two

Before the next morning's briefing, Tim and Jane knocked on the door of Hunter's office.

"Do you have a moment before we go through, boss?" Tim asked.

"Yes, of course. What are you two up to?"

"As if, boss."

"Tim, you forget, I have known you a long time and known your father longer. On top of that, Jane is looking decidedly shifty and uncomfortable. You two have something on your minds. Probably something you want me to smooth over with the esteemed DCIs, so just spit it out."

"Funny you should mention it, boss. Remember I suggested yesterday that if the two deaths were linked, they were probably not the only ones?"

"Yes, Jane. Go on."

"Well we were chatting about that yesterday and we all agreed."

"Who is 'we all'?"

"The usual suspects. Us, Rache, Bear and Mel."

"And what did you lot agree on?"

"Well, boss, a lot of people who are transgender, or even pre-op transgender, or gay move away from their home areas to get away from cruelty, discrimination and start new lives," Tim said. "So, if they subsequently disappeared, many of them might not be reported. Their family and friends might not even know which part of the country they were in."

"Surely they would have friends within their community wherever they had moved to?"

"Yes, but might they not just think they had moved again?"

"It's possible. But even if those friends thought it was strange, the police are hardly a trusted service to the communities transgender people inhabit," Jane said. "Not all the disappearances would be likely to be reported."

"But some of them would be. I think we need to start with those. We could look back over the last thirty years at the reports of disappeared people and see if Jane is right. Find out if these are not the only two instances."

"I would also like to find the body that you saw. We might have a chance of doing that," Hunter said.

"Alright, Tim, you make your point at the briefing. I don't want Jane to incur any further wrath from DCI Inglis. I want to concentrate on a plan to find the body, but I'll back you up if necessary."

***

When the briefing started, it was clear that DCI Mackay was bristling from having to hand over briefing of his team to Inglis, again. However, it was Inglis who called the meeting to order and asked for an update from Hunter.

"I have arranged that DC Angus McKenzie and DC Rachael Anderson go today to interview the stable hands that we still need to speak to, sir."

"Can't one interviewer do both?"

"One lad is in Peebles in the borders and the other is at home over the bridge in Dunfermline, sir. It seemed more time efficient to have separate interviewers."

"I can see that, DI Wilson, yes. What else is on the go?"

"I want to find that corpse that Myerscough and Zewedu saw. I plan to have DS Colin Reid and DC Nadia Chan follow the blood trail as far as possible and then see what lies ahead within a reasonable distance."

"Good. It might well be worth re-visiting the site, Colin," Mackay said.

"We will, sir. I thought we might also look again at the photographs of the scene so we can compare."

"Ask Sam Hutchens for a copy and take them with you," Mackay said.

"DS Renwick and I will be co-ordinating, of course," Inglis

said.

"Of course, sir," Tim said to Inglis. "Would you like DC Zewedu and me to follow up on DS Renwick's idea that these two victims may not be the only ones?"

"Yes, yes, splendid. Report directly to DS Renwick, whatever you find."

"Of course. Will DS Renwick require to supervise the lads, sir?" Hunter asked.

"It would be for the best, DI Wilson. MIT in charge, and all that."

Hunter winked at Tim.

Chapter Twenty-Three

Sir Peter enjoyed waking in his own bed. He found it strange that he could have breakfast when he wanted, and he could eat whatever he felt like. More than that, now he was home, Kenneth and Alice acted as if nothing had happened. They cared for him as they always had, ignoring his fall from grace.

He liked showering in private, choosing his own clothes, drinking proper coffee and reading the paper without some unwashed illiterate looking over his shoulder asking what it said.

This morning he was sitting eating breakfast when Ailsa and Gillian wandered into the dining room. He didn't like the green patch at the front of Gillian's hair. It looked ridiculous in a woman of that age. What was Tim thinking? What was she thinking? She wasn't a child, for goodness sake.

"Hi Dad. How are you this morning?"

"Good morning, Sir Peter,"

"Good morning ladies. I thought I'd get Kenneth to drive me into town. I'm going to go shopping for Christmas gifts. Do you want to come with me?"

"How can we come with you, Dad? You might see something for us!" Ailsa laughed.

Sir Peter didn't want to admit that going into the city alone was daunting. He had been in such a structured environment for so long that now the loud noises of real life startled him. He also found it frightening being amongst the crowds of people moving this way and that, also the hustle and bustle of people pushing past each other in the German Christmas market was intimidating. It was all so unfamiliar and, because he was not used to it now, he would rather have company, minders, carers. He had no intention of saying that.

He didn't realise that he had become quiet as he waited for

a response, but he saw a strange expression pass over Ailsa's face. He wondered if she had understood his issues. No way he would push her to come with him. He had never shown weakness and had no intention of starting now.

"But, if you would like some company, Dad, you could just tell us to go away for five minutes if you wanted to buy for one of us. Would that work?"

"It would work for me," Gillian said. "I still have a few presents to buy. A trip into town would be useful for me. We could have lunch in the Christmas market."

"I was thinking more of lunch in the Number One in the Balmoral. I think it has a Michelin star now."

"Oh gosh, Dad. That would be lovely, but we would really have to dress properly for that and dressing for dining and dressing for shopping are not the same thing at all. Why don't we compromise and go around the corner to the Alain Roux Brasserie for lunch?"

Sir Peter smiled. How typical of Ailsa to find a compromise that suited nobody but was agreeable to everyone.

"I'll just finish my coffee and then I'll go and speak to Kenneth. If I tell him we'll leave in thirty minutes, will that give you ladies time to finish breakfast?"

Ailsa looked at Gillian. "Make it forty minutes, Dad."

"Yes please. Forty minutes would be great," Gillian said.

***

Sir Peter asked Kenneth to drop them at the West End of Princes Street. This would allow them to start their search for gifts in Frasers and walk east visiting other department stores like Debenhams and Jenner's and the stalls at the Christmas market and then walk through the Waverley Mall, before they went for lunch. Sir Peter asked him to return for them at three o'clock. He was confident he would manage being out in town for those few hours, until he stepped out of the car.

A young man running for a bus bumped into him, a baby was screaming, and the traffic raced around the corner from Lothian Road into Princes Street. It was noisy, unpredictable, and unfamiliar. Sir Peter held the car door open for Ailsa and Gillian and then took Ailsa by the arm as they moved towards Fraser's windows to look at the display.

"Is this too much for you, Dad?" Ailsa whispered.

"No, no not at all," he said. He was sure she knew he was lying. He garbled on to cover his embarrassment. "I just wanted you to see these fine handbags. What do you think?"

He saw her smile at him, and they walked together into the store.

"Let's go and have a look, shall we, Gillian?"

"Yes, I love the perfume departments. They smell so lovely."

Sir Peter was grateful to Ailsa who made sure that she and Gillian stayed close to him, except for the few occasions that he asked to be left alone. He did not want them to see the gifts he bought for them or Tim. They all stopped for a warm glass of glühwein in the German market and he relaxed enough to buy some decorations, ham, sausage and a large Stollen cake.

He noticed that Gillian spoke to the stall holders in fluent German. He recalled that Tim had told him that she was an excellent linguist.

The journey along Princes Street was slow and far more unnerving that Sir Peter had ever expected. His time in prison had affected him more than he was willing to admit.

Then he saw him. Sir Peter and the girls were wandering through the perfume counters in Jenner's when Sir Peter saw the tall, thin man with the walking stick and the limp. He recognised him immediately and did not want to be noticed by him.

Sir Peter dodged behind a display stand.

"What are you doing, Dad?"

"I would like to leave, now. May we go over to the Waverley Market? Right now? We should do that."

"Yes, of course, Sir Peter. Whatever you want. Follow me." Gillian cut a swathe through the other shoppers to make a quick exit.

But he turned just a second too late. He caught the man's eye and saw him raise his cane in acknowledgement.

Sir Peter followed Gillian out of the store. He was glad when the lights turned green for pedestrians right away. He held tightly on to Ailsa as they crossed the road. He looked back, but the man was not there.

He tried to act normally as they walked around the underground Waverley Market. He bought two bottles of good malt whisky. One for Kenneth and one for himself. When he heard Ailsa and Gillian talking about Scottish gins, he bought a bottle of Edinburgh Gin and a bottle of the Caorunn raspberry flavoured gin before going into the perfume shop and choosing a large bottle of Marc Jacob's Daisy Eau So Fresh that he thought Gillian would like.

Ailsa and Gillian darted into different stores to complete their Christmas shopping, but he noticed that one or other of them always stayed with him. Maybe he had misjudged Gillian. What business was it of his how she did her hair?

Finally, they arrived at the Brasserie. There were only two tables left, one by the door to the kitchen and one in the window. Sir Peter uncharacteristically chose the one away from the window. He did not want the man to see them if he passed. He did not want him to cause a scene. He could not be bothered making polite conversation. He did not want to end up on the front pages of the papers, for all the wrong reasons, again.

Chapter Twenty-Four

Angus set off from the station. He was pleased he had been charged with interviewing the stable hand in Peebles while Rachael was heading north to Dunfermline in Fife. He liked the road to Peebles and planned to stop in at the Peebles Hydro to pick up a voucher for afternoon tea. He would give that to his godmother for Christmas and bring her down to make use of it in the spring when the weather was fine, and they could enjoy a walk in the grounds too.

He arrived at the stable hand's home just before lunchtime. It was a neat little bungalow with fake snow on the windows and a small Christmas tree with flashing lights on a table in the bay window. Angus rang the doorbell and a young woman answered the door.

"I'm looking for Mr Rowan Sprigg," Angus said. "Have I found the right house?"

"No. But you have found the right house for Miss Rowan Sprigg. Will that do?"

The detective's face turned as red as his hair. "I'm so sorry, of course. Are you a stable hand at the riding school in Liberton?" he asked. He noticed the long scar down her cheek but didn't comment on it.

"Yes, I am. I live in mostly at the stables. I'm home to have the Christmas holidays with my folks but they're not in. I don't suppose it matters, after all, I'm over twenty-one. You must be the cop. They phoned to say you'd be coming. I suppose you better come in. Do you want a cuppa or owt?"

"Thank you, yes. A tea would be good."

"Milk and two?"

"Just milk please. I am Detective Constable Angus McKenzie."

"You don't sound like you're from Edinburgh. You from up

north?"

"Yes. Spent most of my life in Lewis."

Angus took a mug of tea from Rowan and searched for a coaster to avoid putting it on to the table.

"Don't worry about the table. It's old and stained already. Mum always says she's going to get a new one, but it's not happened so far."

Angus held his cup.

"Did the officer who phoned you tell you why I was coming to see you?"

"To interview me about a murder. But I didnae do owt like that. I may have pocketed the occasional riding fee or snaffled a coupla bottles a beer, but I never did a murder. I don't care who says I did."

"Oh no. You are not being interviewed as a perpetrator. We wondered if you might have seen anything out of the ordinary. You may have seen something that you didn't even realise was important. So, do you mind me just asking a few questions?"

"Go for it."

Angus put his mug on the carpet and pulled out his notebook. He spent almost an hour questioning Rowan but heard nothing he thought would be useful. However, just as he was leaving, Rowan said something unexpected.

"You know you asked if I saw anybody pushing a shopping trolley across the fields. Well, I didn't. But I did see a buckled Sainsbury's trolley at the side of the path, beside the fields and behind a bush when I was walking down after I finished work. It was disgusting, all brown crusty stuff at the bottom of the trolley and the wheels were covered in grass and muck. It might still be there."

***

Angus got back into his car and called Nadia. He knew she and Colin planned to go to the scene of the crime and follow the blood, so they could just walk a little further and see if the shopping trolley Rowan had spoken about was still there.

***

Rachael was heading out of the city towards Dunfermline. She drove across the Forth Road Bridge and glanced across at the old red rail bridge to her right.

It did not take her long to find the home of Stewart Brown. It was a top floor flat. Rachael rang the bell and a harassed, dumpy little woman came to the door with a howling toddler hanging onto her dress.

"Come in, lass," the woman said. Then she picked up the child and shouted in his face. "If you don't shut the fuck up, I'll throw you out of the window. Do you hear me?" She turned again to Rachael smiled and spoke in a soft voice. "He's teething poor little mite. It's our Stew you're wanting to see, I think."

"Yes please. Do you think it's a good idea to shout at the baby?" Racheal asked tentatively.

"Don't have kids do you, dear? Well, you come back to me when you've got three under ten in a two bedroomed flat and your good for nothing teenager comes back to sponge off you at Christmas. You tell me then that you don't shout."

Rachael walked in the direction that she pointed and opened the door into a small living room with a large plastic Christmas tree in the corner. There were Christmas cards strung up all over the place and tinsel around the pictures. A teenage boy was draped over one end of the couch. He stared at the television while he played a computer game.

"You've met me maw, I heard. Fresh out of charm school she is. What do the cops want with me, anyway? I've no' done anything." He never took his eyes off the screen until Rachael sat down at the other end of the couch.

"This will be faster if you're not playing that game while we speak."

He sat up, looked at her and grinned. "You're bonny."

"I'm spoken for."

She asked all the introductory questions and then sat back a bit.

"You must get up pretty early to feed the horses. Did you

79

see anything out of the ordinary that day?"

"What sort of thing do you mean?"

"Well did you see anybody you don't usually see or see someone doing something unusual?"

Rachael waited as Stewart thought for a moment then he looked back at the television and she could tell his attention was wavering. She saw the remote on the table in front of him. Reached out and switched the screen off.

"Fuck's sake. That'll no' save my game."

"It won't harm your game. I've only turned the screen off. Now, could you just think about anything unusual you saw."

"Well, Rowan was away earlier than me, so I had to do all the feeding, but I didn't have time to clean out all the stalls before I left. Mrs Bossy Boots the owner wanted me to, but it was too much to do. I got three of them done and then I had to leave for my train."

"It must have been quiet with nobody else about early in the morning," Rachael said.

"It always is quite quiet. But I did hear a loud scream. I looked about, but I couldn't see anything."

"When would that be?"

"I'm not sure. I don't wear a watch when I'm doing the stables and my hands were dirty, so I didn't look at my phone. If my hands were that dirty, I must have been doing the mucking out. It would have been after seven, probably nearer eight o'clock."

"When you finally left for Christmas and went for your train, did you see anything different from usual?"

"Nah, not that I remember. There was a broken, dirty old shopping trolley and a couple of plastic carrier bags caught in the hedge, but nothing unusual."

"So had the shopping trolley and the bags been there for a while? Had you noticed them before, Stewart."

"I don't go out that much. I don't get paid a lot and I have to pay for me digs an' that. I don't remember if they were there the last time, I walked down the lane, but it's not very surprising to see that kind of trash, is it?"

"You said the shopping trolley was dirty and broken. How

was it broken?"

"I think some of the wheels were off."

"Do you remember how many?"

"Maybe one or two, I suppose."

"And Stewart, what part of the trolley was dirty?"

"All of it. It was manky. Especially the carrying bit where you would put your shopping. That bit was all dirty with mud and yuck."

"Could that mud have been blood, Stewart?"

"What? No! There was nobody near it. Nothing in it. And there was too much of it to be blood. It had to be mud." The lad screwed up his face and pursed his lips.

Rachael looked at him and realised he had never thought about the dirt being anything but mud until that moment. She decided not to dwell on this further as it would probably give him nightmares. She thanked Stewart for his time and stood up. She handed him back the remote control.

"Thanks. I only saw one old bloke on my way along the lane. An old man with a white van. He was shoving a big thing into the back. But I didn't see what it was. And there can be the odd person in the lane. At this time of year, it was probably a Chrissie pressie, I thought. Anyway, I was in a hurry, so I didn't stop to help."

"Stewart, what did the man look like?"

"Old, dark hair, quite tall. I don't know."

"What time was that?"

Stewart thought for a minute. "Must have been about ten, maybe eleven o'clock. I wanted to get the train about noon, and I hate being late."

"If I sent a police artist here to meet with you, would you be willing to work on creating a picture of the man for me?"

"What's in it for me?"

"I won't do you for failing to help with my enquiries," Rachael said.

"That's a made-up thing." Stewart grinned at her. "But go for it, I'll help best I can. What did the man do?"

"I don't know yet, but I'd like to find out."

Rachael left Dunfermline and spoke to Hunter on her hands

free to get the police artist to Stewart Brown's flat as soon as possible.

Chapter Twenty-Five

Frankie noticed that Jamie was not at all keen to go to the showroom that morning. He and Donna almost had to push him out of the house and when the girls were dropped off at their nursery, Frankie thought Jamie was going to drive straight home.

"Don't be an arse, Jamie. We've got to go to work. If the man comes in, I'll speak to him and you go to hide in the garage with Mark and Shug," Frankie said.

"Aye okay. I'm going out to see my pop this afternoon anyway."

"That's good. Uncle Ian will be glad to see you. Are you going to tell him about the dead body we didn't see?"

"Aye, nothing like a story about a corpse to cheer up the old man while he's in the big house, is there?" Donna asked."Shut it, Frankie. There goes the phone, I'll get it. Fuck, he's here, I'm off." Jamie scuttled into the garage to speak to Mark and left Frankie to talk to the thin man from the previous day.

Frankie watched as Donna walked slowly back to the reception desk and answered the ringing phone. He thought, not for the first time, that it was a good thing she was there.

"Good morning, sir, how nice to see you again, did you want to take a better look at the limousine?" Frankie asked.

"Yes indeed, and I wondered if I might have a talk with the other young gentleman. I think we may have had a misunderstanding yesterday."

"He's busy right now. Can I give him a message?"

"That's alright. I'll wait. And can you arrange for me to take this car out for a test drive."

"I can do that. Give me a minute." Frankie was about to turn around when he saw Jamie drive away from the showroom. Piss. Frankie still did not have a driving license, that meant he would have to get Mark to clean himself up and take the man out.

"Jamie can be a right arse sometimes," Mark said. "Aye give me ten minutes, Frankie and I'll clean up, shuffle the cars and take the bloke out for a run."

"Thanks Mark. I'll get Donna to make him a coffee and he can have that and wait until you're ready."

"I hope he buys the bloody thing."

"Me too. He says he needs it for his business. He runs a funeral place and it's their busy time."

"Lovely. Okay, Frankie. Give me ten."

Frankie went back to the customer to explain the test drive would be in about ten to fifteen minutes. Frankie was glad when the man accepted the offer of a coffee and walked back to the limousine with him to discuss the dimensions and features of the car. Then Frankie was surprised. The man asked if there might be a finance deal available. Frankie had never come across a funeral director who couldn't pay cash, but he nodded and agreed that they did have finance packages available.

When Mark came out, Frankie noticed he had cleaned up nicely. He moved the limousine out of the showroom, onto the forecourt and out to the street. Frankie waved them off and took the mugs, still half full of coffee to the kitchen to wash them.

"Strange, that man says he runs a funeral place, so he must be loaded, but he asked about finance, Donna."

"That's not so strange. Lots of rich folk are canny with their money."

"I suppose so. I hope he buys that thing now, especially wi' Jamie being such a chump."

She kissed him on the cheek and said, "oh, your cousin is one of a kind, I'll give you that."

***

When Mark and the man came back, he handed the keys to Mark. "I think that will do nicely, but I want to think about it," he said. "I'll be back if I'm going to take it. Will the other young man be in then?"

Mark shrugged. "Frankie will Jamie be in later today or tomorrow?"

"Who knows? Who cares?"

"Well I don't know, but I do care," the man replied.

"Sorry, I didn't see you there, sir. I think Jamie will be back soon, but at this time of year, it is difficult to be sure exactly when," Frankie said. "I hope we'll see you later, anyway." He shook the man's hand and watched him limp down the road leaning on his stick.

Chapter Twenty-Six

Nadia and Colin arrived at the site that the corpse had been found. Crime scene tape isolated the area but there was a group of teenagers standing discussing what they had heard on social media. The detectives stood back, unnoticed, to listen.

"It was a lad who had all his blood pour out into the river. There was such a lot of blood all over, you could practically swim in it," said the tallest boy.

"And then he disappeared. Aliens took him," the girl said.

"I don't think it was aliens, I heard he was eaten by vampires. They need the blood," the tallest boy said.

Colin nodded at Nadia. "Time to move along now, people. Nothing new to see here," he said.

"Who made you the boss of us, man?" the tallest boy asked.

"The queen," Colin said sourly. "We're police."

The kids made to run. Nadia blocked their way. "Do you come along here often?" she asked.

"That's a question folk don't ask now," the girl said. She grinned an impish smile at Nadia but noticed the detective didn't return her humour. She went on more seriously. "Not often, but there's nowt to do right now, so we come to look at the horses, sometimes."

"Did you see anything the day this happened?" Nadia pointed to the police sign by the edge of the tape.

"Nah, it was right early. I was in bed." The tallest boy nudged the girl.

"Aye, but mind we saw that van when we came out to meet Matt that morning. We were earlier than usual so we could go and get holly for the Christmas tables," the girl said.

"I dunno. Was it that white one up the lane?"

"Aye, mind we'd never seen a car, or anything stopped up

there and that man, he was pulling something into the back of it. Remember, Matt?"

"Oh aye. I remember."

"What was the man putting into the back of the van?" Nadia asked.

"I didnae see. It was big. But couldn't see much because it was in a big black plastic bag or a towel or whatever. Must have been a Christmas present or something like that."

"Did it seem heavy?" Nadia asked the tallest boy.

"Well, aye, he was puffing trying to get it in. I offered to help, but he barked at me, so we just moved along."

"Did he have an accent?"

"He was loud but not like foreign."

"What did he look like?" Colin asked.

"He looked taller than me," said the tallest boy. "Course he was in the back of the van, so it was hard to tell."

Colin saw he was about the same height as the tallest boy was.

"And he was skinny," the girl said. "Sorta feeble looking."

"And thin, quite thin," Matt said.

"Would you be able to help a police artist draw a picture of him?" Nadia asked.

"Fuck off! Would we like be famous and be in the papers and have to go to court and everything?" the tallest boy said.

"I doubt it, but it might help with our investigations. Could you all be in the same house, so you could work together with the artist?"

"Aye, they'll come to my house. They always do," the girl said.

Colin and Nadia took a note of their names and addresses and watched the kids wander away towards the Liberton end of Hermiston of Braid. They were chatting excitedly about this new-found diversion.

Nadia called for a police artist to meet with the kids and did not understand desk sergeant Charlie Middleton's anguished cry of 'not another one!' Then she and Colin began to look at the scene carefully themselves.

"Look, there, the light marks of that shopping trolley,

Colin."

"The ground is extremely hard, because of the cold. So, I'm surprised there are any marks at all."

"Yes, but the ground by the river will be a bit softer because of the water, and I guess if the body was transferred into it, the trolley would be quite heavy, not just because of the body but the mud and water would add to the weight too."

"It would suddenly get heavy. Look, there, the wheel marks are much more obvious there by the river," Colin said. He pointed towards the river and showed Nadia the area he was looking at.

"Yes, we're lucky it hasn't rained because maybe we can follow the blood. Oh dear, look the tracks seem to run out quite quickly," she said.

"True, but to be honest, the morning dew will have diluted the blood, even if there isn't much rain. I think the flattened grass might give us our best indication of the direction the body was taken. Shall we see what we can see?"

The two of them wandered across the grass in the field, following what they could see, slowly and methodically.

"Crossing the field must have been an afterthought, because it would have been easier for the assailant to drive up to the end of the road and take the body in the trolley that way," Nadia said. "This must have been a nightmare with grass choking the wheels and blood dripping through the wires."

"He must have seen Tim and Bear come along and had to change his disposal plans."

"Horrible thought, just disposing of a body in a shopping trolley. Is it more likely he saw them leaving the park, because remember, Tim said the body was quite cold?"

"Yes, whoever the murderer was he wouldn't want to risk making himself obvious to any witnesses, so perhaps he went around to the lane over there. The lie of the land would obscure him from the scene of the crime," Nadia said.

Colin held the fencing on the other side of the field so that Nadia could get over it.

"Can you see the trolley?" she asked. "Angus's witness mentioned it and so did those kids we spoke to."

"I don't see it. We should take a walk up and down here and see if we find it." Then Colin shouted. "It's there! I see it, behind that gorse bush. Someone has tried to hide it."

"But not very effectively. I'll call the station and get some uniforms with a van to pick it up and get it to forensics." Nadia pulled out her phone and dialled the call. While she and Colin waited for the uniformed officers to get there, they got very cold and swung their arms across their bodies to try to warm themselves up.

"It's hard to believe the city is just over there, isn't it? You could be right out in the country here. I'll need a hot green tea when we get back to the station, I think," Nadia said.

"A coffee for me. I wonder if the boss has some of his good coffee, I could charm from him."

"Good luck with that."

Chapter Twenty-Seven

Jamie waited in line to go through security. He submitted to the body search and put all his valuables, including his phone, into a locker. He just kept a few pounds in coins to buy him and his pop a coffee and a snack from the machines.

He chose a table in the far corner so that he could chat properly with his pop and be overheard by fewer people. Jamie noticed that the visiting room smelled of a heady combination of disinfectant and furniture polish. It caught him at the back of his throat and made him gag. He knew that one of the jobs inmates could get was cleaner of all the public areas in the prison. He thought this must be quite a good job because you could get out of your cell and find out what was going on. He also knew that his pop was aware of anything important that was going on, whether or not he was assigned a cleaning job.

Jamie watched the prisoners enter the room wearing their brightly coloured strips to distinguish them from the visitors. Should he tell his pop about the man who was interested in the limo? Should he tell him about seeing him later in the dress?

Jamie stood up as Ian walked towards him. They shook hands then hugged briefly.

"No Frankie today?"

"No Pop. Frankie and Donna are minding the showroom. The girls are at nursery, so you're just stuck with me."

"Not at all, son. Get us a coffee and a packet of cheese and onion, will you?"

Jamie went to the machines and chose two white coffees, two Mars bars and a bag of cheese and onion crisps.

"You can fleece poor old Irish Mick out of another phone with those chocolate bars."

"Aye and I probably will. Has my friend Les been in to see you?"

"Dunno, what does he look like?"

"Ah, well, that all depends," Ian said with a smile. "He's tall and thin and always elegant, but he got into a lot of trouble in here, because he likes to dress up."

"Dress up? It's hardly worth it in here, is it? I mean, you're not going to get a date or go out for a fancy meal."

"You don't really think things through, do you, son? Not all the men here are like us."

"What, you mean they're not all on the rob?"

"Oh God." Ian sighed. "No, son. Not every bloke in here likes lassies. Les likes both lads and lassies and he sometimes dresses like the elegant gent he can be but sometimes, when it suits him, he chooses to wear a wig and a gown or a skirt and high heels. He got a lot of stick in here and not just from the lags. Some of the screws have very old-fashioned prejudices. Especially one called Bernard Inglis. He's a sadist if he doesnae like you."

"You're not prejudiced as long as there's something in it for you, right pop? But surely your pal didn't show himself up like that in here. If he did, he must be mad."

"Well, he had a long sentence, so, the longer you're in for the more difficult it is to hide your true self. He's actually okay, Les, and he's loaded. His son's wee Gerry, great wheels guy, I'm told that's why he wanted a job at our place."

"Your pal never said wee Gerry was his son."

"No, he'd want to suss you out first, without giving too much away. The family runs a funeral parlour and so they tend to buy expensive vehicles for the business. That's a good contact for our business. He lives with his sister and wee Gerry up Wilton Road. Nice houses up there."

"I think I know where he lives, Pop." Jamie told Ian about Les coming into the showroom and then his evening walk and coming face to face with Les through his window.

Ian threw back his head and laughed. "Who was more surprised, you or him?"

"I dunno, Pop. But he came back to the showroom today and I didn't know all this. I had no idea how to explain to him why I was in his garden."

"He probably thought we'd spoken, and I'd told you where he lives. It'll be okay if you just let him think that. And sell him a bloody car, we could do with the money."

The men continued to talk, business and pleasure until the bell rang to end visiting hour. As he got up, Jamie turned to his pop.

"You said he got a long sentence. What did he do?"

Ian shook his head and drew his finger across his neck.

Chapter Twenty-Eight

When Jamie went back to the showroom after the visit, he told Frankie and Donna that his pop had asked after them and sent his love to the girls. Then he explained all his pop had told him about Les.

"Well the man says he's coming back to speak to you, and you better bloody be here," Frankie said. "I'm sick of having to make excuses for you."

"And Mark had to do the test drive cos me and Frankie can't drive," Donna said.

"Aye right, I hear you. I'll be here. I'll even make the coffee now."

"With biscuits," Frankie said. "Oh, and Gerry's back."

"Gerry's back? Where the fuck has he been? And has he phoned his auntie? Do you know he's limousine guy's son?"

"How the hell would I know? Ask him when you take the coffee through."

"Make Gerry a fucking coffee? If I'd been here, he'd be bloody sacked."

"But you weren't here. He was and you're making the fucking coffee."

Jamie grinned at Frankie and wandered to the office to make the coffee. He couldn't think where Gerry could have been or what he had been doing. Jamie also didn't think he would get any sense out of wee Gerry if he asked him, but he would try.

***

Wee Gerry wasn't looking forward to seeing Jamie. It was lucky Jamie had been out when he got in to work. Frankie was much kinder and at least he didn't shout so much. He hoped he didn't get asked any questions. It would be difficult to answer any without outright lies. Would Jamie mind lies? Probably not, unless he found out he'd been lied to.

He looked up from the car engine he was working on and saw Jamie talking to Mark. Jamie had brought coffee. Wee Gerry decided to stay put. Perhaps if he kept his head down, Jamie would not notice him. No such luck.

"Gerry, good to see you. Want a coffee?"

"Aye, thanks, Jamie," he stuttered, and opened his eyes wide in surprise.

"Good. And I want an explanation. Grab a coffee. Come through to the office. We need to talk."

Wee Gerry took a mug of coffee and followed Jamie to the office.

"Is Frankie coming?" he asked Jamie.

"No chance. He's too bloody soft. If I'd been here when you came in today, there's no way I'd have let you back into the garage. You'd have got the sack there and then. I don't care who your pop is."

Jamie held the office door open for wee Gerry and then closed it quietly and firmly behind him. It was unlike him to be so calm. Wee Gerry found that even more scary than shouting Jamie.

"You sit down, Gerry and now tell me what the fuck is going on. How come you don't seem to realise that the opening hours of the garage apply to you as well as to everybody else? And how do you manage to go missing for days at a time? Your Auntie didn't even know where you were. She thought you were here. You're such an arse, Gerry. How come you're here one day and off the next?"

Wee Gerry sat down and waited patiently while Jamie finished his tirade. When the wall of words stopped, he took a sip of his coffee and looked at Jamie.

"You wouldnae believe me if I tellt you."

"Try me. I'm a big boy, not much surprises me. Why do you skip coming in so often? And you never phone in."

"I've got another job."

"You what? I hadnae seen that coming. You've got another fucking job?"

"Well, it's not so much a job as a responsibility. It disnae pay. I help out with Les's funeral place when we're busy. I need to. And sometimes I have to help another guy to make numbers at funerals."

"You what? Look I really don't bloody care. Do you no' think you've got a responsibility to turn up here, and actually do the job that pays you? You could take a day off properly or you could always come to your right job, Gerry?"

Wee Gerry looked across the desk at Jamie and began to cry.

Chapter Twenty-Nine

Hunter rarely left the station early, but today he made an exception. Parvati had a cancellation. One of her students had called off a tutorial, so when he got a call offering him extra time, he jumped at the chance. He enjoyed being with her. It did make him feel a bit guilty. He had never lied to Meera before, but this secret was fun, exciting, and made his heart flutter when he thought about it. It was worth the guilt.

He smiled at Parvati. She was always dressed immaculately and there was no doubt she was a beautiful woman. She turned heads wherever they went. Today they were meeting in the Central Library. He saw she had found a little corner upstairs where they would not be easily noticed. That was clever, he didn't want anybody to overhear them or see them together. It could ruin everything.

When he had finished his session with her, he had learned so much, but how much would he remember? He couldn't practice on his own and he didn't know anybody who would be able or willing to help him. He didn't want to make a fool of himself. He looked nervously at Parvati. His heart skipped a beat with the excitement. She was wonderful.

"I think that's enough for today," she said at the end of their hour. "I'm not sure you could cope with much more of this, could you?"

"No. I am exhausted. That was hard work, and I am so nervous that we will get found out. I'm sure I'm getting an ulcer. My insides turn somersaults every time we meet."

"That sounds really uncomfortable. Are you sure all this deception is worth it?"

"Oh yes, I can't stop seeing you, now. I need you. I'll never manage without you, Parvati. You know that."

He saw her smile up into his eyes. And his stomach flipped again.

***

Hunter left the Central Library as secretively as he had arrived. He crossed the Royal Mile and dodged into Deacon Brodie's. The bar was busy. It was almost always busy, so nobody paid him any attention. He ordered a pint and stood at the bar.

"Any tables upstairs for dinner?" he asked the barman.

"Dunno mate, you'll need to go up and ask them. Take your beer with you. It's no problem."

Hunter climbed up the old staircase at the back of the bar and walked into the restaurant. It was quiet right now, and he was lucky, there were tables left for the evening. He chose to take a table by the window. He called Meera and agreed to meet her in the bar for a drink before dinner. Hunter couldn't remember the last time he had taken Meera out for a meal. He spent so much of his time with Parvati now.

He went back down to the bar and ordered another pint. He stood and slowly drank it at the bar looking around his fellow drinkers. The clientele at Deacon Brodie's was always eclectic. The pub was just across from the High Court in Edinburgh and there were often groups of advocates and solicitors huddled around tables muttering and whispering about their day in court. There were other groups of people, mainly tourists chatting in a variety of languages. Hunter recognised Italian, German and French, but there was a Scandinavian looking group behind him whose language was unfamiliar.

Suddenly, Hunter noticed a face in the pub that he recognised. Or at least at first, he thought it was. There was a tall slim man at the far end of the bar with a loud voice. Hunter thought the group of men around him seemed like sycophants, hanging on his words, laughing at his jokes, and nodding their approval. He heard his voice boom out across the bar. He thought for a moment that it was DCI Arthur Inglis, but then he noticed the face was a little thinner, the man's tone was a

97

little deeper and his language a little rougher. On second glance, it wasn't Inglis, but this man was every bit as self-important. Hunter lingered over his pint because he didn't want to order another drink before Meera arrived, so he watched the people around him enjoying their evenings and observed the familiar looking man in the ambience of the old central city pub.

He did not notice Meera arrive, she caught him by surprise. She approached him from the back and put her arm around his waist.

"You're under arrest, mister," she whispered in his ear.

He turned around and smiled. "Lovely to see you. It seems ages since we've been out."

"It's true. I can't remember the last time I was in this pub. It's always so busy, down here though, do you mind if we just go up to the restaurant? I'd rather have a drink at our table there."

"No problem. We can do that. Shall I lead the way?"

Hunter downed the dregs of his beer and turned to head back to the restaurant. He held his hand out behind him and she took it to stay close to him as they weaved their way through the groups of other drinkers and went upstairs. He held the restaurant door open for her and they were shown to their table right away.

"Oh dear, that waitress looked about twelve. I must be getting old," Hunter said.

"No, you're not getting old, Hunter. You *are* old."

"You meanie." Hunter laughed. "Do you want a gin and tonic?"

"Yes, make it a large one, will you? It's been a long day. I'm going to go to the ladies' room to smarten up before dinner."

"You look good to me. But by all means do that, if it makes you feel better. I'll get the drinks in. Wine with dinner?"

"Yes, please. A nice red."

After they had ordered, Meera began telling Hunter about her day. She had been giving a guest lecture in pathology at The University of Edinburgh Medical School in the morning and already regretted giving out her e-mail address to the students. Parvati did warn me against it, but I thought she was exaggerating the enthusiasm of the students. She wasn't."

"She said you were a big hit."

"You spoke to her? She never said. When did you see her?"

Hunter blushed furiously and, if he could have got away with kicking himself, he would have done. He was incredibly grateful that their starters were served at that point. The scallops were put down in front of him and Meera had chosen the pate. When that waiter left them to their meals, Meera turned to him again.

"When did you say you saw Parvati? My boyfriend with my best friend. That would be a classic romantic drama."

"I didn't. I didn't see her." The lie made him blush again. "We spoke briefly. She meant to call you to say how well you had done and hit my number instead."

"Ooh, she never called me. Should I be worried?"

"She probably realised I would tell you. Anyway, I'm glad it went so well. Shall I pour you a glass of wine?" He picked up the bottle of Merlot from the table and poured them each a large glass.

Chapter Thirty

DCI Mackay was the first senior officer to walk into the briefing room. It smelled of bacon, coffee and sweat. He looked around and identified the source of the bacon as Tim, Bear and Mel finished their breakfast rolls. He saw Hunter standing talking to Colin drinking coffee and he opened the windows to try to get rid of the smell of sweat.

"Ah, come on, sir. It's far too cold to open the windows," Rachael complained.

"The heating's on. It's a waste of public money," Nadia said.

"The windows are staying open for at least half an hour to air this place and wake us all up."

"Good God! Where's that howling gale coming from," DCI Inglis said as he marched into the briefing room ahead of Jane. Shut the bloody windows, McKenzie," he said to Angus.

Angus looked at Mackay. He didn't move but watched as the two DCIs had a brief discussion and then Mackay waved to Angus to close the windows.

"Now what do we know today that we didn't know yesterday?" Inglis asked.

"Well, sir, I went down to Peebles to see the stable hand Rowan Sprigg."

"Ah yes, did the young lad have anything useful to tell us?"

"Well the young lad is a lass, sir. She didn't see anybody she didn't know and didn't see anybody pushing the trolley."

"So, no help at all then," Inglis said dismissively.

"Perhaps, perhaps not. When she was leaving the stables to come home for Christmas, she noticed a beat-up old shopping trolley at the side of the path. She said she thought it was from Sainsbury's and that it might still be there because it was hidden a bit behind a bush and, as Colin and Nadia were going to the scene anyway, I asked them to have a look for it."

"How did your site visit go, DS Reid?" Inglis asked Colin.

"Well we had hoped to follow the route taken by the perpetrator by following the blood stains because there hadn't been much rain, but I think the morning dew and the wildlife must have seen to most of that, we ended up following the flattened grass."

"Yes, but only after we'd spoken to that group of kids," Nadia said.

"That's right. There was a group of teenagers at the scene and they were talking about the crime, so we asked them if they knew anything. In the course of our conversation with them, it transpires they had seen a man putting something large and heavy into the back of a white van. We thought it could be the white van that we had seen leaving the Sainsbury's car park."

"The one you lost track of," Inglis said.

"Yes, sir. We asked the kids if they could describe the man and they were willing to meet with a police artist to do that. This is the result," Nadia handed the identikit picture around.

Bear laughed. "It could be you, sir," he said to DCI Inglis.

"Well, obviously it isn't. And that comment is neither funny nor helpful. Clearly this picture is no bloody use."

"Maybe not, sir. But we did find the trolley. It wasn't immediately obvious because of the bushes in front of it. Still, it had certainly seen better days and we waited for uniforms to come and pick it up and take it to forensics," Nadia said.

"Has it been fast tracked?"

"Of course, sir."

"Did they get a registration number for the van?"

"No sir. They offered to help the man, but he shouted at them, and they just went on their away."

"DC Anderson, can you save the day? Did your witness have anything useful to tell us?"

"I went up to Dunfermline to see the stable hand Stewart Brown, sir. He left at a different time from the other stable hand and witnessed a man struggling to get a large thing into the back of a van. It is possible that this was the same man that Colin and Nadia's teenagers saw."

"That would be a coincidence and I prefer evidence to coincidences, Rache," Hunter said.

"I know boss, but I got a police artist to go over to Dunfermline and meet with Stewart. This is the result of that meeting." She passed around copies of a picture of someone who looked absolutely nothing like DCI Inglis.

"Now we're talking. This is much more the thing," Inglis said.

"I don't suppose when he saw the van, he noticed what kind of van it was. Or better still got a registration number," Hunter said.

"I didn't ask my lad that kind of detail, boss. He didn't sound like he'd paid enough attention."

"When the man told my teenagers to move along, they did exactly that," Nadia added.

"I'll phone Stewart this morning and find out if he remembers any more details."

"He's a teenage boy, make it after ten o'clock," Hunter smiled.

Chapter Thirty-One

There are always going to be things you prefer to keep to yourself. For Fraser and me it is that night when we found the dead man. It is no wonder that Fraser went into accountancy. No corpses to worry him there. But he tells me he finds plenty of skeletons.

I did not even feel able to talk about the scene with the mother of my children. Of course, Alison and Cameron are grown up now and the marriage is long dead. Maybe that's why it died, because I was not able to talk to her about the things that mattered and worried me most.

I think the fact that the body was never found made it worse for Fraser and me. After that, I never liked ghost stories. I could always see the body of that man rise up in front of me and float around because he had not been laid to rest.

Meera is a pathologist and spends most of her day with corpses but I haven't even told her about that first time I saw a victim of violent death.

I have seen many corpses, of course. It sort of goes with the territory of being a detective. But none of those have bothered me the way that first one did. And now, modern science has revealed the victim was a woman, not a man. They wore masculine clothes. I would have sworn it was a man. Maybe the person identified as a man. I don't suppose I'll never know, I just know that I saw a man. But perhaps I was wrong, and my eyes were fooled.

It would be wonderful if science could help me now and that might allow me to lay to rest in my mind that first victim I ever saw.

Chapter Thirty-Two

"Dad, I don't have long. The boss has given me a couple of hours because I'm waiting for info coming from forensics."

"Excellent. He's a good man, Hunter Wilson."

"You've changed your tune."

"He's been good to you. For all he was a pain in the arse to me."

"Well, you did have an affair with his sister-in-law."

"Enough of the history lesson, Tim. Can we talk about the here and now? I want to buy a car from Ian Thomson's place. He was an invaluable guardian to me. Especially when I first went inside and didn't know the ropes. There I was, a naïve toff, ripe for the picking. But he stood up for me. He taught me a lot. And I wasn't the only fellow Ian Thomson stood up for. He protected skinny Les Littlewood many a time."

"The Thomsons are an interesting family. They go in and out of Saughton like there was a revolving door, but they're not all bad."

"No, but they do have a knack of getting caught."

"They do, don't they? Anyway, what kind of car do you want?"

"I thought maybe a Bentley or a Roller. Something that would give me some status when Kenneth is driving me about the city."

"Dad, your status is that of an ex-con. You don't need a car like that. Honestly! Why don't we see if Jamie can get you one of the hybrid BMW 3 series? Or even a Range Rover if you must, you can get that in a hybrid too."

"What's all this about hybrid? Have you become an eco-warrior since I've been away?"

"No. But I think we should all take a little responsibility for the future of the planet, don't you? I can see electric cars being a common sight on the roads within twenty years. Cleaner air, fewer asthma sufferers."

"What a lot of bloody nonsense. Don't forget your money comes from Wills Tobacco."

"I know. But I don't smoke or promote the goods. That was Mum's family background and there's nothing I can do about it."

"I suppose that's true. Anyway, we should go and see what Jamie can offer me."

Tim shrugged his shoulders and accepted that it would take more than one conversation to change his father's fixed views. He led the way to his hybrid BMW 7 series motor.

"I could get one of these." His dad patted the leather upholstery and fondled the dashboard. "This is nice, very smart."

"You do not need a car this size, dad. Be honest. You need a car to get you from A to B and that's it. You're not going to be going far for a while especially while you're on the tag, are you? You have to be in the house between seven at night and seven in the morning."

"But I would like a nice car."

"And I will get you a nice car, just not a huge gas guzzler. Understood?"

Tim smiled as it was his father's turn to shrug. He had not wanted to emphasise that he now held the purse strings, but if his father was going to be stubborn, it was his weapon of last resort. He drove to the showroom and when he pulled up outside Thomson's Top Cars, Tim saw Jamie in the office with a young man in the chair opposite him. The young man looked upset. Tim wondered if he had had his car repossessed. He followed his father across the forecourt of used cars and into the display of expensive new vehicles in the showroom. He smiled. His dad would never change. He had lived a privileged life for too long, but nevertheless, Tim was not going to buy him a Bentley.

"What do you like the look of, Dad?"

"This Bentley is very fitting, don't you think?"

"No, I don't. I think that second-hand Jaguar is rather smart."

"Or what about the silver Aston Martin? I like that?"

"I'm sure you do, but I'm not going to spend that much on your car."

"Oh, for goodness sake, Tim. You could buy it out of a couple of month's interest from your trust fund."

"That's as may be."

"And you are living in my house."

"No, Ailsa and I own the house now, remember? After you spent so much of our inheritance it was agreed we would accept that house and not make a claim against you."

"You wouldn't have done that anyway."

"I admire your confidence, Dad. Now, let's not argue. Can we get back to the cars? What about this Range Rover?"

"It's bright red. That's a bit common."

"I'm sure Jamie can get it for you in a different colour, if that's the only problem."

Tim saw Jamie pat the young man on the shoulder. They walked out of his office together and the young man turned to walk away towards the garage. Tim noticed that he seemed to have composed himself.

"Gerry!" Sir Peter shouted across the showroom. "Fancy meeting you here, my lad. How's life going for you and your family? How's your dad and your aunt?"

"Sir Peter. Hello. We're all well, thanks. A bit of re-adjusting now my dad's home. I thought you got out after Christmas. Good to see you."

"No, no, here I am out and about with my son, Timothy here. He's a copper you know."

Tim was sure he could see Gerry blanche at the word.

"Don't worry, he's one of the good guys. He's going to buy me a car from Jamie, today. Are you working?"

"Yes, I'm a garage hand here. Jamie and Frankie keep me busy."

"Excellent, that's exceptionally good. Well, I don't want to be accused of holding you back. And remember, Gerry, do not be afraid to be yourself."

"Thanks, Sir Pete." Gerry shook hands with Sir Peter and walked away.

"Now Jamie, I need a suitable car to get me about. What do you have for me?"

"Who's paying, you or Blondie, Sir Pete?"

"I'm paying, Jamie, so no up-selling. Alright?" Tim laughed.

"Don't tell me, let me guess. Sir Peter, you need a fine fancy car to meet your standing. Blondie, you want a decent car but for you it'll have to be hybrid. Am I right or am I right?" Jamie grinned at his own cleverness.

Tim suggested the BMW 3 series or the hybrid Range Rover, then he wandered over to talk to Frankie and Donna at the reception desk while Jamie talked his dad into the kind of car he had suggested and made his dad think it had been all his idea. Tim knew Jamie was good at that.

He watched his father wander amongst the cars and talk about the advantages and disadvantages of each in turn. Then he saw a thin, elegant man walk into the showroom.

"Sir Peter!" The man shouted. "I saw you the other day but missed you for a chat."

"Les, how good to see you. What a shame we missed each other," Sir Peter lied. He really couldn't be bothered making small talk with this former inmate, so he changed the subject. "Do you know Ian's son, Jamie?"

"We've met, but not been introduced."

Chapter Thirty-Three

Hunter avoided eating in the station canteen as often as possible. The food was uninspired and repetitive while the room smelled of grease and bleach in equal measure. The trays were almost always sticky or wet and the staff were scarily authoritarian. However, today, there was little choice but to brave the cooks.

He was waiting on the forensic report for the details of the trolley. It wouldn't help with the murder that haunted him, but it might bring justice for somebody else.

He opened the door to the canteen and walked in. A wall of noise met him as he joined the line waiting to be served. He looked at the chalk board with the day's offerings. Lentil soup, mince and potatoes, spicy sausage casserole or fish and chips with baked beans or mushy peas.

When he got to the front of the queue, he saw the last portion of mince being scraped off the bottom of the dish to be dropped onto the plate of the uncomplaining young PC in front of him. He saw her look at her plate.

"Baked beans or mushy peas?" the caterer asked.

"With mince?" Hunter said, incredulously.

"Are you complaining again? It's not even your dinner, DI Wilson."

"I know, but did nobody think about the veg when you planned the menu?"

"Do you want spicy sausage, fish and chips or fish and mash?"

"Oh God." Hunter sighed. "Fish and chips, I suppose. Beans." He pre-empted her next question. He paid for his lunch and looked around for a table. None was free. He saw Bear and Mel get up and walk towards the tray racks. Bear nodded to Hunter.

"Seat for you here, boss, if you don't mind sitting with the proles." Then he whispered to Jane. "See what you can find out about his new woman, Jane."

"Aye, right. I'll do that and I don't think."

Hunter smiled and moved carefully between the other tables to reach Colin, Jane, Nadia and Rachael. He put down his tray and joined the group.

"So what's the chat?" he asked.

Jane looked down at the table.

"Just wondering what we'll get from forensics and when, boss," Nadia said.

"And wondering if Tim will disown his dad or get him the flash car he wants," Jane said.

"I don't think Tim believes a big, fancy car is appropriate for his dad right now. And he holds the purse strings, Jane," Hunter said.

"Yes, and bear in mind, Tim is a bit of a petrol head himself and he can buy what he wants since he got his Mum's inheritance. Anyway, I must go for a walk before I get back to me desk. You coming Rache?"

Hunter watched the two women leave and turned his attention to his fish. It looked greasy and unappetising. He ate a few mouthfuls and then pushed it away.

"Did you notice anything else helpful, when you found the trolley?" he asked Nadia and Colin.

"Nothing we could see, boss. But we talked about how much better forensic science is than it was thirty years ago. There must be something the science can tell us," Colin said. "And Nadia and I are going to help searching for reports of missing people. Surely some kind of lead must turn up."

"I hope so. Who's working on the missing right now, Colin?"

"All of us except Tim. But he'll be back this afternoon."

"Good. Chase up forensics too will you, Colin?"

"I'll try boss. But they're pretty snowed under at the moment. I think they want to clear the decks as far as possible before Christmas."

"Very good. Snowed under at Christmas. Tell them there won't be any Christmas until after I've got my forensic report on that bloody shopping trolley."

"That's a style of persuasion I haven't used yet, boss."

Hunter got up to go back to his office, at least there he would get a decent cup of coffee.

Chapter Thirty-Four

The man's eyes were cloudy. He looked as lost as I felt. Fraser and I didn't know what to do. I was looking at death for the first time. Dad dealt in death. He would know what should be done. We rushed home. Covered in the dead man's blood.

When you look into the eyes of a corpse, many people do die with their eyes open, it is like looking into the eyes of the lost. I didn't know that before I saw the dead man. I stared at him and the pool of blood he seemed to be swimming in. It made me feel sick. I couldn't see him breathing but I had to feel for a pulse, just in case. Someone had to check if he was alive and Fraser wasn't going to do that. He made that perfectly clear.

Suddenly, I understood the old practice of forcing eyelids closed immediately after death, sometimes using coins to lock the eyelids closed until rigor mortis intervenes. Open eyes at death may be interpreted as an indication that the deceased is fearful of the future, presumably because of past behaviours. Those open eyes stared upwards. I remember it yet. I wondered if it was an indication that the deceased was fearful at death because of the way he died or because of the way he conducted his life.

Even now, that memory returns to me in the middle of the night. I dream of him alive, dancing, drinking, discussing matters of no import with friends. And then I wake with a start, sweating and shrieking because he is dead and alone in the dark.

I cannot share the memory; it is too real. It is my secret nightmare that recurs too often in my dreams.

Chapter Thirty-Five

"What brings you here, Sir Peter?" Les asked. "Did you see my son, wee Gerry? He's here too. Works here now, full-time in the garage. It's a wonder he's never been caught for robbing cars."

"It's good to hear of a young man putting his dodgy motor skills to a lawful use. My son, the tall one over there, is going to buy me a car. I've been talking to Jamie and I told him I thought this BMW would suit me well. Good car and I like this metallic blue. What do you think, Les?"

"Handsome lad. He looks genuinely like you, Sir Peter, but I think you're a lucky bastard if he is buying you a car after all you said you put him and his sister through. I need a new limousine for the funeral parlour. I wanted to support Ian's business, after all he protected both of us from the mob and me from the screws on more than one occasion in the big house. And decent of the lads to give Gerry a job."

"Your family kept the business going then, all these years?"

"Aye, they did. You know I was set up. I did not kill anybody. You must believe that I wasn't involved at all."

"Les, everybody who's inside says that. I swear I was the only convicted man in there who admitted to what they had done. I'll leave you to your musings while I just go to have a word with Tim about a couple of extras for the car. Good to see you."

Les watched Sir Peter walk towards Tim and saw Jamie give the big detective the thumbs up. He saw Tim smile and return the sign. Jamie turned away from the father and son. It was clear he had that sale in the bag. Tim would pay the full price. Les knew it would be his way of thanking Ian for looking out for his hapless father while he was in prison.

"Jamie, isn't it?" The tall thin man put his briefcase into his left hand with his cane and held out his right.

"Yes, I believe you are a friend of my pop?"

"I have that honour. I'm Leslie Littlewood. Your father protected me often in my former abode and I will never go past this excellent establishment for my vehicles from now on."

"Thanks, Les, but just about the other night…"

Les held up his hand. "No need to mention that, dear boy. I was on my way out to a gathering and I do like to get dressed up. It hasn't been possible to do so properly for some years. But how did you know where I live?"

"Pop must have mentioned it."

"Indeed, he must. And I suppose you have Gerry's address on file. Good of you to give my son a job. Now, about the limousine. Can I get it on a business credit card, or do you prefer cash?" Les tapped his briefcase.

***

"Chips and rice tonight, Frankie boy," Jamie said. He was grinning as he walked over to Frankie and Donna. "Chips and rice."

"A good sale then?"

"Not at all. Two good sales. And the limousine sold in cold hard cash."

"Cash? That was over a hundred grand!" Donna exclaimed.

"I gave him a discount for cash. I don't usually give discounts."

"You don't ever give discounts, but that much cash deserves one, right enough," Frankie said.

"He'll be back to pick it up tomorrow. Get Gerry to polish and valet it for his pop, will you, Donna?"

"Shouldn't we declare that much cash for what do they call it, money laundering?" Frankie asked.

"Aye, sure an' we will. Don't be such an arse, Frankie. We'll get it written off in the books over the next year."

"Okay, if you're sure that'll work, Jamie. Are we getting a

Chinese to celebrate tonight?"

"You bet we are. Just let me finish the paperwork for Blondie's dad's car while you two go and pick up the twins from nursery. I'll see you back home."

"I bet he's put that new car in his own name. He'll no' let his dad away with much."

"Spot on cuz. And he vetoed the extras his pop wanted."

"I don't really blame him."

"Neither do I Frankie."

Chapter Thirty-Six

Tim added the new car and his father to his insurance policy before they left the showroom and they drove home separately. When they arrived back at the house, Kenneth opened the door and informed them that Alice had a cold buffet waiting for them in the dining room. Tim knew he should really get straight back to the station, but as his stomach was rumbling, he decided to risk Hunter's wrath rather than grab something to eat from the canteen.

The choice of sandwiches was Alice's standard fare. There were rounds of thick cut roast beef and horse radish, salmon and cucumber and a sharp cheddar cheese with tomato. She had also made a sultana cake that Tim noticed was still slightly warm. Tim and his dad chose from the delicious selection and Tim smiled as Kenneth brought in a fresh pot of tea.

"I really don't want to go back to the station after this."

"Well don't go. Phone DI Wilson and tell him I'm being a pain and you are afraid to leave me alone."

"He would certainly believe that, but I think I'll save that for the days when it's true."

"Thanks very much," Sir Peter said sourly. "It was a bit of a surprise to see Les again. He had an even harder time than me inside. Both cons and screws were out for his blood."

"That's harsh. What was that fellow Les convicted of, Dad?" Tim asked.

"He got a long sentence. Nearly sixteen years. He was charged with murder."

"I'm amazed he got out at all. Murder? They'd throw the book at him now."

"The problem was, we couldn't prove it, because there was no body. He ended up being convicted of attacking that vulnerable victim and others and perverting the course of justice."

"That's awful. How did you solve the murder case?"

"We never could properly solve it because the victim wasn't traced. Les admitted to a lesser charge because he was being threatened, he said but he would never say by whom. The death went back over fifteen years and there were many other attacks before he was caught."

"That murder would have been about thirty years ago. But Dad, what if Les was right, what if he didn't kill anybody and what if he was being threatened by the person who did? That means the guilty person is still out there, thirty years on and may still be getting away with murder."

Chapter Thirty-Seven

Jane put her cardigan on when she got back to work. She found the room a bit chilly. She took charge of distributing the responsibilities for the cold cases. She had Bear and Rachael review the original report from Hunter's corpse find so many years ago along with the new forensic report on it that had been received. Colin, Nadia, and Angus were charged with searching through unsolved cases of missing persons over the last thirty years while she and Mel collated all the evidence and statements in the recent case that Tim and Bear had witnessed. Jane wanted as much ground covered as possible before tomorrow morning's briefing.

As the afternoon wore on, the incident room got colder and colder. Jane got up to check all the windows were shut and felt the radiators.

"Fucksake. There's no damn heating. Angus, go and see Charlie at the reception desk and find out what the hell has happened to the heating. It's too bloody cold to work in this."

Jane watched Angus leave the room and Tim enter it. "Good of you to join us, Tim. Manage to agree on a car with your dad?"

"I did. It took us a while, but eventually he chose something sensible and Jamie managed to get him to believe it was all his idea. That boy is really amazingly persuasive."

"I think that's what gets him into as much trouble as he gets out of," Mel said. "How is the bold boy?"

"He didn't even mention you, Mel. I think he has a new love."

"That's good news," Mel said with a grin.

"God, it's cold in here. Have you numpties had the windows open?" Tim rubbed his hands together.

"No, these numpties have been working their arses off while you've been skiving," Jane said sourly.

"I am entitled to time off, you know?"

"I know. I'm sorry. I'm just cold and cross."

"Let me make it up to you all. I've got some of Alice's sandwiches and cake for you and I'll make hot drinks." Tim took the drinks orders and went across to the kettle.

It was several minutes before Angus braved returning to give his news to an angry Jane.

"Charlie says the boiler's broken and it will be tomorrow morning before it's fixed. The engineer needs a part."

"Fucking hell, Angus. This is likely to be an all-nighter for us. We can't work in the freezing cold. What are we meant to do? I'll go and speak to the boss."

Jane grabbed a sandwich and left the room. She marched along to Hunter's office, knocked sharply on the door, and walked in. Hunter was meeting with Mackay and Inglis. The men looked serious.

"Perhaps not right now, DS Renwick," Mackay said. "DCI Inglis, DI Hunter and I all have something important to discuss." He turned his back to her and carried on speaking. "We can move most of those in our cells to Gayfield Square station, and just release saggy Aggie with a caution. She doesn't really cause any trouble, just sings too loudly when she gets drunk."

"Are you still here, DS Renwick? DCI Mackay said not now," Inglis shouted.

"I know what he said, sir. However, I and the other detectives working on the murder case will need to work long hours tonight, perhaps all night, to prepare for the briefing tomorrow morning and there is no heat. The boiler won't be fixed until tomorrow morning."

"Didums. We know that. Have a coffee and put on a sweater DS Renwick," Inglis said.

"Sir, that is unacceptable."

At that moment, Jane noticed Tim pop his head around Hunter's door.

"Oh, for goodness sake," Hunter said. "This isn't a game of

sardines, you know, young Myerscough."

"I do know that. Yes, boss. But I have an idea that may allow us to get the work done without freezing our bollocks off. Sorry Jane."

"Okay spit it out and then bugger off," Hunter said.

"If You and the DCIs will sanction the removal of records from the station overnight, we can go and work in my dad's study in the house. He isn't using it and it's big enough for us all to have desk space. There are at least six laptops in the house. Dad also had an old printer in there that still works. We would be warm enough to work and I undertake to bring all the records back here in the morning and Kenneth can run everybody home when we're finished. What do you say, boss?"

"This is most irregular," Inglis said.

Tim continued to look at Hunter.

"It is also irregular to let out saggy Aggie with only a caution," Jane said. "We cannot think properly when the room is as cold as that, sir. I don't know how long the heating has been off, but it was clearly off for a long time before we noticed."

"Jane, Tim, give us a minute, will you?" Hunter asked.

When they had left the room Jane asked, "Do you think they'll agree?" She munched her sandwich solemnly.

"Probably. Reluctantly but probably. What choice do they have? They want this sorted before the papers go mad about it over Christmas."

"They could send us down to Gayfield Square."

"And get other coppers involved. I can't see them wanting to do that."

"They might think it better than getting your dad too close to it."

Hunter's office door opened, "Jane, Tim, come back in," Hunter said.

"Tim, your plan is acceptable on strict conditions: first that your father does not touch the records and is kept well away from the work, second that you and Jane are jointly responsible for the records and their safe return to the station in time for the briefing at eight tomorrow morning and third that copies of reports are emailed back to the station and none are retained on your home computers. Is that acceptable to both of you?"

"It's fine by me, boss. I'm just trying to help solve a problem."

"Yes, there's no problem with any of that for me, boss," Jane said.

"Fine, I'll stop by on my way home to see how it's working in practice."

"But you live in Leith, boss. That's miles away."

"Bugger off, both of you and tell the others the good news."

"It'll be warmly received, boss," Tim said with a smile.

Chapter Thirty-Eight

Jamie's phone rang a little after ten in the evening. He didn't recognise the number and guessed that his pop had won a contraband phone from a habitual loser in a card game. He was right.

"Hey Pop, who did you do over for the phone this time?"

"Nobody, I bought it fair and square." Jamie thought his pop sounded offended.

"Aye, and what did the poor schmuck want so desperately as to swap for their phone?"

"Two KitKats, a Mars bar and a couple of fags."

"Thought so. Anyway, I'm glad you called. We had a right good day in the showroom today. Your pal Les bought the limo for cash. He's going to pick it up tomorrow. And before you say it, yes, I gave him a discount and no, the money didn't go through the books."

"Good. We'll write it off before the end of the next year. No need to trouble the tax man with that. I'll tell you how to do that each month as we go. How much did he give you?"

Jamie told his father with glee. "With the discount, one hundred and eight thousand. I thought we could get rid of it through the books at nine grand a month over the next year."

"Aye, but never in round figures, mind. They stand out to the tax man like a sore thumb. Put one hundred grand of the money in the safe for just now and you and Frankie take four thousand each for a good Christmas."

"We really don't need that much, pop, but thanks. I'll put all but a thousand in the safe and we'll each have a monkey for just now. Then we'll see how it goes."

"Whatever works for the both of you, son. But that was a good day."

"Nah, pop, it doesn't end there. Blondie brought Sir Peter in because the old man needs a car for a run around and Blondie bought it for him."

"What did he choose. Please tell me it was the Bentley."

"No can do, pop. Blondie is holding the purse strings, so it had to be something green and sensible."

"For fucks sake, that lad could buy and sell the city with the money his mam left him."

"I know that, you know that, Sir Peter knows that, even Blondie knows that, but, as I say, pop, he holds the purse strings and the old man had to accept that."

"Okay, what did they buy? Don't tell me it was a used one."

"No, it's new. I got Sir Peter to think the car choice was his idea and he took the hybrid BMW 3 series in metallic blue off the showroom floor. Just under thirty grand. And of course, Blondie pays with a credit card, so it's money in the bank."

"Aye, you did alright today, son. And the books'll look good for the end of the year."

"They will, we'll need to shuffle the motors in the showroom when the limousine has gone, so it still looks good and full because we'll be two cars down."

"Aye do that, Jamie. How's the garage going?"

"Mark and the lads have been really busy in there too. Mark wants to get the repairs and MOTs all done and out of the place before Christmas so we're no really taking in any new work, unless it's a kent face or an emergency."

"He's a good lad, Mark. We were lucky to get him. Give him and Shug a wee cash bonus for the end of the year."

"And wee Gerry's back. I know you're going to tell me I'm a soft touch, pop, but when he told me what he's been through. And I didn't know his dad was in the big house with you but for much longer."

"Wee Gerry? I've never actually met him. I only know what you and Les told me. I've never clapped eyes on him. The job for him was just a favour to Les. Gerry was going right off the rails; I can assure you of that."

"Well, Les said he was."

The line went dead. Jamie realised he was now talking to

himself. The credit in the phone his pop had won had run out. It had lasted longer than usual and that was lucky, but it always seemed to drop when he was hearing something right interesting from his pop.

Chapter Thirty-Nine

The briefing was to start promptly at eight in the morning. Hunter noticed that most of his team, except for Tim, were wearing the same clothes they had worn the previous day. He also saw that none of them was eating breakfast. He walked over to Tim.

"How did it go?"

"I think you'll be amazed when you hear about all the information we've found. I worked with Angus, Colin and Nadia on missing persons reported and not traced over the last thirty years. I tell you, boss, Colin and Nadia are the dream team. They work so methodically. Angus and I were the gophers." Tim smiled.

"Nobody's eating this morning. That's unusual."

"Well, boss, we finished about six this morning and instead of getting everybody home, we utilised all four showers in the house and then went into the dining room where Alice had prepared a selection of cereals, fruit salad, bacon rolls, fried egg sandwiches, fruit juices, tea and coffee. She cannot help herself when there is a group of people in the house. So, to be honest, boss, I think we have all eaten far better than usual this morning."

"Good. Hopefully, you'll be firing on all cylinders, with Alice's help, of course."

"Yes, no excuses this morning."

Hunter heard Mackay slamming his pile of files on the desk and he walked towards the DCI and explained quietly what Tim had said to him. He stood back as Mackay called the room to order and asked if the forensics report was in regarding the shopping trolley.

"It is, sir, but would you mind if we heard from Bear and

124

Rachael, first?" Jane asked.

"Go ahead, DC Zewedu," Mackay said.

"Rache and me." Bear looked up and noticed DCI Inglis frowning. He started again. "DC Anderson and I were tasked with reviewing all the evidence old and new regarding the cold case.

"From the statements given by you and your brother, boss, the victim was dead, but probably recently so because the body was not completely cold when you checked for signs of life."

Hunter nodded. "That seems to fit the facts as I remember them."

"You and Fraser helped the sketch artists prepare a picture of the deceased and also confirmed the victim's height at about five feet four or five inches. So, somewhat below the average height of five feet eight inches for men in Scotland."

"You said then that you couldn't see the wound but, of course it was dark, but you were aware that there was a large loss of blood." Rachael took up the report. "A sharp serrated knife was found near the site where you found the corpse. The blade was just over six inches long and would have easily caused a fatal wound. There was also a fingerprint on the knife, but we had no match for that."

"I remember that, although I was only a humble PC at the time," Inglis said.

"He was never humble," Tim whispered to Bear.

"You have something to share, DC Myerscough?"

"Not at all, sir. I'm listening carefully."

"Zewedu, carry on," Inglis said.

"The more recent forensics have analysed the blood in a way that was not possible when the original crime was committed, and there were two types of blood on the knife. It seems as if the victim may have drawn blood from their attacker."

"The blood results show that the victim was female, but their assailant was male," Rachael said.

"We also have a match for the fingerprint now," Bear said.

"Excellent! Don't keep us in suspense, Bear. Who is it?"

Hunter asked.

"That's just the thing, boss, we don't have a name, we just have a match with a print on the shopping trolley in the modern case. It looks like the attacker was the same person in both cases."

"That's shocking," Hunter said. "You're sure the print is not on our database?"

"Nor on the international database held by Interpol, boss."

"That means this man could have been attacking victims, untraced, for thirty years. What else have we found out, Jane?"

"I worked with Mel, DC Grant, on the modern case that Tim and Bear witnessed. Again, the victim, originally identified as male, was, in fact, at birth, a female. There were high levels of testosterone in the blood, but that doesn't mask the chromosomes XX present from birth."

"What else did the trolley tell us, DS Renwick?" Inglis asked.

"The report from forensics has been rushed through, sir. Bear rather stole my thunder on the finger print, but because we have the shopping trolley, we have a full set of prints, there, It seems as if the attacker had to change their plans because Tim and Bear came along unexpectedly and the assailant had to move the trolley across the field. I doubt very much they intended to do that."

"If the victim has had gender re-assignment surgery, might we be able to check medical records? The cases are relatively few," Mackay said.

"Yes, sir. That is today's challenge. We don't know if they had had the full surgery, but it would seem from the blood results that they should certainly be in the system."

"It would also appear that these attacks are both LGBTQ hate crimes. Don't you think, DCI Inglis?"

"Oh, for God's sake, DCI Mackay, these gays and queers are no better than they ought to be. You can quite understand a decent red-blooded person losing the plot with them, can't you? They deserve all they get."

The silence in the room was palpable. Hunter looked around at the team and saw their reactions. Each and every one of them was horrified by DCI Inglis's prejudiced speech.

"So, let me check this through with you, sir. You think a victim is not a victim because of who they love or how they identify themselves?" Jane asked quietly.

"I suppose that's not quite right, but I can understand a decent person being so horrified by these creatures that they lose control."

"What if I was attacked and killed, sir?"

"For goodness sake, DS Renwick, you are an outstanding police officer with an impeccable record. Any attack on you, or any one of us, would feel the full force of the law."

"But a person attacked or killed who is LGBTQ would not?" Jane asked.

"I think you are rather diverting the briefing, DS Renwick, and to no good purpose. What else did your team discover?"

Hunter looked straight at Jane. She blushed slightly. He shook his head, imperceptibly, and she replied with a slight nod.

"DS Reid, could you tell us what your group's investigations found?" Hunter asked to move things along. He would have to get Mackay to speak to Superintendent Miller about Inglis. The man's attitude was unacceptable.

"Yes of course, boss," Colin said. "I was charged, together with Tim, Nadia and Angus with looking through the missing persons' register. As the cases we had already identified were in the old Lothian and Borders area of Edinburgh, we concentrated our search there. We also knew that both victims had been originally identified as male by those who found their bodies, but were, at birth at least, female. We further concentrated our search for missing persons who might be gay, cross dressers or transgender."

"Those are quite different things, Colin," Hunter commented.

"That's true, boss. And we were not trying to mix up or belittle the differences. It's just that we wanted to identify groups that seemed most likely to be targeted by this murderer in light of what the two known cases showed us. We tried to ensure that the likely victims were properly and fully identified."

"Alright. What did you find?"

"Why did you bother, more like?" Inglis laughed.

"Hunter, will you continue the briefing while DCI Inglis and I take a few moments out?" Mackay asked.

"Of course, sir. Colin, what did your group find?"

"We found eleven unexplained disappearances over the thirty-year period."

"The problem we identified, boss, and it's been a problem here before, is that we are hardly the most trusted emergency service of that part of the population," Tim commented.

"I wonder why that could be?" Rachael said sarcastically.

"What I mean is that people within the LGBTQ community who move into or out of an area may well live under our radar and are not always likely to come to us if they have a problem being bullied or threatened. So, while we identified eleven missing persons who met our criteria, there may be more."

"That is a dreadful thought, but I understand," Hunter said. "Do we have any identifying feature on record for any of those eleven people?"

"Yes, but most importantly, we have death certificates for two. One died of cancer in the Western General Hospital in 1989 and another died in a hostel of a heroin overdose in 2004. So that left us with nine people reported missing and unaccounted for."

"Of those nine, three were gay men with no history of cross dressing, two were lesbian women who did not cross-dress as far as we know. The importance of this, we thought, was that they would not be mistaken for the other gender if approached and were therefore less likely to be targeted by the aggressor we have identified," Nadia said.

"But they might suffer attacks because of their sexuality," Jane said.

Hunter nodded.

"The other four consisted of one woman who did wear men's suits, ties and trousers, one woman who had started female to male or FTM transgender re-assignment and two men who had had male to female or MTF transgender reassignment," Angus said.

"Dates, Angus?" Hunter asked.

"They were all reported missing in the period from 1985 to 2011 by worried parents or partners. In every case, disappearance without telling anybody or without getting in touch for a prolonged period was quite out of character."

Mackay and Inglis re-entered the room. Hunter looked at the two men. Mackay looked perfectly calm but Inglis seemed furious.

"Just for the avoidance of any doubt, DCI Inglis and I have agreed that whatever our personal views, every individual is entitled to our respect and the full protection of the law."

"That was never in any doubt here, sir. It is how this team has always conducted itself," Hunter said. "Is there anything else we need to share right now?"

There was a knock on the door. Sergeant Charlie Middleton stuck his head around the door. "A witness has phoned to say they've found a body at the Mortonhall crematorium. We think it might be Myerscough and Zewedu's missing corpse. And he saw a group of men walking away from it and getting into the back of a scruffy white van. No registration, before you ask, and not much of a description. He noticed the last one to get into the van had a thin face and dark clothes. I suppose it's a start."

"Get him in to take his statement and show him those sketches we have from the other witnesses, Charlie."

"Will do, Hunter."

Chapter Forty

The corpse had been found in the garden of remembrance in the larger city crematorium at Mortonhall. Hunter asked the CSIs and Sam Hutchens, the police photographer, to record the site and Meera went up to examine the body before it was moved. Hunter also instructed Tim and Bear to go across the city to the mortuary to see the body and identify if it was the same one, they had seen in Hermitage of Braid.

When the detectives got there and observed the body carefully, Bear spoke quietly. "God! A few days out in the winter weather haven't been kind to him, have they?"

Tim looked at the corpse. The face was scratched and bitten and two of the fingers were missing. It looked like they had been bitten off, probably by rats, he thought. The clothes were ripped and the area about the crotch torn right through. The animals had attacked that area viciously too.

"What a bloody mess, but it is the same person."

"Yes, it is poor sod. He smells ripe, doesn't he, Tim?"

"Meera, when do you want to conduct the post-mortem? I think Bear and I should attend."

"Are you sure? Bear didn't exactly cover himself in glory the last time Hunter asked him to witness a post-mortem?"

"I know what to expect now. I'll be fine."

"Okay, it's up to you. Clear it with Hunter and if he gives the green light, that's fine with me. Shall we say two o'clock this afternoon? I know Hunter wants it done quickly."

"We'll see you then and I'll make sure Bear doesn't eat lunch!"

"Thank you, Tim. I'd appreciate that."

***

Meera looked at the body in front of her. It was cold, but well out of rigour so the individual had been dead for more than two days and nights. Their features had been fine and their hair that indeterminate length that could pass for male or female. The clothes had been smart, and the hands looked like those of a white-collar worker. An office worker of some sort, probably, Meera mused.

She stood back to let Sam Hutchens take the photos she needed. The two women had worked together so often they rarely had to say much. Sometimes that was best when the scenes they visited were as grim as this one.

"You'll want close-ups of the animal damage to the body," Sam stated.

"Yes, Sam, but can you also take a wide angle from each direction? It might help the detectives to work out where the body was transported from."

"I can tell you that," a young CSI said. "It was dragged off the pathway there and across here. See. They knocked the flowers over there. And they weren't killed here. No blood, see?"

"Thank you. I meant where the body was brought from, but a bit further afield than just those few yards. And I know about death. I am the pathologist," Meera said.

"Okay. I thought you were the photographer's assistant."

Meera smiled at Sam and watched as she took the last photos and put her equipment back into its cases.

"Do you need a ride, Sam?"

"No thanks, Meera. I've got the van. I'll be fine. I'll get the photos over to you by lunchtime. I think I heard you say the post-mortem is early afternoon, so you will have everything by then. Do you want me to send them to Hunter too?"

"Yes please. Then at least we'll have something to talk about."

"What do you mean?"

"He's been very quiet and secretive lately and keeps telling me he's working late or playing darts."

"Well, to be fair, he usually is."

"Yes, but on the occasions when I have called the station,

because his phone is off, he's not there and when I popped into the pub on a supposed darts night, there was no match at all."

"Oh dear. What are you thinking?"

"I'm thinking there may be somebody else."

"Then he's a bigger fool than I took him for. Talk to him, Meera."

"Where do I start?"

Chapter Forty-One

"Good afternoon, Les," Jamie shouted across the showroom. "I've manoeuvred the limo out of the showroom for you. It's on the forecourt, especially valeted by your own lad, wee Gerry, and it's ready to go. Look, I've got your keys here. Do you want to give the vehicle a final look over?"

"I'm sure it'll be fine, Jamie, but let's take a look together."

They went out to the limousine and Les sat in the driver's seat while Jamie perched on the front passenger seat. Jamie wasn't quite sure how to approach the subject of wee Gerry, so he decided on a direct approach.

"Les, I hope you don't mind me asking, but you said my pop knew wee Gerry?"

"Aye, that's right, Jamie. It was good of him to take my lad on. It's just like your pop to look out for his pals."

"Well, that's just the thing, when I mentioned it to my pop, he said he didn't know wee Gerry. He said you told him about your boy and wanted us to take him on because he was going off the rails."

"That's right. It was a favour to me. My wee Gerry is a wheels man through and through. Always has been. He can drive anything, make a getaway car go faster than a jet on cobble a discreet getaway with a shopping trolley if you want to go unnoticed. He's not really a bad lad, just no' on the side of the angels."

"I'm glad but I'll not be needing any getaway rides from him here. Do I need to keep an eye on him?"

"Well, I wouldn't leave him alone with a set of wheels for too long. He might find a use for it that you don't want to be involved in."

"He told me about how he lost his nephew, he got right

upset. It must have been awful."

"It was a shock for all the family, but at least he got a niece out of it. Come to think of it, I don't believe Rowan even changed his name."

"What do you mean, Les?"

"Wee Gerry's nephew, my daughter's boy, my grandson, went the whole hog and had the operation to become a woman. Gerry really couldn't get his head around it. The whole family found it hard. But I don't think much else changed. She had always worked with horses and still does. After the op, she moved to work at a different stable. Just to get away from the wagging tongues. She's up here in Edinburgh, somewhere, but my daughter and her family live in the borders, in Peebles. Lovely town."

"What was all that hoo hah and weeping I got from wee Gerry about his responsibility to look after his family and how he had never got over losing his nephew so young?"

"You'll need to ask the lad about that, Jamie. It seems a bit over the top. Mind you, I did my best to help young Rowan, but a lot of the family didn't adjust to it."

"You're bloody right. I'll ask."

***

Jamie marched into the garage and stormed up to wee Gerry. He kicked him on the leg and Gerry appeared from under a car.

"You and me need to talk, Mr," he said.

"What about, Jamie?"

"Your fucking niece. I'll give you responsibility and I've lost my nephew so young. Come on you. The office, now."

Chapter Forty-Two

Tim drove to the mortuary as he had been there more recently than Bear. Nevertheless, the approach through a narrow street of blackened buildings to the Edinburgh City Mortuary still made him shudder.

The building was situated in the historic part of Edinburgh known as the Cowgate. Tim knew the area derived its name from the old practice of herding cattle down the street on market days. Today was grey, cold, and cloudy, and the street seemed even darker than usual. Tim looked along the Cowgate and thought what a canyon of a road it was. The street was narrow with only one lane of traffic passing in each direction and the pavements were not wide either. He stared at the steep gradients leading off to either side. Tim glanced at Bear and noticed he was frowning; he was probably trying to hold the contents of his stomach in place.

There was nowhere obvious to park, so Tim was glad he had brought a small car from the station pool rather than his own large BMW. He lurched the car around and Bear gripped on to the door handle as he swung the vehicle into the morgue car park and drew up at the rear beside the anonymous black 'private ambulances' outside the morgue.

Bear's silence throughout the journey had done nothing to make it more pleasant for Tim but he understood that Bear was attending the postmortem out of a sense of duty to the victim and to Hunter. He entered the building in front of Tim.

***

Meera, and her colleague, David Murray, were the attending pathologists. Meera scrubbed up and disinfected her hands then she made her way over to the examination room where David Murray was already waiting for her. He had wheeled in the body of the victim and had already transferred it to a stainless-steel table that occupied the middle of the spotlessly clean white floor. The victim was lying on his back with his arms loosely resting by his sides.

Meera glanced at David and shook her head. "This is so vicious," she said. "And very difficult when we know so little about the victim."

"Who do you think will attend for Police Scotland today?"

"I believe Tim and Bear found the corpse in its original site beside the Braidburn in the Hermitage, so they have been delegated to come today."

"Well, I hope Bear manages a little better than he did last time. Didn't he faint?"

Meera nodded. She turned her attention to the body on the table. She noted the livor mortis on the man's body caused by the settling of the blood. "He was definitely not killed in the location where he was found."

David frowned. "Yes indeed. Oh, it sounds like the boys in blue are arriving."

As Tim and Bear walked towards the examination room, Tim was amazed, as always, how much it resembled an operating theatre.

The door opened. Meera looked up. She smiled at Tim. "DC Myerscough, DC Zewedu, thank you for coming. It seems we were correct, David."

"It is always interesting, but I would happily never come here again if it meant that people stopped getting killed," Tim looked at the floor then at Bear.

"And I would just quite happily never come here again. We should get gowned up, Tim," Bear said.

"This way," Tim said.

"There really is a distinctive smell in here, isn't there?"

"Yes, a bit like a combination of formaldehyde, antiseptic and industrial soap, isn't it? It's also a bit chilly, just those few degrees below what would be considered comfortable makes all the difference."

When Tim and Bear returned to witness the postmortem, Tim commented, "It's a big room."

"Yes, well by the time I've got my large double sinks along the wall, a metal counter to hold all the tools and the channel leading to the drain, I suppose it has to be big," Meera said. "It also looks a lot bigger without you filling up my space, DC Myerscough." Meera smiled.

"Thanks, Doctor Sharma," Tim replied with a grin.

"When you two are finished sparring with each other, can we get on?" David asked.

The two DCs moved so that they could see the body on the stainless-steel examination table below the powerful circular halogen lights which were suspended from the ceiling. Meera positioned herself on the other side of the table from the two detectives.

They watched in silence as Meera first freed the body from its tightly laced boots. There were cuts and grazes on the body's hands possibly from the fight he put up against his attacker and the animal bites and scratches he had suffered since death. Meera also noticed the tiny abrasions and colour changes to around neck.

"David, look at this," Meera said.

"His neck was bound, held or restrained in some way, by the looks of things. He might have been throttled into unconsciousness before he was stabbed." David pulled a face as he watched Meera remove the clothes from the top of the body to get a better look. "There's bits of grass and dirt stuck to that," he said.

"Probably from after he was dumped at the crematorium," Meera said.

"Yes, that would be right. He was just beside the river when we first saw him," Bear said.

As each piece of clothing was taken from the body, Meera methodically gave them to David. He put each item carefully into plastic evidence bags which would be handed over to the forensics experts for further examination. Meera then took blood, urine and hair samples as well as oral and anal swabs before removing the victim's underwear – the first thing she

137

noticed was the long stab wound slicing from the belly right round to the side of the body.

"Look at this, David," she said.

"Nasty!" David Murray frowned.

"I don't suppose there's much doubt about the cause of death." Tim grimaced.

"No doubt at all. The poor soul would bleed out from that in minutes. They would never have recovered consciousness from the strangulation either. There wouldn't be time. So they wouldn't have felt the pain from the cut."

Bear gasped.

Tim closed his eyes.

"Monster!" David whispered. "I'm not surprised you saw such a large pool of blood. This attack was vicious and deliberate."

David reached for the digital camera and documented everything as Meera finished undressing the body. She scraped gently underneath the nails of the remaining fingers.

"I have fragments of skin here that might give us DNA from the attacker," she said.

Then she sprayed the body with fungicide and used a hose with a powerful water jet to methodically wash and disinfect the corpse fully. When she was finished, she turned on her voice recorder and dictated the official examination. She began by stating the date and time, followed by the case number then she described the general state of the body, before she moved on to describe the grisly details.

Meera checked that the directional light in her headset was switched on, although she knew it was, it gave her a couple of seconds to compose herself discreetly before she began checking the skin around the corpse's neck.

"No other suspicious bruises," David commented.

A touch check of the neck revealed that both the larynx and trachea of the victim had collapsed. "And his hyoid bone in the neck is fractured, so it suggests that he was strangled probably before he was stabbed, the strangulation would have been used to subdue him," Meera said glancing at David.

"When we found him, that paisley patterned tie looked too

tight and off centre," Tim said.

"The paisley patterned tie is certainly a blast from the past," David said.

"It is but in light of these wounds, it would appear to be the strangulation weapon." Meera then turned her attention back to the body.

She checked for signs of sexual or any other kind of aggression. She began with the mouth: pulling it open and checking for any trauma or skin and teeth colour alteration in case a poison had been used that discoloured the teeth or tongue or perhaps burned the skin inside the mouth. Meera found no primary indications of poisoning, but samples would be sent for a toxicology report in any event.

Then she moved to the chest. "The nipples have been repositioned, probably after the gender realignment surgery, it has been done carefully to try to avoid nicks or tears."

***

In the car on the way back to the station, Bear and Tim were exhausted.

"Did you notice how neatly his nipples had been detached and repositioned?" Bear asked. "Delicate work."

"Makes me think the surgery was done here in a British hospital. I wonder if we could get hold of the medical records, now the victim is dead, I can't see it breaching confidentiality, because he's dead. I'll ask Ailsa tonight. She'll be glad of the respite, she's in charge of Dad today."

"Lucky Ailsa, a little slice of heaven." Bear smiled.

Chapter Forty-Three

Hunter was sitting in the canteen at the Western General Hospital, waiting for Parvati to arrive. He had chosen a portion of lasagne and some salad. It was the only time he would have for lunch today. When she arrived, he waved across to her and saw her go to pick up a packet of sandwiches and a bottle of water. He noticed people's heads turn when she sat down close beside him, rather than opposite him. He knew many of the men would be envious, she was such a beautiful woman.

"I would never have thought about meeting here. It is inspired, Parvati."

"I'm not just a pretty face. Now I think we are at the stage when you should be able to talk to me and we can have a discussion about something, anything."

"Are you sure? I am so nervous. Hearing my voice speaking that truth is so strange."

"I know, but I think you should try. We will start with something easy."

He listened carefully and was thrilled when he could answer her first question without faltering. He had understood her to ask him what his name was. She smiled when he replied and asked her what her name was. She then asked him if he was enjoying his lunch and, again he was able to reply. The conversation crept on over lunch and at the end of their time, she told him to ask any question he liked. Hunter took a deep breath and asked the only question that really mattered to him. He listened carefully as Parvati corrected his pronunciation and then he repeated his question. A doctor walked by.

"Her daughter? How old can her daughter be?" he asked.

"Old enough for you to mind your own business," Parvati replied sharply.

Hunter led the way out of the canteen and Parvati hailed a taxi to take her back to the university.

"Thank you again for your time and patience, Parvati. Do you think I'll be able to do it properly?"

"Just one or two more practices and you'll be fine. Term is over for me anyway, so I am only working on my research. Let me know when next suits you."

"I will, thank you."

He held the door of the taxi over for her and watched her drive away. He walked back to the station with a spring in his step. He was pleased to have been able to conduct an honest conversation, albeit a simple one. That was an achievement of which he was proud.

***

When Hunter got back to his desk, he turned immediately to his computer. No report from Meera, yet. But he did have a list of the names and last known addresses of the missing persons he read through it and didn't recognise a single individual. Yet each of them represented a life lost, a family broken, friends in despair. Why had none of these individuals been traced? Hunter couldn't help wondering how people got so far under the radar that they went missing and were never found.

There was a knock on his door and Jane walked in. He signalled to her to take a seat as he continued to stare at the list.

"Boss, I've had an idea."

He looked up at her. And what would that idea be, Jane?"

"Well, I've been trying to think why that body turned up in the grounds of the crematorium. I mean, we obviously weren't meant to find it, because it wasn't meant to be there. It is a very public place to leave a corpse."

"I agree. It is most unusual. But what do you mean, we weren't meant to find it?"

"If you murdered someone you wouldn't want the police to find the body, would you?"

"Of course not, but I wouldn't leave it in public grounds

141

either."

"Exactly my point. I don't think our attacker wanted to do that either, but they weren't left with any choice. Our witness came into the garden of remembrance at the crematorium because they were early for a funeral and went to pay respects to their aunt while they had a few quiet moments. And Charlie says both sketches look like the man they saw."

"That's not helpful. Anyway, what are your thoughts, Jane."

Hunter sat and listened to Jane as she developed her theory. He had to admit that it made perfectly good sense and he suggested that she phone the crematorium to enquire as to whether her theory held good. If it did, they would have to do even more digging to solve the murder.

Chapter Forty-Four

That evening, Sir Peter sat down to dinner with his family. Alice had made a splendid meal of steaks, baked potatoes and seasonal vegetables. She had especially made a tasty vegetable burger for Gillian and for pudding Alice had made one of her specialities, a fruity apple and blackberry crumble with home-made custard.

"I haven't eaten this well for so long. I really can't explain how much this wonderful food in the company of my family and, of course, you, Gillian, means to me."

"Notice the food comes first and we are a distant second," Ailsa said. "Have you remembered to give Kenneth and Alice the evening off, Dad?"

"Yes, just as you asked me to, and I brought two bottles of delicious Malbec up from the cellar. It has had plenty of time to breathe. Shall I pour?"

"You know, I read somewhere that leaving a wine to breathe makes no difference at all. It is just an affectation," Gillian said.

"Indeed?" Sir Peter looked at Tim in bewilderment. He was not used to being contradicted. He was angry with her. "I find it enhances the taste considerably. Would you like a glass?"

"Yes, thank you, Sir Peter." Gillian said quietly.

"Come on, Dad, don't sour the mood," Tim said. "Gillian is only telling us what she has heard. She is entitled to do that and even, God forbid, to disagree with any of us if she wants to."

A silence fell amongst the group.

"Vegetables are cooked just the way I like them, slightly *al dente*," Ailsa said. "And the steaks are delicious. How is your veggie burger, Gillian?"

"It is really tasty and flavourful, thank you, Ailsa."

How like his daughter to change the subject away from conflict. She reminded him so much of her mother in character, but both Sir Peter's children resembled him physically: tall, blond, and long limbed. He was immensely proud of both them, but Gillian was still not a puzzle to him.

"Oh, Ailsa, I wanted to ask you something. Are hospitals permitted to release medical records of dead people?"

"I know if the person has left a Will, the executors or personal representatives can ask to see them. If there is no Will, the next of kin can demand them, but I suspect that's not what you mean."

"No, we have a murder victim whose identity is a mystery, but they have had major surgery. We might be able to work out their identity if we could find their surgical notes."

"Goodness, that could take forever, unless it's most unusual surgery and you are extremely lucky. You would need a warrant, but how could you get a warrant if you don't know the identity."

"Meera and David are the attending pathologists, could the medical notes be released to them without a warrant?"

"In the circumstances, I think they could. Can you tell me what kind of surgery it was?"

"I don't see why not because I can't tell you the victim's identity. Dad, may I have another glass of wine?"

"Of course, Tim. Hand me his glass, will you, Ailsa?"

"The surgery is extensive, but not unique. He has had gender reassignment FTM. The quality of the work makes Meera think it may have been carried out here."

"There are not that many specialists carrying that kind of work. Had he had the full re-assignment?"

"Yes."

"It is not carried out all at once. Such extensive surgery would take too long. The individual would be under anaesthetic for longer than would be safe and it would be too much of a shock for the body."

"Do we need to discuss surgery over dinner?" Sir Peter asked.

"We're not really discussing the surgery, Dad, it's more the strategy of such complex work and the legalities affecting the deceased," Tim argued.

"Tim, the upper body surgery is done first. I think you might find it easier to look out the records for the lower body re-assignments. There will be fewer of them. I don't think there are more than a handful of specialists in Scotland who can give trans people hormones, authorise surgery or provide gender recognition certificates. I think you will be able to get it online, Tim."

"Will you help me with that after dinner?"

"I will, but let's have pudding first."

"Again, food comes first," Tim said.

Sir Peter tucked into his pudding and the talk around the table turned from surgical operations to the benefits of fruit and vegetables in a balanced diet. The portion of fruit in front of him was smothered in thick, creamy custard and, although it might not be balanced, he found it delicious.

***

After dinner, Ailsa and Tim sat with their heads together over a computer screen in their father's study.

"Only last year the Scottish Government issued the Gender Reassignment Protocol (GRP) to Health Boards. It applies to primary and secondary care services in Scotland and its purpose is to provide a treatment pathway for gender reassignment. Of course, not all patients will want or need all the services offered, Tim."

"There are both non-surgical and surgical treatments, aren't there?"

"Oh yes, of course. Every patient is different. But from what you said at dinner we only need to consider those who have had full surgical reassignment. Shall we have a look at the list of specialists?"

"I'm amazed, there are only five doctors mentioned here. The waiting lists must be long," Tim said.

"I believe so, the waiting period can be a year or more."

"I'm going to take a note of these specialists names and contact details. The boss will want me to get in touch with them. Thanks for your help, sis. Now I'm off to meet the team for a pre-Christmas drink."

"No problem. I'll go and rescue Gillian from Dad."

Chapter Forty-Five

Frankie and Jamie were sitting together in their living room. They were pleased with the bonus from Thomson's Top Cars.

"What you going to do with your money, Frankie?"

"I think I'll spend most of it on driving lessons. I think I should try my test again.

"Aye, right. You've failed your theory test at least three times."

"I know that, Jamie. Don't rub it in. What you going to do with yours?"

"I thought I might get a wee holiday with Linda. A few days in the sun, you know, Magaluf in Spain or Ayia Napa in Cyprus."

"That sounds good. I'd only thought about a nail session for Donna."

"A nail bed? Yuck!"

"No, like a manicure and pedicure thing."

"Hark at you and your pedicure."

"Well Donna used to work in a beautician's, and I know about these things."

"It's a good idea. I could get Linda one too and Donna could talk her into coming to us for Christmas."

"I'm not making any promises on that score. You'll need speak to Donna about it, Jamie."

"Can we see if we can get appointments for tomorrow. We can do it online. The longer we wait the less likely Donna is to talk Linda into it."

"What did folk do before computers and mobile phones?"

"Oh, don't start that, Frankie. You sound like my pop. Give Donna a shout and I'll see what she says before I book anything."

Donna was in the dining room, ironing Frankie and Jamie's shirts and hers and the girls' dresses. She had the radio on and was singing along to a Little Mix number when Frankie opened the door. She smiled broadly.

"Hello, Frankie. Do you want to make us all a cup of tea?"

"Yeh, no problem. But can I ask you something first?"

"What are you up to, Frankie Hope?"

"I wondered if you'd like me to arrange a manicure and pedicure for you tomorrow?"

"Really? That would be great. I'd be all pretty for Christmas."

"You're always pretty, Donna. I'll make the tea because I think Jamie wants to speak to you too."

"Now I *am* suspicious." Donna looked up into his eyes and laughed her light tinkly laugh. "You make us a cup of tea and I'll go to find your cheeky cousin and speak to him." She switched off the iron and went next door to hear what Jamie had to ask.

***

Jamie, Donna and Frankie were sitting drinking tea and eating Jaffa cakes while the girls were sleeping soundly in their beds.

"Is there no *Corrie* tonight?" Frankie asked.

"Aye, but no' for half an hour, cuz. Did you hear that wee Gerry had me going on the sympathy telling me he'd lost a nephew very young?"

"Aye, sad."

"Well, yes and no, Frankie."

"That's a bit harsh."

"No, it's no', the nephew had an operation and became a niece so the person didnae die. But wee Gerry's never got his head round it, so Les said."

"You must be really unhappy to go all the way and have big operations," Donna said. "But what's it got to do with wee Gerry? I mean, if you love your nephew and then you get a niece, surely you still love them and hope they'll be happy in

148

their own skin going forward. That's what I think, anyway."

"You'd think so, wouldn't you? Anyway, the niece works up at that stables in Liberton, you know, near where Blondie lost the corpse," Jamie said.

"I saw on the news they've found a body up by the crematorium. I wonder if that's the same one or a different one. It might be a dangerous serial killer. It's scary to think of that," Donna said. She cuddled closer into Frankie.

"If you two are going to use this as an excuse to get groping, I'm going upstairs to arrange the treatments and phone Linda. And you can get her to come here for Christmas, Donna." Jamie stomped out of the room and up the stairs to his bedroom.

Chapter Forty-Six

Tim met the team at the National Gallery, near the Christmas market. Mel, Jane and Rachael had chosen to go up to Deacon Brodie's Tavern for a pre-Christmas drink. Angus, Bear and Tim accepted invitations to join them, but Nadia declined. She had to work an evening shift in her uncle Fred's Chinese takeaway. She explained to them that it was so busy at this time of year, she felt duty bound to help. Colin couldn't go either, because he and his wife, Maggie, had Christmas gifts to wrap for their wee ones, Rosie and Adam. He told the girls it was something he and Maggie liked to do together.

As the group walked up the Mound towards the bar, they passed a Salvation Army band playing loud brass instruments and singing popular carols to the passing crowds. The Christmas tree on the Mound was perfect, as always, and beautifully decorated with bright, white lights.

"Did you know that tree is always gifted to Edinburgh by Norway?" Jane asked. "Their present marks Edinburgh's historic and cultural links with Norway since the Second World War."

"I've been told that, but I'd forgotten," Mel said as they arrived at the pub. "Shall we push our way into the bar? Bear, you lead the way and get the round in. I'll get a table."

"Good luck with that, I'll bring up the rear and will you help Bear with the drinks, Angus?" Tim said.

There was a large, noisy group of tourists just about to leave their table and some young lads were hanging around to take it after they had gathered all their jackets. Mel slipped into one of the seats and patted the one beside her to indicate that Rachael should take it.

The boys groaned and started to argue with Mel about her

tactics.

"Gentlemanly of you to give the ladies a seat, lads," Tim said. They turned around and looked up into his smiling face. They groaned again and began to move away. Nobody wanted to start a fight with Tim.

Bear was forcing his way across the room.

"These lads have kindly given the girls a seat, Bear."

"That's good of you lads, merry Christmas, to you." He put down the four pints he was carrying in his large hands on the table. "Angus is bringing the wines for Rachael and Jane. He's also got some snacks, Tim, before you ask."

"Make a space lads." The tall red-haired highlander moved towards the table.

Mel smiled sweetly at the young men and ignored the unpleasant names they called her. She had heard much worse in the station.

"Ailsa helped me out with our investigations. Did you know there are only five specialists in Scotland who can help those who need gender transition surgery?"

"Yes, it has been a problem for years, "Jane said.

"Can you imagine how awful it must be to live in a body that doesn't represent who you are?" Rachael asked. "It must be a living hell. And to make matters worse, the trans community suffers appalling prejudice."

"I don't understand it. Can't everybody just live and let live?" Mel said.

"I don't know but believe me it is not just trans people who suffer prejudice," Bear said quietly.

"Don't you worry, pet, just you leave the people who are nasty to you and I'll sort them out." Mel patted Bear on the knee.

"Yes, do that. They'll come off much worse if Mel gets hold of them than if Angus and I get started." Tim laughed. "Tomorrow I'm going to phone around the specialists and see if I can get an identity for our victim."

"Aren't there privacy issues?" Angus asked.

"Not now he's dead, no."

Conversation around the table lulled momentarily and the

detectives became aware of a group of smartly dressed men at the far end of the bar. A tall, thin man who looked vaguely familiar and a shorter, younger man were both dressed in black suits and ties, as would traditionally be worn at a funeral. The others were less formally dressed, but still wore black ties. The tall man was in the middle of the group and clearly liked the sound of his own voice.

"Terrible that, no decency now, no respect. Imagine cancelling a funeral. Dreadful." He spoke loudly as if addressing the whole pub, rather than just his friends. "And then that person finds a dead man in the garden of remembrance. What is the world coming to? I ask you that. Police crawling all over the place. No respect."

"I heard it wasn't really a man, it was one of those who've had an operation to look like a man," a bald man in the group said. "These creatures make me sick."

"Too right my friend, that kind of creature casts a blight on the human race. It's disgusting," the self-important man agreed.

Tim saw Jane turn red with fury. He stood up and walked over to the group.

"Could you tone it down, guys? You're speaking so loudly everybody in the pub can hear you, and we all just want to enjoy a quiet drink."

"What you going to do, call the cops on us?" the tall man asked.

"That won't be necessary." Tim showed his identity card.

"Detective Constable Myerscough. Any relation to the fallen idol, Sir Peter Myerscough?"

"My father."

The man laughed. "He was a guest at my establishment in Saughton until recently. We could tell you a few things about your old man. And you'll be working with my brother DCI Arthur Inglis. Don't try to pull rank, laddie. I'll win every time."

The barman came over. "Is there a problem, gents?"

"Yes, these patrons are speaking so loudly, they are disturbing the whole bar. Do you want to deal with it, or shall I arrest them for causing a breach of the peace?" Tim asked.

"I don't think that's necessary. These men are regulars and I doubt their banter is disturbing anybody."

"I think you'll find they are. There may be several complaints."

Tim looked around and smiled. He noticed that Angus was standing at the middle of the bar speaking seriously to the manager of the pub. He also saw that Jane was at the other end of the bar with Rachael getting the next round in and talking to the young woman serving them and pointing at the group of men.

"If you speak to your colleagues, you have at least two other complaints," Tim said.

Bear walked up and whispered in his ear. Tim smiled. He walked to the back door that led to the restaurant and watched while Bear and Angus stood at the front door of the pub. The three big detectives waited in silence until the uniforms that Bear had called for arrived and arrested the whole group of men.

A cheer went up around the pub as the obnoxious customers were led away and bundled into the back of a police van.

Tim helped Jane and Rachael back to the table with the drinks and joined his friends for the rest of their evening. He was amazed at how many people bought them a drink, and a bottle of bubbly was even sent over by the manager. He felt quite lightheaded as he left the pub, so he took a taxi home.

Chapter Forty-Seven

Keeping a secret is difficult. If it is something good, you want to share it with people because it is lovely. If it is something awful, you want to share it and get it off your chest.

As soon as you share a secret, it is not a secret, it is a confidence. If it is something happy, those you have shared it with will undoubtedly want to tell others. If it something unpleasant, those in the know are likely to disclose it to others too.

I have always been good at keeping secrets. By nature, I am quiet. I tend to think things through. I have done so ever since I was a child. My brother, Fraser, was always more outgoing than me. He still is, but on the night we found that dead body, he was a little boy again.

Of course, it was he who tripped over the dead man's leg and fell head over heels from his bicycle, he who thought he had broken his arm, he who was mostly covered in the blood.

As teenagers, we had our own bedrooms, but the memory of that horrific sight, ghastly smell and sticky feel of the blood gave us nightmares. When he woke up after a nightmare, he would often slip into my room to find me staring at the ceiling, trying not to go to sleep so the dreams would not come.

Equally, when I did fall into a troubled sleep, I would often wake with a start and slip into Fraser's room. There he would be, lying in his bed with tears rolling down his cheeks.

Now we are adults, and I know more about that body than I knew then, I called him to tell him the man we thought we saw was a woman.

"How difficult life must have been for him. Have you ever talked about that night with anybody else, Hunter? Talked about how you felt or how you coped. I haven't. I just keep it wrapped up like a seeping wound."

"Me too, Fraser. It's my secret. I wouldn't know what to say."

Chapter Forty-Eight

"Fucking wee Gerry is late again. I am bloody sick of this and we don't have Donna today because she and Linda are off to get their nails done."

"To be honest, Jamie, we're hardly run off our feet and you wouldnae put wee Gerry on reception to cover for Donna."

"I know. I'm just sick of being taken a lend of. He acts like we're daft and you may be, Frankie, but I am most definitely not."

"Thanks very much, and I don't think. I was going to make us a coffee, but you can whistle for it."

Jamie started whistling. The phone started to ring, and Jamie whistled louder as he walked towards it.

The usual recording from the prison phone ran through its announcement and Jamie pressed the button to accept the call. When the line went through to his pop, Jamie heard his old man roaring with laughter.

"What's so bloody funny, pop? You're spending another Christmas in the big house and Harry is stuck in Afghanistan. It's not funny."

"Oh, but son, I've just heard something really funny and I had to call to tell you. It's meant to be a secret, but all us lags know. Wait till I tell you." Ian went into more hoots of laughter. Jamie was worried that his pop might run out of breath and die he was laughing so hard.

"Come on then, what's so bloody funny, pop?"

"You know the screw Inglis, the one I've talked about?"

"Aye, pop, the bully."

"Well, he was meant to be at a funeral yesterday and it was cancelled apparently, and he was sounding off in a pub. Sir Peter's lad was there and got him taken to the cells for breach of the peace. So, the arse is in the clink."

"How do you know this?"

"One of the other screws had to come in to cover for him and he's no' best pleased. He's telling anyone who'll listen."

"Fuck! That is funny. But I'll tell you what's no funny, wee Gerry's no' turned up this morning. I'm getting bloody sick of it, Pop."

"I'll have to go, son. Irish Mick wants to share the news with his folks. This is the best laugh we've had in ages. If you see Sir Peter or his lad, do thank him from all of us."

***

Tim had been for a run around the Hermiston loop before he came home. He had a coffee and showered and was in the process of getting dressed for work before Gillian was out of bed. She held her arms out to him and drew him towards her. Her scent and soft kisses aroused him immediately.

"I can't do this, I'll be late for work, pet," he said. He sat on the bed to kiss her.

"And I can't do another day with your dad. And Ailsa's working today, so I will be alone with him. He drives me crazy. I'm sorry, Tim."

"Why don't you make yourself an appointment to get your nails done and a massage and it'll be my treat?"

"I don't suppose I could get a facial, too, could I?"

"My pleasure, Gillian. Make sure you book it early so you get an appointment."

"Thank you, Timmy, that would be lovely. You are tops." She threw the covers off and sat up. She had a cheeky glint in her eyes when she swept back her hair and then Gillian closed her eyes and rubbed her breasts too close to his face for him to ignore her pert pink nipples. He took one in his mouth and sucked it for a moment until it was hard. He caressed her belly and his erection began to throb. He stared into her green eyes.

"I don't care if I'm late for work."

"Neither do I."

Chapter Forty-Nine

"And what time do you call this?" Jamie shouted at wee Gerry across the showroom.

"You'll never believe what happened. I was meant to be helping Les at a funeral late yesterday."

"You were meant to be here, yesterday too." Jamie cut him off.

"Aye, but no' that late."

"All day."

"Listen, Jamie. It was up at the crematorium, but there was some sort of a problem and I got told the funeral was cancelled at the last minute. Some of the folk that were going went for a drink and Les and I were invited along. Les said he wouldn't go cos he had things to see to, but I went."

"Gerry, is this going to be a long story? If it's too long and I lose interest, can I record it and play it back later?"

"No, that's the thing, Jamie. One of the older blokes starts on about men becoming women and gays and stuff and he's in the pub talking louder and louder. Then your pal, the police guy who got his dad a car, he comes over and has a word. The old bloke gets lippy with him and before I know it, we're all in the back of a police van and off for a night in the cells. Les had to get me out this morning."

"That's a good excuse. You've no' used that before."

"I knew you wouldn't believe me, but it's all true. I had to go home to get a shower and change my clothes but I suppose I'll get the sack now, because you don't believe me. I couldn't come it here in my good suit."

"I do believe you, wee Gerry. I know it's true. One of the men you were with was an officer at my pop's prison and the story of him getting locked up in the cells has gone around there like wildfire. My pop can't stop laughing about it."

"Aye, that was the old guy, Inglis, he tried to pull rank on your pal. To be honest, that's when it all went wrong."

**

"What time do you call this, young Myerscough?" Hunter asked as Tim walked into the incident room.

"The briefing starts at eight, doesn't it, boss? It's only three minutes to."

"You're cutting it rather fine. And I believe Inglis wants to start the briefing by taking a shot at you. It seems we ended up with his brother in the cells last night with a group of his pals. They were all processed and fingerprinted before Mr Bernard Inglis, prison officer at HMP Edinburgh was allowed a phone call."

"Oh dear, boss." Tim did not sound at all contrite.

"And it was almost six o'clock this morning before DCI Arthur Inglis was able to be raised to come and authorise the release of his brother and his friends. That DCI is looking for a scape-goat, Tim."

"Where is he now?"

"He's in DCI Mackay's room, letting off steam. I think Mackay is trying to calm him down."

"That's good of him, boss. But his brother's as much of a bigot as DCI Inglis."

"I suggest you join the others in my office and grab a coffee, get your stories straight and come through for the briefing, pronto. Here, take the post-mortem report from Meera. If you are all a few minutes late, you were bringing them up to speed and didn't see the time."

"That's more than decent of you, boss."

"I know. You owe me a pint and the full story once we've got rid of DCI Inglis."

Tim smiled and walked towards Hunter's office. The rest of the last night's drinkers were in there muttering amongst themselves. Tim noticed they fell silent when he walked in.

"What are you all looking so glum for?"

"Because you are going to get the bloody book thrown at you by Inglis and we'll all be collateral damage," Bear said.

"I doubt it."

"You have a plan?"

"Yes, and it's the easiest to operate."

"Go on then, tell us."

"When Inglis comes after us, and he will, we tell the truth. Exactly how it happened. His brother is not the kind of man who should be in charge of anybody, especially not in a prison where there's no way out for his victims."

"Tim, you are a genius," Bear said. He slapped his friend on the back and they all walked quietly to the briefing room.

Chapter Fifty

Only Mackay, Hunter, Nadia, Colin and Inglis were sitting in the briefing room as Mackay watched the other detectives walk in. They entered quietly and stood at the back in a semi-circle facing him. Unusually, nobody was eating, and only Hunter had a mug of coffee. Mackay thought he had done a good job of defusing Inglis' ire, but as soon as Tim walked in, he realised how wrong he was.

"You impossible, liberal upstart," Inglis shouted as he got up and raced towards Tim.

The big detective simply raised his arms to his chest and put his hands out to stop the angry man before he reached him. Inglis was swinging punches at him, but Tim's reach was so long all he did was hit the air between them. It was very funny. Everybody in the room laughed and even Mackay and Hunter smiled as Inglis became increasingly impotent and furious.

"You ignoramus! I suppose you think that's funny, Myerscough," he shouted, taking a step back.

"No, sir. But I was only saving you from yourself. I wouldn't want to have to arrest you for assaulting a police officer. May I suggest you back away from me, sir, because I don't see this ending well for you if you attack me."

"Are you threatening a senior officer, DC Myerscough?"

"No, DCI Inglis. You were attempting to assault me. If I have to defend myself, it won't take me more than one punch to end the fight."

"I don't think that will be necessary, DC Myerscough," Mackay said. "I suggest we concentrate less on our differences and more on our common goal, to find the killer." He watched as Inglis returned to the front of the room and stood glaring at Tim.

161

"This is not over, Myerscough," Inglis said.

"Indeed it is, Arthur," Mackay said quietly. He noticed that Tim had not moved, nor raised his voice. He was impressed by that.

"In the circumstances, I will be chairing the briefing today," Mackay said. "I know we have information to share about the murder, but I want to start with the elephant in the room. DCI Inglis will inform us what he understands happened last evening. Arthur, over to you."

"Thank you, DCI Mackay. My brother was planning to attend a funeral yesterday, however, when he arrived at the crematorium, only the funeral director was there to turn people away. The funeral had been cancelled."

"That is most unusual. I've never heard the like," Mackay said.

"Neither have I," Inglis agreed.

"That evening, my brother joined his friends for a drink in Deacon Brodie's Tavern. He is a regular there and known and liked by all the staff and frequent patrons, of course."

Mackay noticed that Bear was about to comment, but Tim put his hand on his friend's arm to silence him. Mackay thought this was wise and allowed Inglis to continue.

"Bernard, that's my brother, was chatting quietly with his friends over a pint when Myerscough approached him and threatened him. Bernard realised he was Sir Peter's son and was severely intimidated. Before he knew what had happened, DC McKenzie and that one, who's name nobody can pronounce, joined the attack. Even DS Renwick was bullied by her companions to complain about my brother and his friends. This resulted in them all being arrested. It is a shocking attack on a group of upstanding citizens. I really thought more highly of you, Jane. I am most disappointed in you."

Mackay noticed that Tim was staring at the ceiling. He seemed to be biting his lip so hard, it might bleed. The rest of the group were staring at the floor. Hunter, Nadia and Colin were all looking at Inglis in disbelief.

"If all that wasn't bad enough, Bernard and his friends were photographed and fingerprinted and charged before I could get here to sort this out. Bernard has been suspended from duty, pending an investigation. I am horrified that any police officer should act with such an extreme abuse of power."

"Says the man who won't learn to pronounce my name and stated recently that attacks on members of the trans community were understandable," Bear said. "Now that we've listened to the fairy tale, which of us would you like to tell what really happened, sir?"

"Thank you, DC Zewedu, let me just check with DCI Inglis in case he has anything he wants to add at this point. Do you, Arthur?" Mackay asked.

"No, thank you, Allan. Shall we hear from DC Myerscough? It seemed to Bernard that he started the attack and personally, from what I have seen this morning and what I know of his background, that would not surprise me at all."

Mackay nodded at Tim. He was standing at the back of the room and before he started to speak, he moved the chair beside Colin and sat down so that his eyes were level with the others who were seated. Mackay was fascinated by this unthreatening move which reduced the feeling of hostility that Inglis had created. He thought it was clever.

"Should I just start, sir?" Tim asked Mackay.

"Go ahead, Tim."

"If any of my colleagues who were actually present last night and witnessed what happened think I am getting this wrong, please let me know. But this is the evening as I remember it.

"Jane, sorry DS Renwick, DC Anderson and DC Grant had all arranged for the team to go for a few pre-Christmas drinks. They had chosen Deacon Brodie's because it is central. Nadia and Colin couldn't go because they had other things planned, but Bear, sorry, DC Zewedu, DC McKenzie and I were able to join them. Can I just use people's first names, sir?"

"Of course. Go ahead, Tim."

"The pub was busy, but Mel managed to get a table because some people left just as we arrived. Bear and Angus got the drinks in and we were chatting about this and that, when a

163

group of men at the far end of the bar became loud. Their conversation became increasingly rowdy and then deteriorated into a booming monologue by a tall, thin man at the centre of the group, whom I now know to be DCI Inglis' brother," Tim paused and looked at Arthur. "You and your brother do look alike, sir. Anyway, we were not interested in what he had to say, but it was impossible to avoid hearing it.

"He was speaking in a most derogatory way about minorities and that was offensive to us. After all, Jane, Rachael and Bear were at our table."

Mackay nodded but noticed Inglis looked confused. Tim carried on.

"I went over and asked the men to lower their voices. The loud one, Bernard Inglis, threatened to call the police and I showed him my warrant card to explain that would not be necessary.

"Angus complained to the manager about them and Jane mentioned her concerns to the girl behind the bar when she bought the next round of drinks. Bernard spoke in a derogatory way about my dad and threatened me with a report to DCI Inglis, as this senior officer was his brother and out-ranked me. He became increasingly obnoxious, so Bear phoned the uniforms for back up. After that he, Angus and I blocked the exits so the group could not leave and when uniforms arrived, we charged them all with breach of the peace and they were packed into the back of a van.

"A great cheer went up around the pub because everyone was glad to see the back of them and we spent the rest of the evening on free drinks.

"That's about it, sir. Did I miss anything out, Jane?"

"No, I don't think you did, Tim. That was a fair explanation of what really happened."

"Thank you, Tim. Does anybody have any questions?"

"Why do DS Renwick and DC Anderson count as minorities?" Inglis asked.

"We are gay, sir and in a civil partnership." Jane held Rachael's hand. "We love each other."

The team burst into a round of applause.

"But that can't be, you are a good officer, DS Renwick."

"Thank you, sir, and I am gay. That's all there is to it."

"Bloody disgusting. Nobody told me that," Inglis exploded.

Hunter stood up, "May I suggest that we take a half hour break before we start the real briefing? I think we need to rethink our objectives to treat each other with respect and courtesy. The atmosphere in here is far too highly charged at the moment to go straight onto other business."

"Good idea, Hunter. Let's do that," Mackay said.

**

When the briefing reconvened, the feeling in the room had changed completely. Mackay had suggested to Inglis that he meet with his brother and discuss the other view of the previous evening's events that his colleagues had put forward. Jane would represent MIT at the briefing and Mackay undertook to report everything that was discussed to Inglis. Without his presence, Mackay felt the team would be more unified and focussed.

"I have some information that may be useful," Tim said.

Mackay and Hunter agreed Tim's information should start the briefing. They listened carefully as he explained what he had discovered last night about the small number of relevant specialists who operated on transgender patients.

"Only five, are you sure?" Hunter asked.

"As far as I could tell, boss. It means the waiting times to see a specialist can be up to a year or more."

"I suggest you contact them all and send a photo of our victim, to see if any of the specialists in Scotland recognise him."

"I will, boss."

"Nadia, have you had an idea?"

"Yes, boss. I just want to go over the fingerprints again. From the old case and the new case. If Colin can be spared, he and I might see something that has been overlooked to date. I want to make sure that all fingerprints were checked at the time of the historic case."

"I'm sure my dad would have instructed that, but it is a good idea, to double check, Nadia," Tim said.

"Rachael and I will go over the statements again, boss."

"Do that, Bear. Rachael, can you also go through the list of nine missing people again? See what you can find out about any of them."

Rachael and Bear nodded.

"Of course, boss," she said.

"I want to find out more about Bernard Inglis, boss. I'll check his record. I'll also try to find out who the other men were with him yesterday," Jane said.

"That's fine, but I want a word with you when we finish here."

Jane blushed and nodded at Hunter.

"Jane, I recognised one of them, the shorter man in the suit, He's Gerry Littlewood, his father is Les Littlewood the undertaker and former prisoner who served time with my dad. Gerry works at Thomson's Top Cars," Tim said.

"Be still my beating heart. I'll go and interview him, boss."

Hunter smiled at Mel. "Take Angus with you. You might need a bodyguard if Jamie Thomson is around."

***

Hunter led the way to his office and Jane followed him. He held the door open for her and indicated that she should take a seat. He sat beside her, rather than on the other side of the desk.

"You didn't need to do that, you know."

"Do what, boss?"

Hunter raised his eyebrows and stared her. "There is not a single member of the team who would have made Inglis's comments personal to you and Rachael."

"I know that. He just made me so fucking angry."

"I realise that, the man is a bigot and a luddite. It is a long time since I met an officer quite as detestable as he is. His views and his attitudes reprehensible."

"Exactly, boss. I couldn't stand it any longer."

"You know he will gossip all around MIT?"

"Yes."

"And try to use it against both you and Rachael?"

"Yes, boss. I know I should probably have bitten my lip, but I just couldn't anymore."

Hunter smiled and said, "Jane, we will just have to work a little smarter. Bernard Inglis is not at the prison today, so I suggest you and Tim make an appointment to meet Ian Thomson. Find out a bit about him. Then, get Tim to take you to his house, discuss the Inglis brothers with his dad. After all, he worked with Arthur and was subjected to Bernard's rule."

"Okay, boss, doesn't Tim have some calls to make?"

"Yes, but I doubt it will take him more than an hour. You and Rache go and have a delicious cup of tea in the canteen and catch up with Tim after that."

"Delicious and canteen are two words you rarely hear in the same sentence." Jane smiled. "Thanks boss."

"Don't worry, we'll sort this. I plan to phone Superintendent Miller at MIT and explain what happened. I have no doubt he will come at Inglis from above. Attack is the best form of defence."

Chapter Fifty-One

Hunter realised that, with the team working on the murder, he could slip off for a couple of hours over lunchtime. He went to his office and grabbed his coat and phone. He left the building, noticed only by the desk sergeant, Charlie.

"DI Wilson," he shouted. "If anybody asks, where are you?"

"None of their business."

"Charming, and I don't think. I make a polite inquiry and get my head bitten off. Sooner I retire from this shit hole the better."

"Agreed," Hunter said as he strode out of the station.

He phoned Parvati from his car and was thrilled that she could give him an hour of her time, provided he could get to her flat. He drove out of the car park and joined the stream of traffic heading towards Comely Bank.

He arrived at the door of her tenement and rang the bell. After she buzzed him into the close, he noticed it was a beautiful nineteenth century entrance, with original ceramic tiles at the front door and the stair-well was lit by a large glass cupola in the roof. There were only two apartments on each landing and Hunter bounced up the stairs two at a time until he reached the second floor. She stood in the doorway and smiled broadly at him.

"Hunter, how good to see you."

"It's kind of you to give me this extra time, Parvati."

"Not at all. It is fun to be involved in this subterfuge, although I'm not sure Meera would approve. Never mind that. I think that our meeting should be entirely my way today. I want you to practice exactly what you want to." She smiled at him. Her soft, brown eyes danced with joy.

"I'll try."

"Are you nervous?"

"Never more so Parvati. I am bloody terrified. Wait a minute, that's my phone. I'll turn it off."

Hunter looked at his screen. It was Meera. He paused then switched his phone off and settled down on the sofa with Parvati. He held her hand as he spoke, quietly, then listened carefully while she corrected him and repeated herself again, and again, and again until he got it right.

He didn't listen to Meera's message until he was back in the car. Shit! He should have taken the call. He tried to phone her back, but her phone was off.

Chapter Fifty-Two

The phone in the showroom rang. Jamie answered the call with his usual lack of enthusiasm. He listened and his expression changed when he realised Les Littlewood was on the other end of the line. He hoped the man had found he needed another expensive vehicle for his business, or even for himself. He could certainly do with a new one, that old van in his driveway was in a shocking state. Unfortunately, Les only needed a hearse serviced.

"No, we're not really taking on any new jobs, Les. Not till after the holidays. We close on Christmas Eve and open again after New Year. I could book the hearse in for a service then. Is that any use to you? Aye, well you have a think and let me know. No worries, Les."

Jamie finished the conversation and turned away from the reception desk. His face broke into a wide grin.

"Well if it's no' my darling, Mel. DC Grant, how the fucking hell are you? It's been far too long. I know you've missed me; you don't need to tell me."

"Enough of your cheek, Jamie Thomson. I know you and Linda are an item and you never give me a second thought these days. This is my colleague, DC McKenzie."

The men shook hands.

"As soon as you come to your senses and ditch that big copper, you'll still be in with a chance here." He thumped his chest with a flat hand. "What brings you to this neck of the woods anyway, Mel? You want to buy a car or do Edinburgh's finest need my help. Again?"

"I hate to burst your bubble, Jamie, but I'm looking for one of you employees, Gerry Littlewood."

"Mel, you really don't want Gerry. He's not nearly as good

looking as me and his hands are always dirty and covered in grease."

"I know it would be impossible for him to come between us, but it is Gerry we're looking for. He may be able…"

"…to help you with your enquiries. I know, I know. Hold on a minute." Jamie walked towards the garage and shouted. "Gerry. Police."

He watched as Gerry slid out from under a car, stood up and turned to run out the back. Jamie grabbed him by the collar.

"No, you don't wee man. You're going this way." He marched Gerry through to Mel and Angus. Are you okay to talk here or do you want to use my office?"

"If it's okay to use the office that would be good, Jamie."

"Aye. I think Frankie's in there. If he is, we'll just throw him out!" Jamie led the way to the office. He was right, Frankie was in there chatting quietly to Donna. "Come on you soft tart, wind it up. He took the receiver from Frankie. "Sorry, Donna, love, he's got to go." And Jamie hung up.

"Bloody hell, Jamie. What would you say if I did that to you and Linda?"

"You wouldnae dare. Now the very lovely DC Grant and this other plod need to talk to our wee Gerry here. So, shift your arse, Frankie."

"Hi DC Grant. How you doing?"

"Fine Frankie. All set for Christmas with those wee girls of yours?"

"Aye. They're growing right fast."

"Enough of this blethering. Can we please get the interview done, if you don't mind Mel?" Angus asked.

Jamie and Frankie left the office and went for a wander around the showroom to pass the time.

***

Mel sat on the far side of the desk and Angus took the seat by the door. She signalled to Gerry to sit beside Angus.

"Gerry, we want to talk to you about the friends you were with at the pub yesterday."

"They're no' my friends."

"We saw you with a group of men yesterday at Deacon Brodie's."

"Aye, so, it's no' against the law to have a drink with a few mates."

"They are your friends, then." Angus said.

"No' really. I just know them."

"How do you know them?" Mel asked.

"One of them was a guard at the big house when my dad was there. Inglis his name is. He gave my dad a really hard time at first. He's no' like other folk, my dad. It sort of runs in the family."

"So, if he gave your dad a hard time, why is he a friend of yours?"

"He's *not* a friend. We just came to an understanding. I help him out occasionally and he left my dad alone. Of course, Ian Thomson helped dad too. That's how I got my job here. I don't want to lose it, but I've had to take a lot of time off recently to attend to funerals and Jamie's no' got a lot of patience left with me."

"Wind that back a bit, Gerry. An understanding. What kind of understanding did you come to with Inglis?" Mell asked.

Gerry blushed. He looked at the floor and bit his lip. "It's a bit difficult to explain, DC Grant."

"Try."

"If there's a funeral and he needs help, I give it."

"What sort of help could he possibly need at a funeral?"

"Oh, you know. A discount from the family business, arrange the body, turn up and fill up the room, help with flowers. My family does run a funeral parlour you know."

"But this man isn't a professional mourner. He is a prison officer. How many funerals can he possibly need help with?" Angus said.

"And I'm sure he passes enough corner shops that he can pick up a few flowers if needed, Gerry. You'll have to do better than that."

"I suppose it all started when his wife went. Of course, I didn't know him then."

"Just a minute, Gerry. Mel, look at that man!" Angus said. "He looks familiar."

"That's my dad, Les. Les Littlewood from Littlewood's the undertakers."

"That's the man in the other picture."

"I think you're right, Angus. Les, did you say, Gerry? I think you and Les better come back to the station with us for a little chat."

"Am I under arrest?"

"No, not if you co-operate. We'll just all go to the station," Mel said. "Let's go and tell your dad the good news."

Chapter Fifty-Three

Donna met Linda outside the beauty salon. It was the same one Donna had worked in, and where she had met Frankie. She still knew a lot of the girls who were there.

"Jamie's never done anything like this for me before," Linda said.

"No Frankie hasn't either, but I hope they get into the habit of it. Shall we go in?"

They pushed the heavy glass door and walked over to the welcome desk. The whole place was bright white and spotlessly clean. Donna remembered how much work it took to keep the place that way. She knew the girl who checked them in, and they had a chat.

"Your men have arranged a really lovely pamper for you. Bubbly and everything, Donna. You are really lucky. And they've booked you for fingers and toes. You'll have a good time."

"We're looking forward to it, aren't we, Linda?"

"Ooh yes. Can we be close together so we can chat?"

"Of course, we thought you'd want that. Follow me and I'll get you a wee glass of bubbly before you start."

They all giggled, and Donna and Linda followed the girl across the wide area leading to the cubicles at the back. Theirs was set up for two clients. It was lovely. They laughed when the bottle of Cava opened with a 'pop'. It was exciting.

"Please come to us for Christmas, Linda. I need the support. You know Jamie is just going to get drunk and be a pain to me and Frankie if you don't."

"I don't know, Donna. I've said to my mum that I'm going to her."

"You could come over on Christmas eve and stay over at

ours for the morning to watch the twins open their presents. The girls are so sweet."

"I suppose," Linda said. She sipped her drink. "But I've told my mum."

"Well, stay with us for lunch and then drive over to your mum for the evening."

"And not drink? That's not happening!" Linda took more of the Cava and frowned. "I'll talk to her and see what she says. She might be okay to go to my sister and have time with her kids."

"Is that a yes?"

"Alright, it's a yes."

"Cheers, Linda. You're a star." Donna smiled and topped up their glasses of fizz. Now that she was confident Linda would join them for Christmas, she decided to change the subject.

"I didn't know if I was going to make it this morning, Linda because that wee Gerry was late again."

"Goodness, what was it this time? I don't know why Frankie and Jamie put up with that grubby wee toe rag. All Jamie does is complain about him."

"His dad was in the big house with Ian, so I don't think they want to sack him. But really, I phoned Frankie when I was waiting for you, and he told me Gerry said he was late because a funeral had been cancelled."

"Cancelled? Who cancelled it? Can you cancel a funeral? I've never heard of that."

"Then Gerry said he'd been carted off in a police van last night when he was at the pub with his mates and the coppers were there again today to interview him."

"Really, Donna? That can't be good for business. I wonder what he's been up to. Of course, Jamie and his pop are hardly squeaky clean, I suppose."

"I don't know, what's going on, but his dad is an undertaker. That's creepy enough at the best of times."

"It is, isn't it. What happened when he was inside?"

"The family ran the business without him for years, Frankie says."

"I wouldn't like to do that. Makes me feel right queasy."

"And he dresses up."

"Well, we all like to dress up sometimes. Especially at this time of year, Donna."

"No, I mean dresses up. Wears dresses sometimes. And he's very tall, I think he must have a problem getting dresses to fit. It wouldn't be so bad if it was wee Gerry, he's quite wee. Well he would be." Donna started laughing.

"Do you think those bubbles are going to your head?"

The girls heard the door of the cubicle next to theirs open and close. Then they heard the conversation drift over the partition.

"I'll do your massage and then your facial and after that I'll do your nails, Dr. Pearson. You get ready and I'll be back in a minute."

Then their own beauticians entered the cubicle and both Donna and Linda decided to get their pedicures first.

"It will be much easier to continue drinking the fizz while we're getting our toes done. I wouldn't want to smudge my fingernails, but we can finish the fizz before we get to them," Donna said.

"So, as I was saying, who can cancel a funeral? I mean it's not as if the person came back to life."

"I don't know, Linda. The family might postpone it, or there could be a problem with the funeral parlour or the crematorium, but I don't know. Have you ever heard of that happening, Tracey?" Donna asked her beautician.

The girl shook her head. "Never heard of it."

"Did Gerry know who cancelled it? Was it a friend or a member of his family? I mean if he was meant to be there, he would know."

"No Linda, wee Gerry's hopeless. He never knows anything or says he doesn't. He told Jamie and Frankie that his dad was the undertaker, but he was there to 'make numbers' for a pal. When it didn't go ahead, they all went off to the pub, except his dad. He had things to do, according to Gerry. But the world according to Gerry is an odd place. He's okay with his dad wearing dresses but won't speak to his nephew who became his niece. It's all mixed up if you ask me."

"His nephew became his niece. You don't hear that very often. But at least nobody died."

Donna poured them each another glass of Cava and they clinked glasses.

"Do you get many men in here, Tracey?" Donna asked.

"Yes, male grooming is growing noticeably more popular, now. Why do you ask?"

"We heard the person in the next cubicle was a Dr. Pearson and I just wondered."

"Dr Pearson is a woman." Tracey lowered her voice to a stage whisper. "She's going out with a very wealthy, good looking policeman. He's treating her today. She did well. The manager says he could buy and sell this place."

"It must be Tim Myerscough. He's one of the good guys in the police force. He's a friend of Jamie and Frankie."

"I don't know his name. What colour do you want? Do you want toes and fingers the same?"

***

Donna and Linda were settling their bill at the desk with the cash Frankie and Jamie had given them.

"So, you'll spend Christmas with us," Donna said.

"Alright, I've said so. I'll sort it with Mum. You've talked me into it."

"Good. Today has been fun."

Then Donna looked over at another woman who came up and stood beside them. She had a green flash at the front of her hair and paid her bill with a Black American Express card.

"I think you were the ladies discussing my boyfriend, Tim Myerscough," she said in a matter of fact tone of voice. "If you know anything about the cancelled funeral, you should tell the police."

"We don't really know anything, just what we were told. Is it true they found a body up at the crematorium? Is that why the funeral was cancelled?" Donna asked. She felt defensive.

"Creepy isn't it? Finding a dead body," Linda said. "I read in the paper your man found one and then lost it. How do you

177

lose a dead body?"

"I don't know anything about it, but if you have information, do tell the police." Gillian sounded bossier than she felt and smiled as Donna watched her leave an enormous tip and picked up her card receipt. She walked out of the door smartly.

"Funny having a bit of your hair green, isn't it?" Donna muttered to Linda.

Chapter Fifty-Four

Tim did not have a long list of phone numbers in front of him, but he wanted to make the calls to the experts before he went on to undertake the interviews with Jane. He needed talk to each doctor and send them copies of the pictures of the deceased. The man did not look pretty, but if he had consulted any of the doctors, the chances were good that they would recognise him.

When Tim spoke to the first two specialists, he drew a blank, but the third one, although she had not operated on that particular individual, was sure that she knew who had done so.

"How can you be so sure?"

"Because of the precision of the stitches and the neatness of the scars, it can only be Hugo Karlsson. I trained with him. The handicraft is like seeing the work of a master painter. You just know whose work it is if you are familiar with their style. He's working in England now, but I can give you his number if it helps?"

"It would help very much, thank you."

Tim noted down the number and took a few moments to look up the surgeon's profile on the internet. The accolades paid to Karlsson were many and various and his patients seemed to praise his work and his compassion. Tim smiled. This man seemed to be dedicated to his profession. He lifted the phone to call.

A woman's voice answered the phone. "Mr Karlsson's office," she said in a clipped voice.

Tim explained who he was and asked to speak to Mr Karlsson.

"You may just catch him. He has a full day of surgery planned today, but I believe he is on a short break between operations. He might be at his desk. I will try to put you through. If he is not available, you can leave a message."

The line flicked over to a different ring tone and almost immediately the call was answered. "Karlsson."

Tim introduced himself and explained the case he was involved in. He heard Karlsson sigh.

"I'm sorry to disturb you, Mr Karlsson, but I wonder if I could enlist your help. We fear the most recent case may be the latest in a series of attacks against transgender people that have gone unnoticed for some years."

"That would not surprise me at all, DC Myerscough. My patients are amongst the most misunderstood members of society. I have never suffered the body dysmorphia that they do, but still I can sympathise and want to help. Am I so very unusual?" He paused.

Tim feared that he might be more unusual than he would wish but chose not to answer the question. He asked Karlsson if he would be willing to look at pictures of the victim and, if he could, identify him.

"Send me what you need me to look at and I will respond today, when I can. I cannot promise a timeframe because today is a busy day."

Tim guessed that most of Mr Karlsson's days were busy. He thanked the surgeon and concluded the call.

***

Jane had made the appointment for them to interview Ian Thomson at HMP Edinburgh. Before they left the station, Tim confirmed with his father that they would meet with him over lunch. He saw no reason for them to miss Alice's cooking.

Tim took his own car when they left the station. Jane, sitting beside him, decided to confront the elephant in the room.

"I doubt you'll need me to act as navigator on our way to Saughton."

"I think the car could make its own way when I think of the number of months dad was in there. I know HMP Edinburgh is known as Saughton, but it's actually in Stenhouse Road. It's such a quiet residential area to house a prison."

"Yes, the homes are modest, except for Stenhouse Mansion, of course. But it's a decent place to live. Do you think Ian Thomson will be able to tell us much?"

"I hope so. At least he should be able to tell us how Bernard Inglis treats the inmates, especially the minorities."

"If his attitude is anything like his brother, I don't fancy their chances."

"Well. Here we are. I'm looking forward to seeing how this goes." Tim got out of the car quickly and waited until Jane was beside him before he locked it."

"I doubt any harm will come to it with all these cameras about, Tim."

"I'm a creature of habit." He smiled and led the way to the reception.

This visit qualified as a police interview, so it did not reduce the time with his family to which Ian was entitled. Tim knew well that the two hours visiting permitted for convicted criminals each month was precious, and no inmate would be willing to cut that short to meet with the police.

Tim and Jane were sitting with their backs to the window in a private interview room. Ian was brought to them by a prison officer who nodded to the detectives. When Ian was seated, the officer left the room and closed the door. But Tim, Jane and Ian all knew he was right outside and straining to hear anything that was said, even if it was meant to be confidential.

"I hear you bought your pop a nice motor, but you could have done me a favour and given him the Bentley. I've had that on my books for months."

"That was the one he wanted, believe me, Ian." Tim smiled.

"I do."

"But Jamie did a great job of talking him into thinking the hybrid BMW was his idea. He's incredibly happy with it, thanks."

"That boy. I'm going to have to sack him." Ian grinned. "And how's your pop coping with his newfound freedom?"

"He keeps leaving the house uncomfortably close to his

curfew times. He's a pain in the arse."

"No change there then. But, please, tell me the rumours going around this place are true. Someone is telling us you got our own dear Bernie Inglis banged up last night. Is it right?"

"Yes, it is true, Ian. Only on a breach of the peace and his brother got him out this morning without charge," Tim said.

"Without charge? Pity."

"But we did manage to photograph and fingerprint him and even swab him for DNA," Jane said.

"Excellent. You have done a fine job. That man is a nasty piece of work."

"Tell us about him."

"What do you want to know? He's a tall, skinnymalinky longlegs but as strong as an ox. A bully."

"What kind of bully?" Jane asked. She took her notepad out of her bag and began to write down what Ian was saying.

"He picks on all the ones that will find it most difficult in here. He tried it with your pop, Tim, but your old man just called whoever took over from him as Justice Secretary and complained. He got no more trouble from the screws after that." Ian laughed at the memory.

"How like my dad," Tim said. "Anyone else you know had a problem with Inglis?"

"He always gives the youngsters a hard time. especially the good-looking ones. Then there's the gays, the blacks, generally anybody not like him. Like most bullies. My friend, queer Les, had a really bad time with him."

"Les Littlewood the undertaker?"

"Yes. There's no harm in him, and he's loaded so I helped him out with Inglis and his cronies a bit and Jamie gave his son a job. He got his lad to put money into my spending account here. He's okay. But he swings both ways and Inglis especially doesn't like that. But I remember after a particularly bad time, Les's boy wee Gerry, waited till the end of Inglis shift and apparently had it out with him. It was brave mind, Gerry's no' the brawniest of blokes, but it seemed to work. Les had no more trouble off him after that."

"What was the deal?" Tim asked.

"I don't know, and if Les knew, he wasn't saying. But after that if he felt the need he'd walk around in his dressing up clothes, as I called them, and none of the screws gave him any grief."

"I bet the lags did," Jane said.

"True enough, lass, true enough. That's what kept my money from him rolling in. He still needed protection.

"Did you know Les and wee Gerry have a relative that went the whole hog and had a sex change?"

"Oh. Right that makes sense, we were told the stable hand's name was Rowan and we thought it was a man, but when my colleague got there it was a young woman. He just thought we'd made a mistake; I don't think he knew the person is trans." Jane said. She wrote another entry into her book.

"To be honest, it didn't put Les up or down, but he said wee Gerry found it difficult. Shame really, I mean, she's not hurting anybody. Just being herself. It's nobody else's business as far as I can see. Still, that's not what you want to know. You want to know about Inglis."

"Is there more?"

"Only that he's really the ringleader of anything nasty the screws do in here. He has a group of officers that follow him around like sheep."

"Why has nobody complained?" Tim asked.

"Who's going to believe us against them? It'll just be worse in the long run."

Tim and Jane left the prison and walked slowly back to his car. They were both deep in thought and wondering what Sir Peter would have to add to their picture of the Inglis brothers.

Chapter Fifty-Five

Nadia had made herself a cup of tea and Colin sat with a large glass of water as they arranged the evidence and statements gathered to date.

"Shall we start with the most recent and work backwards, Colin?"

"We might as well, it'll make a change. What I do not understand is why the two sketch artist drawings are so different. I mean they are both thin faced, but one is a dead ringer for Inglis and the other looks nothing like him."

"DCI Inglis isn't so thin in the face as that drawing suggests. Too many fancy dinners, I suspect."

"Do you think Angus's witness and our teenagers saw two different men?"

"It's more likely that our group each wanted input and we've ended up with the sketch version of Chinese whispers."

"You can say that DC Chan. I couldn't possibly comment." Colin grinned at Nadia and they finished sorting out the evidence.

"Dr Sharma's post-mortem report indicates that the witness was throttled with the tie that was found at the scene of the crime and was stunned or became unconscious before the fatal attack. Do you think the tie would be heavy duty enough to be used to do that?"

"I wonder who the tie belonged to, the victim or the attacker? And the victim had dirt and scrapings of skin and under their nails, they did not go quietly, Nadia."

"No, they put up a fight. That's probably why they were strangled to make the attack easier for the assailant."

"I don't think it's unique to this case. Remember a Paisley patterned tie was found near the scene of the crime the boss witnessed."

"That's right, Colin. It must have been a horrible thing for young boys to see. I'd never heard the boss talk about it before this recent murder, had you?"

"Not at all. But what would he say? It was thirty years ago."

Colin and Nadia continued sorting out the evidence and made a comprehensive report of the findings that were supported by it. They were just finishing when the incident room door burst open and Angus stood grinning at them.

"Guess what. No, you'll never guess. I'll tell you."

Colin and Nadia had never seen the normally quiet highlander so animated. They suggested he sit down, but he was much too excited for that.

"We've found the man in your picture."

They looked at each other blankly. Neither Colin nor Nadia could make sense of what they were being told. Then Mel walked in and added to the confusion.

"Has Angus told you?"

"I think he's trying to communicate something, but we're not quite speaking the same language yet," Colin said.

"The man in the sketch made from those teenagers' descriptions walked into Thomson's Top Cars. We've got him downstairs waiting to be interviewed."

Colin grinned. "That's amazing,"

"Well done you two," Nadia agreed.

"I said that, what's so different when Mel says it?"

The four detectives went along to Hunter's office to share the good news. Halfway along the corridor, Nadia pulled at Colin's arm and they stopped. She whispered in his ear and he nodded. They walked back to the incident room to give Angus and Mel their moment of glory.

Hunter was amazed by the news and immediately agreed that Mel and Angus would interview wee Gerry while Colin and Nadia questioned Les. They could all collate their findings before this evenings' briefing.

Tim's information would be available then too and Hunter planned to do a little investigating of his own. There was a niggle in the back of his brain, and he had no wish to leave the thought unheeded, even if it did mean allowing some members of his team to hurry along a blind alley. He hoped they would forgive him if he was right.

Chapter Fifty-Six

"Mister Timothy and DS Renwick," Kenneth said as he opened the door. "Sir Peter told me you were coming for a meeting and Alice did hope you would be able to stay for lunch. She's made a shepherd's pie to try and tempt you both."

"That was my cunning plan all along, Kenneth. Please thank Alice. The shepherd's pie sounds delicious. It's so cold outside. I think I'll see if dad is ready to eat now and we can have our meeting over lunch."

"I think you'll find Sir Peter in the dining room waiting for you. I'll bring up the lunch."

Tim watched Kenneth walk along the corridor to the kitchen while he and Jane climbed the stairs to the dining room. The carpet's thick pile gave under their feet and Tim noticed the smell of cigar smoke had returned to the house, now that his dad was home.

Sir Peter greeted them warmly. It was obvious to Tim that his dad was glad to have some company. Jane stood with her back to the radiator and rubbed her hands together to try to get them warm before lunch was served.

"I believe this is not a social call, but that I may be able to be of some assistance."

Kenneth brought in the lunch and Tim indicated that he would serve. Sir Peter, Jane and Tim took their places at the table and tucked into the delicious meal.

"Homemade shepherd's pie, carrots and cauliflower. You really can't beat it, can you?" Sir Peter said. "Now how can I help?"

Tim listened quietly while Jane told his dad about the previous evening and Bernard Inglis getting carted off to the cells. His was glad to hear his dad laugh genuinely and heartily. He had not heard much of that since he was released."

"That must have been so funny. I wish I had been there. Bernard is a nasty bully you know. He and his gang always pick of the younger and weaker inmates. But there was no point in complaining. Who would believe us?"

"I heard you complained, Dad. We saw Ian Thomson earlier."

"True, but not many inside have the home number for the Justice Secretary. You know I worked with his older brother too. I think he was a young DC when I was Senior Investigating Officer of that murder Hunter witnessed. He's a bastard too."

"Hunter?" Jane asked in surprise.

"No, Hunter Wilson and I have made our peace. I mean the older brother, Arthur Inglis. Arthur is every bit as bad as Bernie. He kept getting promoted to get him out of the way. I was as guilty of that as any senior officer."

"Well Arthur got Bernie and his pals out of the cells early this morning," Jane said.

"I bet he did. He would not hesitate to throw his weight around and get them out. I know that."

"He did, but not before they'd all been fingerprinted and photographed and had their DNA taken," Tim said as he reached for a second helping of shepherd's pie.

"Oh no! You didn't, did you? Now that's funny, son."

"No. it wasn't me. It was the uniforms on duty. They were determined to treat the group just like any other, no matter how loud Bernie shouted or what he said."

"That is hilarious. No doubt both Inglis brothers were suitably furious this morning. Just for a laugh, do me a favour and run the fingerprints and DNA through and see if you can find anything against any one on the group."

"That would be a waste of resources, dad."

"You can't know that, and it wouldn't cost all that much, and wouldn't it be a coup if you tied up an unsolved case."

"That's highly unlikely to happen, Sir Peter. Bernard Inglis may be a bully, but we've heard nothing that suggests he, or any of his cronies are dishonest," Jane said.

Tim smiled as his dad shrugged his shoulders and served himself a small extra portion of the shepherd's pie.

"I tell you what, Dad, if it makes you feel better, I'll ask the boss."

Chapter Fifty-Seven

Les sat in the small interview room and stared bleakly at his surroundings. He had been in enough of these in his life. This room was small and dark. The only window had bars across it and was almost at the height of the ceiling. Les was tall, but not tall enough to see out of it. The smell in interview rooms was never fresh. It didn't seem to matter how much disinfectant the cleaners used or how much air-freshener the officers sprayed around after the rooms were used. They always smelled of dirt, body odour and farts. This room was no different. He felt quite depressed. He could not think of anything he had done to deserve being here, this time.

He heard footsteps coming along the corridor and looked at the young police constable near the door.

"I don't suppose there's a cup of tea going, is there?" Les asked more in hope than expectation.

"How do you take it?"

"Just milk."

"I'll get it when the suits arrive."

"Thanks very much, son. I'm not even sure why I'm here."

"A potential witness I was told. Good of you to come in."

"Do they usually ask an officer to stand guard at the door for a potential witness?"

"How would I know. Only left Tulliallen last week. Passing out parade is well named." The PC grinned.

The door opened and Nadia and Colin walked in.

"Your man here wants a cup of tea. I said I'd get it when you arrived."

"Alright, but in future remember it's not a canteen," Colin barked.

"The young man said I was here as a witness. If that's right, surely a cup of tea is not too much to ask."

"We should get the basics over," Colin said. He explained that the interview would be recorded and introduced himself and Nadia."

"Is it usual to record witness interviews?"

"It happens when we think the witness may be pivotal to a case. We have several questions to ask you and the answers may have important bearings on a murder investigation."

"Murder? Do I need a lawyer?"

"I don't know, do you think you need a lawyer?"

"I don't think so. I haven't done anything, and I am not aware of knowing anything that may be of assistance to you."

"Well, shall we park the lawyer question just now, and, if at any time you feel you do need a lawyer, we can re-assess. How does that sound?" Nadia asked brightly. She smiled at Les, then her eyes wandered around the room. Les followed her gaze. He looked again around the bleak little space and noticed that the fixing for the camera on the wall needed a good clean; it was caked in grease, grime and dust. He stared at the picked paint on the walls and the graffiti inked onto the table and shook his head.

"Get on with it," he said wearily. Then his face broke into a smile as the young PC returned with his tea. He accepted the plastic cup graciously and settled down to answer what was asked of him.

He noticed Colin started by asking about his conviction and the time he had served in jail. Les answered honestly, it was all on record. But he emphasised that he still disputed his guilt. Then the questions took an unexpected turn. Colin asked him who had run his undertaking business while he was in jail.

"At first we didn't think I'd be in for very long, really."

"You were sentenced to almost sixteen years. Why didn't you think you would be in for long?" Nadia asked.

"Because I didn't do it and I thought the police would try to find out who really did. But they didn't." he took a sip of the tea.

"Who looked after the business during that time?" Colin asked.

"My sister and my son, wee Gerry and at first my daughter helped but, after she got married and moved down to Peebles, she stopped being involved much."

"It was a big ask for a woman and a boy."

"Yes, son. It was. And wee Gerry went off the rails a bit. He is a great driver and a keen mechanic, but he went a bit daft, my sister told me. But luckily he never got caught doing anything wrong."

"Where's his mother? Couldn't she have helped him?"

"I doubt it. She left me to join a religious commune in Utah. I believe she's the leader's number three wife and is very highly thought of, apparently. She just couldn't cope with me.

"I like to dress up, you know, pretty in pink and high heels, sometimes. At first Gerry found it difficult too. He didn't speak to me for months after he found out. Of course, he was young, and it was embarrassing. He got teased. But when I was inside my sister made him come and visit me the first time, and I explained. It makes me feel good and doesn't hurt anybody, so what's the harm in it? Eddie Izzard, RuPaul and Grayson Perry do it. What is wrong with me doing it? My wife divorced me while I was inside and left the kids with my sister. I've no doubt that's what sent wee Gerry a bit off in the first place.

"He seemed to calm down a bit for a while. That was after he had a face-off with one of the guards at HMP Edinburgh. I was getting a rough time from this bloke and his cronies and wee Gerry had it out with him in the carpark. I don't know what was done or said. Neither of them ever told me. But I didn't get any more hassle."

"Your son stayed with his aunt to help run the family business?" Colin asked.

"He was a bit wild as a teenager but grew out of that," Nadia said.

"Yes, and yes. He was a real good help and not a bad lad. Of course, he flipped a bit again a few years ago when my grandson had his operation."

"Was he ill?" Nadia asked.

"No. Not at all. But he was a troubled young man and down

there in the borders it is all farming, rugby and horses, isn't it?"

"I don't know. But I would guess there's more than that to the border towns," Colin said.

"So why was Gerry so badly affected by his nephew's operation?" Nadia asked.

"Rowan became a girl. Simple as that. I helped with the finance. She needs to be herself. Gerry and my sister were angry that so much money came out of the family business for Rowan, but she needed it.

"Gerry found my dressing up bad enough. This, for him was a step too far. But Rowan's not hurting anybody, and she seems much happier now. She did leave the borders to work in Edinburgh, but she is still doing the same thing. She's a stable hand, just loves horses. She hopes to become a jockey."

"Les, can you tell me what you were doing on the morning of twelfth December?"

"Just a minute, what day was that? Let me check my diary. Thursday, that was Thursday. In the afternoon, I had a meeting with my probation officer and in the morning. I don't have anything in for that morning. I'm terribly sorry, I just don't remember."

"Perhaps you were in the Hermitage, for a walk," Colin said.

"No, I was not there. I've never been to the Hermitage as far as I can remember."

"Have you ever seen this van before?" Nadia showed Les a photo of the white van from the Sainsburys car park."

"Yes, it's the old private ambulance. We painted it white when we stopped using it for the business. I sometimes use it for a big shop at the grocery store and my sister uses it if we're delivering flowers to a funeral."

"Have you ever put a shopping trolley into the back of the van?" Colin asked.

Les burst out laughing. "Yes. In fact, it was only a short while ago. Wee Gerry bet me that the van wasn't big enough to get a trolley into it and I said it was. I was right. I think we did something really stupid like bring it home to unload the shopping faster. Imagine you asking me that."

"Do you recognise the person in this picture?" Nadia drew out the sketch artist's drawing put together by the teenagers they had interviewed near the scene of the murder.

"My goodness, that looks like Gerry." He held it closer to his face. "On second thoughts it's so bad. It could even be my sister."

***

Wee Gerry had never been in a police interview room before. He was horrified by how musty it was. It made him gag. The tables and chairs were metal and bolted to the floor. There was a recording device on the table and that was bolted on to it and high on the wall was a camera. He stared at it. Could somebody see him now, he wondered.

There was a policewoman by the door. Wee Gerry looked at her and thought in other circumstances he might have a shot at her. She was quite pretty. He moved around on his seat to see the wall behind him. The only window was there, but it was too high up to see out of it and it had bars in front of it with big, thick cobwebs joining them up. This place was nasty.

The door opened and the red-haired detective and the one Jamie fancied walked in.

"Thanks for coming in to talk to us today, Gerry," she said.

"I didn't think I had much of a choice," he said sourly.

"We are talking to all the witnesses who may be able to help us in a murder case."

"Would you like a cup of tea?" The red-headed one asked.

"Aye, that'd do nicely. Milk and two."

He watched the pretty constable leave the room and decided he would definitely have a shot at her.

Jamie's crush explained they would be taping the discussion because of its importance but that Gerry was there as a witness and didn't need a lawyer. She introduced them all for the benefit of the tape and wee Gerry's tea was put in front of him shortly after that. It was how he learned the pretty one was Lindsey Palmerston.

194

He sipped his tea. He hated tea out of plastic cups. He watched Mel carefully. It was clear that she was in charge.

"Where were you on the morning of the twelfth of December?" she asked him.

"Last Thursday? I'd be at work, in the garage at Thomson's Top Cars."

"Not according to Jamie, you weren't."

"Then I must have been poorly and had a day off. I'd have been at home."

"Your aunt told Jamie you weren't there either. Would you like to take another guess?"

"But remember, three strikes and you're out," the red head said.

"Then I don't remember. I've no idea."

"Could you have been at the Hermitage?"

"I've heard it's a decent enough pub. But I've never been there, and I wouldn't go drinking in the morning."

"The Hermitage of Braid Park, could you have been there?"

"No. Can't think why I would be."

"You have a niece who works at the stables near there. Could you have been visiting her?"

"That weirdo? No way. I wouldn't have been visiting that, I can assure you."

"Do you dislike your niece, Gerry?"

"Have you any idea what it's like as a young lad to have your dad prancing around in evening gowns and your mother goes away to be a whore in some commune in the USA? And then your dad goes to jail and that's actually better because everything calms down and people forget. And then comes the body blow, sweet little Rowan all over the page three of some trashy red top showing off 'her' boobs to fund the rest of her operations before my dear old dad stepped in to pay out of the business that me and Auntie Pam are working our fingers to the bone to keep going. She spends all that money, my money, to become a freak and the whole sorry story of my messed-up family is all over the papers again. Really, you have no idea.

"To answer your question, I don't hate Rowan. But I hate what he/she is." He sipped his tea and stared at the table and tears rolled down his cheeks.

"It must have been hard," Mel said.

"Yes, it was. I've had a fucking awful life because of my crazy relatives."

"It's not all about you, Gerry. I meant it must have been hard for your niece to make the decision to have the surgery to allow her to be herself."

"She seemed like a nice girl when I met her. An attractive and self-assured young woman. She's certainly not a freak," the red haired one commented.

"She is from where I am," wee Gerry muttered.

"I take it your mum and dad separated," Mel said.

"It's about the only thing I understand about my family. Mum couldn't cope with dad being better dressed than she was and left for some religious cult in the USA. Her new husband has about fifteen wives, but at least he dresses like a man."

"Bigamy is illegal in America. The man only has one wife and the rest aren't married to him." The red headed one spoke softly. Gerry looked at him and wondered if he didn't want to upset him any more than he had to.

"I know that. She's just kidding herself. But I can see why she couldn't put up with dad."

"Did you help your aunt run the undertakers when your dad wasn't there?" Mel asked.

"You can say when he was in jail. We all know where he was. My poor aunt could not do it all on her own. I left school at sixteen to give her a hand."

"You must be good with cars to get a job at Thomson's Top Cars in their garage. Did you go to college?"

"No, I taught myself. It started with hot wiring and changing tyres and now I'm pretty good. But I got the job there as a favour to my dad. He got to know Ian Thomson when they were both inside. In the beginning, Ian looked out for my dad."

"Why only in the beginning?"

"One of the screws was a really nasty piece of work and he and his gang had it in for dad. I may not like dad dressing like a ponce, but he is still my dad. I had a word with the ringleader, and it stopped."

"Just like magic. That's unusual. How did you do that?"

Wee Gerry felt himself blush. "We agreed he could do what he liked to anybody else, but he would leave my dad alone."

"And you were out with him and his pals at the pub last night, but he's not a friend," Mel said.

"I didn't say it was Inglis."

"But we all know it is. And you said you help him out at funerals."

"It's all part of the service."

"Who cancelled the funeral, yesterday?"

"The family, I think. Their minister was sick, and they wanted him to do the service. It was a pain in the arse."

"Alright, Gerry. Have you seen this van before?"

"I don't know. I can't see the number plate, it's too muddy."

"Could the van belong to you?"

"No, I don't own any vehicles at all."

"Might it belong to your family?"

"We have a white van. It was what they call a private ambulance, you know, when we take bodies away discretely. Originally it was black, but my aunt painted it white a few years ago when we stopped using it for that. We use it to take flowers to funerals now."

"Do you ever use it to go shopping?"

"Me? No."

"Has it ever been used to go shopping?"

"Possibly."

"Could you be a bit more specific?"

"Yes, I think Dad may have used it when we went to get the big Christmas grocery shop, recently."

"You were with your dad, and you used it to go shopping recently," the red haired one said. "Why did you lie, wee Gerry?"

"Wee Gerry, do you recognise the person in this drawing?"

"No. Wait, is it my dad?"

Chapter Fifty-Eight

It was lunchtime. There was nothing doing at the showroom, and wee Gerry had been taken off with Les to the police station to answer questions. Jamie took an executive decision to close the business for a couple of hours to allow him to have lunch with Frankie.

"Are you sure this is a good idea, Jamie? I mean just shutting the place and going for lunch. What if a punter comes along and tells your pop?"

"And what exactly is my pop going to do about it? He's banged up, remember."

"I know, I'm just saying. Oh, and Donna's given me the list to get the makings of Christmas dinner. I have strict instructions to do that today during my dinner hour and not to leave it any later in case the shops run out of things."

"They won't."

"Maybe not, but I'm not risking it, I'm doing that shopping today."

"I'll tell you what we'll do, we'll go over and get our usual at KFC then I'll come to the supermarket with you and we'll get the stuff together. It'll be much quicker with two of us. What have we got to get?"

Frankie handed Jamie the list. He looked down the page.

"What a lot of stuff!"

"Turn over," Frankie said flatly.

"Fucksake. She does know this is for one day and it's only the three of us and the twins, or four if Linda can be persuaded to change her mind."

"She knows. She says Linda is coming. Still want to come with me?"

"Linda hasn't said anything to me, yet but I wouldn't miss this, Frankie lad. I think we should take the car."

As they entered the store, Jamie felt bombarded by Christmas music and forced jollity. All the red, white and green decorations irritated him and a jolly man in a Santa suit shaking a tin at him got told where Jamie wanted to put it.

"Don't be such a pain, Jamie. You're just like the thing in that old movie, the Grinch who stole Christmas. Cheer up."

"I'm fine. I just don't want to be forced to be happy. It's not natural."

The cousins wandered up and down the aisles of the store, crossing things off the list as they went. There was great debate about what type of snacks to get, who could possibly want to eat olives and how many cans of beer would fit into the fridge. Then all of a sudden Jamie punched Frankie's arm.

"Bloody hell Jamie. Piss off!" Frankie rubbed his arm and scowled at his cousin.

"No. Look there, what is that bloke wearing? The lighting up Christmas jumper and those tight, multi coloured leggings are not a good look, especially for a bloke who's six feet tall. Bloody fashion victim."

"Says the king of high fashion." Frankie frowned at the list, not even looking up at the object of Jamie's derision. "When she says crackers, do you think she means for cheese or the ones you pull? Better get both."

"That old guy is following the fashion victim. It's creepy," Jamie said.

"It's a bloody supermarket, Jamie. Everybody goes up one row and down the next. Up and down, up and down. We're all following each other. It's not creepy, It's normal in here."

"Yes, but everyone else has a list or at least things in their cart. That creepy guy has nothing in his cart but Christmas paper and a roll of Sellotape. Look."

"Now you're the shopping police. What business is it of yours what anybody buys? You're a pain today, Jamie. I wish you hadn't come."

"No, look, see. When the fashion victim stops, he stops. He's just looking at him not what's on the shelves."

"Why does it matter to you? It's none of our business."

"Fashion victim guy is going to get a doing. I can feel it in my bones. And he may have no dress sense, but that's not a crime. I tell you, just for fun, we will get our cart between theirs and see what happens."

Jamie grabbed the handle of the cart and swung the vehicle into the middle of the aisle, moving swiftly forward until he was positioned between the two men he had been watching.

"Jamie, I'll miss the mayonnaise and the pickles," Frankie shouted. He rushed up the aisle grabbing jars from the shelves and raced up to where Jamie was standing, smiling. He emptied his arms over the cart.

"Now, if I'm right, creepy guy will try to overtake us any time now," Jamie whispered. He glanced back and saw his prediction come true. He wheeled the cart into the middle of the aisle to block the creepy guy. "Frankie, Donna wants tuna, doesn't she?"

"It's not on the list."

"But I think she said she wanted some." He moved the trolley slightly to the left and felt creepy guy try to overtake to the right. "And butter beans," Jamie said, moving the trolley to the right and putting his hand out to take a tin.

"Will you excuse me?" The creepy guy asked.

"No can do, mate. We're with our pal," Jamie said nodding at the fashion victim. "Have to stay together. We're tight."

"I didn't see you when he came in." The man glared at Jamie.

"Nobody ever notices us when we're with him. But you know we're here now." Jamie watched as the tall, thin faced man left his cart where it was and turned to walk the other way down the aisle. He continued to stare until he saw the man leave the store and cross into the car park.

"Now do you believe me?"

"I suppose I do. But I could swear that creepy guy was one of the officers we've seen at the big house when we go to visit your pop. Why would he be following a fashion victim around a store at Christmas?"

"I think pop mentioned a guard who was a real bully. I think

I might call Blondie when we get back to the showroom and tell him what we saw."

"The man didn't do anything. You don't even know if he was going to do anything, Jamie."

"But I know he was acting oddly and that the stuff in his trolley wasn't important enough to him. He just left it and walked out of the store. That's not normal."

Chapter Fifty-Nine

Hunter was on the phone to Meera when Tim knocked on the door and walked in. Hunter waved him to a chair and swung his chair around so that his back was to Tim.

"Meera, I'm so sorry about your grandfather. Of course, he is a good age. I know. Yes, the whole family must be very worried. Is there good medical provision for him? That's good. Expense? I see. Well keep me posted. Perhaps I can treat you to pub grub at the Persevere? Yes, seven o'clock is good, if it works for you. Call me whenever you need to. Meera, I do take your calls, if I can, honestly, I'm just really busy. Yes, I'm always busy."

He rang off and shook his head as he put his mobile phone into his pocket.

"Sorry about that, Tim. Family problems for Meera. I try to be there for her, but it is not always easy in this job."

"You don't need to explain that to me, boss. Gillian complains that Ailsa is either at the hospital or sleeping and I am always at work and she is left putting up with my crazy father. They are not a match made in heaven. It won't be so difficult when she's back teaching at the University, but I think a decent skiing holiday in Whistler over her February break is what Gillian and I need. She finds putting up with dad exceedingly difficult."

Hunter nodded. "She's not alone. Your dad can be hard work." He thought about the idea of a long, expensive holiday, but didn't see much chance of that happening any time soon. He asked Tim if he would like a coffee and poured them each a mug from his pot.

"Thanks, boss." Tim raised the mug in appreciation. "I have just heard from Hugo Karlsson."

"Who is he?"

"He's the surgeon who performed the transition surgery on our murder victim. He identified him straight away. Our victim was born Jennifer Evans in Cardiff back in 1981. She began transitioning and living as a man in 1998 and Mr Karlsson carried out her surgery after she moved to Edinburgh in 2005 and the final operations were 2007. When Mr Karlsson last knew his patient, she had changed her name to William Evans and was working as a computer programmer for HSBC bank out at the Gyle. He remembered William as a vocal campaigner for liberty and human rights. He thought William had always worked with computers but had no idea where he was working recently."

"That is most helpful. We can check with the Human Resources department at HSBC. The good doctor has taken us forwards by leaps and bounds. Good work, Tim."

"I also had a call from Jamie Thomson, boss,"

"What did the bold boy want now?"

"He just wanted to tell me something." Tim crossed his legs and explained Jamie's story to Hunter.

"My goodness, I've never had Jamie pegged as a social hero."

"Jamie just doesn't like bullies, boss. He has no qualms about robbing from the rich, but he doesn't like violence in any guise."

"In that way, he differs from his father. Ian is not averse to throwing a few punches. Still, this gives us a good reason to get Bernard Inglis back in here for questioning. I will talk to DCI Mackay and find out how he wants us to play this. In the meantime, I am doing a little investigating of my own."

"And what would that be, boss?"

"Do you remember there were a spate of industrial injury claims in funeral parlours?"

"Not really, boss. Before my time, probably."

"Well, I've had a thought and I'm going to chase it up. So far, we have nine people who have disappeared and two murders that we know of over thirty years. But people just don't disappear, Tim. And I want to find out where they are. In the meantime, you get Bernard Inglis in here, as a witness, and I'll speak to Mackay."

***

Hunter and Tim were sitting in the interview room waiting for Bernard Inglis to be brought through to them. Hunter glanced around the room. It had been painted about five years ago. Blue at the bottom of the walls and a light grey at the top, but it was now as miserable and grimy as it had ever been. Bored prisoners had picked off spots of the colour and carved their initials in the paint with their fingernails. The room was small and dark. The only window had bars across it and was almost at the height of the ceiling. Hunter looked up and could only see the dark clouds out of it from his chair. The smell in interview rooms was never fresh. It didn't seem to matter how much time the cleaners spent or how long his officers left the door open after the rooms were used and as this room was one of the smallest, it always smelled of dust, dirt and body odour.

The door behind them opened. Neither Hunter nor Tim looked round. Angus guided Bernard around to the far side of the table and went to stand by the door. The prison officer sat down. He glowered at Hunter.

"This better be good, or my brother will have your fucking badge, DI Wilson."

"We have asked you here to help us with a murder investigation. We are most grateful you have agreed to assist us," Tim said quietly.

"Don't you try to seem all sweetness and light. You are just a fucking Myerscough and no better than you ought to be."

"Mr Inglis, I wonder if we could focus on the questions that you might be able to help us with.

"Go on, and get this over with, then. Can the ginger nut get me a coffee and a biscuit? Not a ginger one. I don't like them."

Hunter didn't give any instruction. He just heard Angus open the door and leave the room. He felt this interview was going to be fun.

"I think we should start at the beginning, Mr Inglis. You are

204

aware that there was a corpse found by two of my officers in the Hermitage."

"And they bloody lost it. Arthur told me. That's fucking hilarious. Yes, I know. You were one of them Myerscough and some black bastard."

"Where were you on the morning of twelfth December?" Tim asked, ignoring the abusive comments spewing from Inglis' mouth.

"I was on duty at HMP Edinburgh. You can check my rota."

"I did, you didn't start your shift until midday. Where were you on the morning of twelfth December," Tim repeated.

"At first, I was in bed, then I had a shower, then I had breakfast and then I went to work. That good enough for you?"

"Can anybody confirm that?"

"My so-called wife left me years ago and I live alone, so unless I spent the night with a whore, no nobody can confirm that, Myerscough."

"Why did your wife leave you?" Hunter asked.

"She went to 'find herself' or so she said. I wouldn't even recognise her now if I saw her."

"People don't change that much. I recognise my ex-wife when I see her," Hunter said.

"Your ex-wife probably didn't fleece you for half of your pension and use it to have thousands of pounds worth of surgery to become your ex-husband, but Ursula did and changed her bloody name to Hamish Jones." Bernard spat the words out. Hunter watched the man's lip curl and his eyes glint with hatred.

He heard Angus come back into the room. The young DC put three plastic cups of coffee on the desk and pulled a packet of three rich tea biscuits out of his pocket. He watched as Angus placed the biscuits in front of Bernard without comment and returned to stand beside the door.

Hunter sipped the coffee and pulled a face. He couldn't help it. He hated instant coffee in all its forms and the liquid that came out of the machines in the station was the worst of all.

"Assuming, we accept what you say about the twelfth, Arthur will have also told you that the body was found up by the crematorium."

"Yes, he did."

"What were you doing that day?"

"I was at work."

"I think your recollection is wrong, Mr Inglis. Wasn't that the day you and your friends were meant to be attending a funeral, but I have heard the service was cancelled?" Tim asked.

"Maybe it was. Days run into each other at this time of year."

"Really, I don't find that," Tim said.

"Why was the funeral cancelled? Who cancelled it? When I called the crematorium, they had no record of a cancelled funeral. They did have a record of a funeral where no family were expected to attend, but they managed to get a last-minute flight from Toronto and were able to be there."

"I don't bloody know, do I?"

"Whose funeral did you plan to attend?"

"I can't remember the fellow's name. A retired prison officer I used to work with, I suppose. I was just going along with some of the other officers. Duty funeral, you know the sort."

"I do. But I would also know whose funeral I expected to attend. Wouldn't you, young Myerscough?"

"Indeed, I would, boss. If that is too difficult a question for Mr Inglis, perhaps he could tell us where he was around lunchtime today."

"I had lunch with my brother and then did a little Christmas shopping. Is that so surprising after you got me banged up in the cells last night?"

"Where did you do your shopping?"

"I don't remember."

"Your memory seems to be causing you a lot of problems Mr Inglis," Tim said. "Why don't you look at your receipt?"

"I don't keep receipts."

"Did you pay by cash or card?" Hunter asked.

"Who cares? I paid for my stuff. Okay?" Bernard shouted at the detectives and stood up from his chair.

206

Neither Hunter nor Tim moved. Hunter said nothing until Bernard sat down again.

"I care. You did not buy anything. And no, it's not okay. Witnesses saw you following an effeminately dressed young man around the supermarket. They believed you were behaving in a suspicious manner that posed a threat to the young man."

"Fucksake. What a lot of rubbish."

"They didn't think it was rubbish, but thought it was important enough to call DC Myerscough about it," Hunter said.

"How would they know it was me?"

"They've seen you before. They know who you are."

"Arthur and I look alike; it could have been him they saw."

"Maybe we should ask your brother," Hunter mused.

"Maybe you should and maybe you should leave me the fuck alone."

"Do you recognise the person in this sketch, Mr Inglis?" Tim asked.

"Yes, it's Arthur."

"Who is this?" Tim showed him the other sketch.

"I don't know. It could be Les Littlewood; he was a fag in the big house for years. It could be his son, wee Gerry he goes by. He's got a lot of guts, that lad. Stood up to me once, you know. Anyway, unless there's anything else, gentlemen, I'm off to the pub." Bernard Inglis stood up again and Hunter watched him as he walked towards the door. Angus held the door open for him and accompanied him to the exit.

"Shall we ask DCI Mackay to have a quiet word with DCI Inglis, boss?"

"Yes, a wee informal chat. I think a full witness interview would be like a red rag to a bull. Did Jamie definitely recognise Bernard?"

"No, boss. He didn't. It was Frankie who thought that's who it was, and Jamie phoned it in."

"Frankie's honest, but not as reliable as Jamie. I'll have a quick chat with Jane and then go and ask Mackay to take forward a meeting with DCI Inglis. I have one other thing to talk to him about and then I'm leaving. I'm treating Meera to a meal at the Persevere Bar this evening."

"That doesn't sound like the height of romance." Tim said. "But what's going on that you need to talk to the DCI about, boss?"

"I've just got a hunch and hopefully it will tie up with an idea Jane has. She should have the results of her enquiries by now. Beyond that I don't want to say, young Myerscough. Mackay might think I'm mad."

"Yes, boss. I mean no, boss. I mean, enjoy your evening."

Chapter Sixty

Hunter knocked on Mackay's door and entered the room. He explained how the interview with Bernard Inglis had gone and that, as he had identified his brother as the person in the sketch, the DCI must also be interviewed.

Mackay sighed. "Have you any idea how badly that would go down, Hunter?"

Hunter agreed that that would be true and then suggested to Mackay that he take DCI Inglis for a drink and a chat.

"All I have to do is casually to ask him what he was doing earlier, if he went shopping and if he was accosted because he was following a brightly dressed young man around the supermarket."

"I'm sure you can think of a way to do it, sir. Invite him out by way of an apology for all the inconvenience he and his brother suffered last night and this morning. Christmas shopping is the bane of everybody's life at this time of year. It's an easy topic to complain about."

"Alright, alright. Shut up, I'll do my best. Give me the bloody sketches to take as props."

Hunter grinned. "There are just a couple of other things, sir."

"My heart sinks when I hear you say that."

"Jane has been looking up the death notices that appeared in the papers at the time of death of the two young people we know about."

"From the original eleven? We ended up with nine missing."

"Yes, sir. Both the funerals were arranged by Littlewoods undertakers, they had two funerals on each of the days in question. When she spoke to the celebrants, they remembered those funerals because there were no mourners and the deceased's names were never used. That is unusual."

"But they had moved from different parts of the country, so maybe not so unusual."

"That might be true, I suppose. But yesterday, when the corpse was found in the memorial garden, there was meant to be a funeral going ahead but Bernard, wee Gerry and Les all said it was cancelled."

"I remember that. I've never heard of a funeral being cancelled. Very strange."

"When Jane spoke to the celebrant, she said that it wasn't cancelled. Apparently, no mourners had been anticipated, but some family members managed to get a last-minute flight from Canada which allowed them to attend, sir."

"So why was there all this noise about a cancelled funeral?"

"She doesn't know. She did say there were more men than usual in attendance with the officials from the funeral parlour, but when the family arrived, most of those men were driven away by a woman. They made a bit of a fuss when they were standing around the back of an old white van that the flowers had been in. The celebrant was greeting the family at that point so didn't pay the men much attention. She did notice that only Les Littlewood stayed and drove the hearse away at the end of the service."

"The woman must be Les's sister. I believe she and his son are integrally involved in the business."

"They are sir. I understand she brings the flowers in the old van. But the celebrant told me she heard a lot of noise, shouting and swearing as the service was about to start. It was shortly after that that our witness found the corpse."

"I wonder if the corpse was also in the van and the men got rid of it when the mourners were inside, and nobody would see their actions. It would be pretty ripe travelling in that old van with a decomposing corpse."

"I thought about that too, sir. To be honest the van would smell ghastly even if they'd taken the body out, but it also ties in with something else."

"Oh God! What now, Hunter?"

"We have particles of skin under the most recent victim's fingernails. Nadia and Colin will check the DNA against all our records."

"Good. Anything else?"

"Just one thing, sir."

Hunter put to Mackay his thoughts about the industrial injury cases and the heavy coffins. The DCI looked increasingly serious. He stared at the desk until Hunter was finished sharing his thoughts.

"Hunter, the only way to prove if you are right, is to exhume the bodies. The only practical way of starting this is to exhume the bodies of the two people from our group of eleven that we know about. It is a truly horrible thought."

"I agree, but I have taken the liberty of preparing the paperwork required by the council. As there are no relatives, we need to ask the judge to grant a licence to exhume. I have one waiting for these papers and then Jane will contact the cemetery administrator to confirm where the coffins we need to exhume are buried. Once the licence is granted the cemetery administrator will arrange the moving of the bodies. I'm seeing Meera tonight for dinner, so I'll ask her if she or one of her colleagues is willing to attend."

"Hardly the most romantic topic of conversation, but I suppose Meera is used to you."

***

By seven o'clock, Hunter had been home, changed his bed linen, tidied the living room, cleaned the bathroom, showered, dressed smartly and was standing at the bar of the Persevere with a pint in his hand, waiting for Meera.

Tom and Jim from his darts team came up to him.

"You've not been doing much practising, Clouseau. We need you on top form for the new year."

Meera walked in and joined them.

"If I had a lovely lady like this, I wouldn't spend so much time here either."

"Your wife will be delighted to hear you say that Tom,"

Hunter said.

"He spends far too much time here, I hardly ever see him," Meera said. She kissed Hunter on the cheek.

Hunter caught Tom and Jim staring in disbelief at each other.

"He must be a busy boy, Meera," Jim said.

Hunter smiled and guided Meera over to a table away from the other men. He didn't want them talking more to her and ruining his cover.

"G and T or a glass of red?" He asked her.

"I'll start with a gin and maybe have a glass of wine when we eat."

He went up to the bar and ordered their drinks. He bought pints for Jim and Tom too and had a quick word with them before turning away from the bar. He walked across the room and when he got back to the table, Meera was speaking on her phone. She rang off as he approached.

"Any more word about your grandfather?"

"No, pet. Dad's going to call me whenever he hears more, but that was Parvati, asking if I wanted to go on a shopping trip for a new outfit with her. She is so wonderful, but I've had to say I can't commit to anything right now until I know what's happening with Grandfather."

"Parvati is a lovely person, inside and out, she'll understand."

"I agree, but I wasn't aware you knew her that well."

Hunter blushed and took a drink out of his beer. "I only know her through you, Meera. But she has always been very pleasant. And you have to agree that she's easy on the eye."

"I'm not sure how happy I am to have you talk about her like that."

"Then let's not talk about her, let's choose what we're going to eat, and I'll go and put in our orders at the bar."

They stared at the menu in silence. Hunter could tell Meera was angry with him. This evening was not going the way he had planned it at all. After their orders were in and paid for, Hunter returned to the table and Meera looked like she had thawed a little. He kissed her lightly on the ear.

"So how has your day been?" he asked.

"Busy, a judge has been in touch with me. Some idiot has requested two disinterments, and wants the post-mortems carried out on the bodies, before Christmas. What a comedian!"

"That idiotic comedian would be me, Meera." Hunter said and explained his theory about the missing persons and those members of minority groups they already knew had died.

"Wow, you do think some dark thoughts. No wonder you wake up screaming some nights."

"It's not the here and now that wakes me up. It's my dark secrets from the distant past."

"Like what, Hunter. I didn't think we had any secrets. Do we?"

"This is from long ago and much too difficult to talk about. Anyway, if I tell you, it won't be a secret anymore."

"I think that would be a good thing, after all what is so bad that you could not confide in me? I find that sad and rather hurtful."

Hunter watched the barmaid walk over with their meals. She took their cutlery and the condiments out of her pocket and said she'd be right back with their wine. He smiled as she came back and put the bottle of Shiraz on the table and placed the wine glasses in front of them.

"Enjoy your meals," she said.

"We will," said Meera. "But don't you think dinner being served will get you out of sharing your deepest, darkest, most scary secret with me, Hunter Wilson."

Hunter tucked into his burger and chips and winked at her. He should explain to her, of course he should share the secret fears that still prowled within him. But not right now. It wasn't the time. This should be a nice evening out to relax together and enjoy each other's company.

"Changing the subject, completely, where do you want to spend Christmas?" he asked.

"Somewhere that the only secret is what gifts we are giving each other."

"Ouch, okay, let me explain."

He put down his knife a fork and faced her. He spoke quietly and continuously because when he started the explanation and described what he had experienced and been through and what he and Fraser had seen; he just couldn't stop. He saw the tears in her eyes as she began to cry, and deep concern for him showed on her face. He knew she was hurting for him but somehow, as he continued to speak, his own pain receded and the secret stress he had carried for so many years lifted.

"And you have never spoken to anybody about this? You've not had any counselling?"

"Meera, I was a teenage boy in the eighties. We didn't have counselling. Fraser and I didn't admit there was anything wrong, not to anybody else. We spoke to each other about the nightmares and the ghosts, but never discussed it with anyone else."

"What about your wife?"

"Ex-wife. We hardly spoke about anything in the end, never mind anything that mattered."

"But you told me. I am honoured. I love you so much, Hunter. We have no more secrets, right?"

"Except what I'm getting you for Christmas." He told himself that this, at least was true.

"I can live with that, but I do think we should get you counselling to lay this to rest. I'll talk to Parvati. She is the best clinical psychologist I know. Is that agreed?"

"I agree. Thank you. Now, shall we eat before our meals are completely cold?"

"Good, idea."

They both began tucking into their meals and clinked glasses before taking a drink of their wine. Hunter couldn't believe how much better he felt already, just from sharing that long held secret. Then he saw Meera frown.

"Wait, is that my phone? It's my dad. That's unusual."

Hunter looked at her with curiosity. She began speaking in Hindi to her father. He knew her dad's English was not good, but it always irritated him that he couldn't understand what was being said. Today, although he didn't understand the fast, foreign words, he knew it was bad news when Meera began to cry, again. This time noiselessly as tears rolled down her cheeks. He put his arm around her shoulder and handed her the napkin from the table to wipe her face. Hunter hated to see Meera even a bit upset, but this grief was far deeper than that.

When she finished the call, she stood up and walked, with her head down, towards the ladies' room. Hunter knew there would be more tears shed in there before she came out with her makeup re-applied and looking as radiant as always.

Jim came over to him. "Everything all right with Meera? She seems to be really upset."

"Her grandfather's ill and that was her dad calling. I'd guess the old boy hasn't got long," Hunter replied.

"That's a bloody shame. Tom and I were concerned, Clouseau. Give her our best."

Hunter nodded and picked up his cutlery to continue his meal. It was almost cold now, but he ate his burger in a determined fashion. He was hungry, and he was sure when Meera returned she would ask to go up to his flat. Neither of them would be eating after that and he wanted to finish as much of his meal as he could before that happened.

It was only a few minutes before he was proved right. He looked over to the bar and picked up the wine bottle to ensure there was no issue that he was taking it with him. The barmaid waved to him in acknowledgement and he followed Meera outside and up to his flat where he could comfort her in private.

Chapter Sixty-One

The team had gathered together thirty minutes earlier than usual. Mackay wanted to get at least some of the business dealt with before Inglis arrived. He looked around the room and saw that everybody was present. Bear, Tim and Mel were tucking into bacon rolls. Rachel, Jane and Nadia sipped on mugs of tea while Colin and Hunter stood at the back holding large steaming mugs of coffee.

"Come on then, grab a seat everyone. I want to run through a couple of things before we have company. Is Charlie going to call your number when Inglis gets to the station, Hunter?"

"Yes, sir."

"Good. Now the first thing I want to say is that, thanks to DI Wilson, I had the most uncomfortable evening that I have had in a long time, yesterday. You owe me." He glared at Hunter.

"Yes, sir." Hunter grinned.

"What I discovered was remarkably interesting. Arthur and Bernard Inglis are awfully close in age. Arthur being the elder by only ten months."

"Irish twins my sister calls that. She's a nurse," Rachael said.

"Arthur never married, but Bernard did, although wedded bliss didn't last very long. After five years, his wife left him, took half his money and pension and set off to enjoy the rest of her life."

"From what Bernard told us, that enjoyment didn't include him, but did include undergoing surgery to become a man," Tim said.

"This may explain the hatred Arthur and Bernard have for the LGBTQ community," Nadia said.

"It may explain it, but it doesn't excuse the way they speak or act," Rachael said.

"No, it doesn't, especially when they are in positions of authority," Jane agreed.

"During our conversation, Arthur became increasingly angry about his former sister-in-law, and then he diverted to discussing the low-life that he and Bernard have to come in contact with while doing their jobs."

"That happens to all of us, they're not special," Tim said.

"He went on a ramble about men wearing inappropriate clothes and how it was even worse now than it used to be, when the worst you might see was a Paisley patterned tie. Apparently, he has a collection of colourful ties."

"Why?" Hunter asked. "They're not exactly the height of fashion now."

"He didn't answer that. He did show me a photo of Bernard's wedding day. He carries it with him."

"Gosh, how long ago was that?"

"About thirty years, maybe more. He married when they were both eighteen. Everybody said it wouldn't last and laughed at Bernard when they were proved right. Her going for a sex change only made the teasing greater."

"How would anyone know about that, if he didn't tell them?" Tim asked. "After their divorce it's none of his business what she does."

"My thoughts precisely," Hunter said. "Sir, that's Charlie."

Nadia jumped and said quickly, "I have a result on the fingerprints from the trolley and the DNA from under the fingernails. I checked them against those we took from Bernard's group of friends and prints we have on the various registers, including the one we hold for elimination purposes. It could be crucial, but I need to discuss with you how and when you want to arrange to interview the rest of the people of interest, boss. I don't want to mention names at the meeting now."

"That's fine, DC Chan. Hunter, the only other thing I want to add is that the woman in the picture could have been the person you and your brother described seeing lying dead along the Water of Leith," Mackay said. "I need to see the sketch that was done at the time again."

"I have that in the original box for the case, sir. I'll bring it to you," Tim said.

"Now break up quickly, as if we haven't started." Mackay waved his hands.

Hunter smiled as the group split into its usual groups and Colin grabbed a satsuma from the top drawer of his desk and started peeling it.

"You can't beat a juicy satsuma at this time of year," he said to Hunter.

"I'm more of a clementine man, myself," Hunter said. It was as if citrus fruit was the only thing on their minds when Inglis walked in.

"DCI Inglis, would you like a coffee?" Hunter asked.

"Yes, that would be good. Had a fine session with your DCI last night. Good times, eh, Allan?"

"Yes indeed, Arthur, always good to talk," Mackay said.

Hunter left the room and went to his office to pour Inglis a coffee from his pot. He wanted a couple of moments to think about how he was going to disclose the disinterments that had been approved this morning. It was done in record time, because the judge wanted to finish up for his winter break yesterday. Hunter understood he was going to the Seychelles. It was alright for some.

When Hunter got back, Inglis had called the room to order. He handed the DCI a mug of coffee and was amused to hear him praise Tim and Bear for not eating during the meeting today. Hunter watched the big men just grin and accept the accolade.

Inglis then called for any updates from the previous day and Tim offered to tell the team about his talks with Hugo Karlsson. The surgeon had now confirmed the identity of their victim as William Evans, formerly known as Jennifer Evans. The victim was a computer programmer and would now be aged thirty-two. All this accorded with the findings by Drs Meera Sharma and David Murray during their post-mortem.

Colin and Nadia reported on their interview with Les who

seemed to think the sketch they had thought of as him might be his son or his sister. Mel and Angus followed on by telling the team about their interview with wee Gerry who thought the sketch looked like his dad.

Mackay then called upon Tim to share with the team how helpful Bernard Inglis had been. Hunter watched as Tim took his lead in deference from Mackay and stressed that Mr Inglis had been requested to come in to assist the team with the victim found near the crematorium. He never once looked at Hunter but emphasised to DCI Mackay that the information Mr Inglis had been able to share was most useful, although he did not recall the name of the former colleague whose funeral he was meant to attend, nor did he know who or why the funeral was reported to have been cancelled, although the celebrant confirmed it had gone ahead as planned. He suggested that the undertaker's old white van should be uplifted and examined by the forensics team. Hunter saw Inglis shift on his chair and then Tim finished up by saying that Mr Inglis thought one of the sketches he was shown looked like either wee Gerry or Les Littlewood while the other looked like his brother.

DCI Inglis paused momentarily and then burst out laughing. "What a laugh. Great sense of humour my brother. My goodness, imagine him saying that."

Hunter smiled and suggested that Jane explain her thoughts.

She stood up to explain to the team for the first time how she was concerned that the eleven missing persons they had found out about might all be dead and not properly buried. She was curious because the two people that they knew were dead from this original group of missing souls had had Death notices lodged with the local papers by Littlewood's undertakers. Littlewood's had also been involved in the funeral recently that had wrongly been reported as cancelled.

"Like the boss, I don't like coincidences. I checked where those two individuals were buried and spoke to the boss about my fears."

"I don't really think we need to worry too much about people like that. After all, they were missing in the first place.

Nobody was going to worry about them," Inglis said.

"They were reported missing precisely because people were worried about them, sir." Jane looked at Hunter and sat down.

"I entirely agreed with Jane, so I have made the appropriate requests. We have permission to disinter both bodies."

"Oh, for goodness sake. That is hideously expensive and totally unnecessary. Don't you agree, Allan?" Inglis shouted.

"I agree that it is expensive. If it is unnecessary, only time will tell."

Chapter Sixty-Two

Hunter stomped up and down beside the grave side. He should have worn his thick winter coat, but it was still hanging on the hook at the back of his office door. He had handed the exhumation order to the cemetery administrator and the woman had left him standing as she took it to her office to check the details.

It was bitterly cold, and he had his hands firmly plunged into his jacket pockets to keep them as warm as he could. He saw Jane arrive on her motor bike and envied her the thick leather gear that would protect her from the wind.

"Hi boss. Wouldn't you be warmer with your coat?" Jane asked. She took off her helmet and replaced it with a thick woollen hat to keep her head warm. "The helmet doesn't do anything for my hair, and this woolly hat Rache knitted does less, but it took her weeks. I wouldn't dare complain."

"Best not under those circumstances," Hunter replied with a smile. "What made you think of this issue, Jane?"

"It's simple, really. Burials are so much more expensive than cremations, so why would they be buried rather than cremated? It doesn't make any sense unless they can be buried at even less than the price of a cremation, and there is only one way I could think of to do that.

"Your recollection about the industrial injury claims just made my suspicions stronger. Where is she? It can't take that long to check the forms."

"She won't want to make a mistake. Can you imagine the noise if we got the wrong casket disinterred? Look here she comes, grave diggers in tow. Did you know that's why the Athletic Arms pub in Fountainbridge is known as The Diggers? It has been nicknamed by the good people of

Edinburgh for generations because it was situated between two graveyards. I suppose it was common for grave diggers to drop into the pub after a hard day of burying the dead."

"I know, boss. One of my foster fathers told me that regularly, almost every time he came back from spending the evening in there. He said it sold the best beer in the city."

"It pours a pretty fine pint, but it has an enviable selection of whiskies too."

"That all seems to be in order, DI Wilson," the administrator said. "Do you want us to wait for your pathologist, or shall we start digging?"

"I'm sure the doctor won't be long. She'll probably arrive with the police photographer. There's no point in making everybody stand around in the cold for any longer than necessary. Can we get started?"

The grave diggers broke the ground with difficulty. Hunter heard one of them ask if he couldn't come back in the Spring when the work would be easier. He decided to pretend he hadn't heard the comment.

A car drew up and Doctor David Murray got out with his colleague Doctor Aiden Fraser. The police photographer Samantha Hutchens jumped out of the back and carried her equipment to the scene. She took a photo of the headstone and one of the grave diggers working. Hunter smiled as she walked towards him.

"I know it's not my business, but did you notice the name you are looking for is not on the headstone?" she asked Hunter quietly.

"Well spotted. I noticed that too, Sam. We have asked to exhume the casket of the person the undertakers are known to have buried and believe we'll get more than we bargained for."

"But you're sure we're in the right place? It would be horrible if we dug up the wrong grave, DI Wilson."

"That doesn't bear thinking about. We're as sure as we can be, and the administrator has checked for us too. I must go and speak to Dr Murray."

"David, Aiden," Hunter said as he shook hands with the pathologists. "I'm always pleased to see you, but why did we get the uglier duo from your department?"

"Thanks very much," Aiden said in hurt tone of voice.

"Meera's grandfather passed away this morning. She has taken some personal time and gone to her sister's house. I don't think the family has got over the immediate shock, yet, but she didn't want to be alone."

"Oh God, no! I must phone her."

"Sorry, Hunter, I told her to switch her phone off, in case the department called her in error," Aiden said. "You are stuck with our ugly mugs, I'm afraid."

"Speak for yourself," David joked.

Hunter hung his head and wandered back to the graveside. He should be with her but there was nothing he could do about Meera's sadness immediately, so he might as well concentrate on the job in hand. He saw a driver from the mortuary pull up in a private ambulance.

"Will we need two of those?" he asked David.

"There's another on the way."

"Could you have got a machine in to move this soil?" One of the grave diggers asked.

"No, I can't risk any damage to the casket, or what's left of it, the contents or the surrounding burial plots. Sorry lads," Hunter said.

After a while, the second private ambulance arrived. The driver had been delayed because he had stopped off to buy a round of hot coffees. This was Hunter's kind of man. Even the administrator and the diggers stopped for a few minutes to drink the reviving liquid. Hunter looked into the hole.

"You're well down already. How long have you been doing this?"

"Nigh on forty years, us two," the older looking one said.

"Aye, not far off," his colleague agreed. "We'll get it finished soon. I want to get this over with."

Hunter took their empty cartons and the men jumped back into the hole to get back to work. Hunter walked over to speak to the administrator.

"We have another exhumation over at Portobello. It is a really grim way to spend time."

"Two in one day? That's unusual," she said. "Big case?"

"I hope not," Hunter said.

They looked at each other and heard the gravediggers cheer. They had reached the casket. Sam kept her camera clicking. Hunter, Jane, David and Aiden all went over to investigate the grave as the men opened the lid.

"Fuckin hell," shouted the older one. There's two dead bodies in here."

Hunter nodded at Jane and left the pathologists and Sam to their work.

***

Hunter and Jane stopped at a café. "Do you want lunch?" he asked her.

"Not really, I've still got the smell in the back of my throat. Maybe a tea would be good. Then we can get on to the cemetery at Portobello."

"We do know how to fill our days."

"I've never found that to be a problem, boss."

Hunter ordered a large black coffee for himself and a chamomile tea for Jane.

"Did you see that old tie in the grave?"

"Yes, it would have been garish in its time."

"It's like that's some kind of mark of derision. I'm not looking forward to going through all that again with another grave, boss."

"It's pretty gruesome, isn't it?"

"Did you manage to speak to Nadia about the fingerprints and DNA that have been identified?"

"Yes. She and Colin came in to speak to Mackay and I just before I left."

"Well, don't keep me in suspense. What did she say?"

"I can't discuss it here, Jane. It is sensitive stuff."

He saw Jane raise her eyebrows and turn her attention back to her tea. He took advantage of the lull in the conversation to try to call Meera. Her phone was still switched off. He tried to call her sister's house phone, but there was no answer. He put his mobile on the table more in hope than expectation that she would call him. He turned back to Jane.

"The post-mortem of each of the deceased may tell us more, but we will have to undertake more interviews."

"Do we have the van from Littlewood's undertakers, yet?"

"I'm sure we will. Mackay was going to speak to Charlie about getting a couple of uniforms to pick it up and take it over to forensics."

"Boss, the examination could take forever."

"That's what they said about the exhumations, but here we are. I think Mackay is going to get DCI Inglis to use his MIT clout to move the van up the line. Anyway, I think we better get going. We don't want to be late for our own disinterment."

"Boss, that's revolting. Don't even joke."

They finished their drinks and drove across town to Portobello, the suburb on the East side of the city. Jane got there before Hunter. He knew she rode that bike like a demon, but Hunter entered the gate of the cemetery and drove through the narrow, paved lanes that wove their way between the graves. He stopped when he saw that the pathologists had already arrived and walked over to David and Aiden.

"The administrator was here a minute ago, but I'm not sure where he's gone." Aiden looked around and then pointed to a short man behind a gravestone. "That's him there." He pointed for Hunter's benefit.

Hunter walked over to give the necessary documentation to the official. The little man gave it a cursory glance. He told Hunter everything appeared to be in order and the work could start as soon as the gravediggers arrived. Hunter nodded his thanks and wandered up and down the path, with his hands in his jacket pocket, wishing again that he had brought his winter coat.

The private ambulances arrived before the diggers did, but eventually the work got started. The administrator berated the burly workers for being late and then insisted the cemetery was closing at four whether they were finished or not. Hunter walked over to the man and whispered in his ear.

"Well, perhaps under the circumstances if you need a little

225

more time, I can arrange that. But it will be dark by then."

"Don't worry, sir. I have lights," Sam said.

"Thank goodness for Sam," Jane whispered to Hunter. "It's bad enough when you can see the results of the dig, it would be horrendous doing this work in the dark."

Hunter nodded. He and Jane walked over to talk to David and Aiden.

"Next time you do this, could we do it in the Summer?" David asked. "This wind is bloody freezing."

"You too, David? I'll try to get the criminals to arrange their diaries more to your liking, doctor," Hunter said.

After a while, Hunter separated himself from the group and took his phone out of his pocket. He stared at it for a moment and then tried to contact Meera again. No luck. He thought for a moment and then phoned Parvati. She answered on the second ring.

"Isn't it awful?" she said without introduction.

"Yes, poor Meera. I know she loved her grandfather dearly."

"Yes, but then her grandmother. How dreadful for the family."

"What happened to her grandmother? I didn't know she was ill."

"She wasn't, but she was consumed with grief at the loss of her husband and set herself on fire. She was declared dead at the scene. Of course, Meera's father must go over, but he does not want to travel alone."

"I can understand that it's a long journey and to travel alone when you are grieving so would be awful." Hunter heard a shout from the graveside. "I have to go, Parvati. I haven't been able to speak to Meera, if she calls you, send her my love."

"Two fuckin' stiffs. Not one, two!" shouted one of the grave diggers.

Hunter ended the call and walked over to the deep hole in the ground. Sam was standing beside the gravediggers, holding her camera so tightly her knuckles had turned white.

"It's another one, DI Wilson. Another coffin with two bodies in it."

Hunter heard the photographer retch and then throw up. He saw Aiden go over to her and guide her away from the grave side.

"My lamp," she said.

"Don't worry about the lamp. The pride of Police Scotland has it in their sights and David will bring it over to you when they're finished. You go and sit in the car, Sam. You've seen and smelled enough for one day." The pathologist gave the car keys to the young woman and walked back to David Murray's side.

"I think we are going to be busy tomorrow," David said. "Did you notice the tie lying loose in the caskets when we opened them? They are somewhat dirty and degraded, but they look like the old Paisley patterned ties we all thought were so trendy, once upon a time."

"No, I missed that. I will look at Sam's photos. The ties seem to be a kind of theme with all the corpses we have found in this case."

"It is odd. Why bother? Oh, and I assume you do want the examination of these remains fast-tracked, Hunter."

"Yes please, David. I need anything you can give me as soon as possible."

"I feared you were going to say that. Who will be attending?"

"I'm not even sure I'll be able to spare anyone from the team."

"I can just send you results if you can't."

"That might be how it is."

"I won't let the lack of a plod hold me back," David joked.

Hunter stood and watched while the corpses were lifted from their resting place and put into body bags. Each private ambulance carried a body to the morgue.

"Will you be able to start tomorrow, David?" Hunter asked.

"Can't think of anything else I'd rather do. I'll take Sam's lamp back to her and I'll make sure Aiden drops her home. I think the poor girl's had enough for one day."

"Thanks, David. Good night."

Hunter turned to Jane. "Will you be alright getting home on

your bike?"

"Of course, boss. I'll see you tomorrow."

"See you then. I'm going to try and find Meera. I don't know about you, but I feel like today has been a long, long day."

Chapter Sixty-Three

Hunter arrived at the station early and tried to phone Meera again. This time she answered her phone and he finally managed to speak to her.

"So why have you been phoning my best friend? What do you have to say to her that can't be said through me?" she shouted.

Hunter held the phone away from his ear.

She had spoken to Parvati and learned that Hunter had her number and had used it.

"I have just spoken to Parvati and learned that not only do you have her number, but you have been using it? That is inappropriate in so many ways. Do you not think I have enough to worry about without you chatting up my best friend? Is my life not quite hard enough? How did you even get Parvati's number, Hunter?"

"You must have given it to me, pet. But I didn't chat up Parvati. I wouldn't chat up your friend, any of your friends, honestly. I was worried about you."

"Why would I ever give you her number? Why would you even need it? My grandparents are both dead and I have to stress about you and your bad behaviour." She burst into tears. "Oh Hunter, did you hear what Grandmother did? My uncle found her burning and shrieking and dying. It is too horrible."

"I know, darling, I'm so sorry. I wish I could make it better. Will you be home tonight so that I can hold you and kiss you and try to relieve your pain."

"Yes, you come. I need you."

"I'll be there. I'll bring dinner."

"I can't eat."

"You should eat. I'll bring Chinese."

"I like Chinese."

"I know, Meera. And Meera, I love you."

***

Mackay knocked on Hunter's door. "I'm sorry to hear about Meera's grandparents. Jane told me. Are you all right to be here?"

"Yes, sir. I have no choice. I think we are remarkably close to wrapping this up. Now that we know how those two bodies were disposed of, and the dumping of that body at Mortonhall, it is, sadly inevitable that those bodies will not be the only ones treated with such contempt."

"Just because the people were trying to live the lives they wanted. I am appalled. We need to find out if all the rest of those missing people have died and been submitted to hidden burials. It is a disgusting thought. How many people are we talking about?"

"At the moment, another nine, all from the LGBTQ community."

"Shocking. Unforgiveable. I want interviews conducted today. DC Chan and DS Reid can start with Les Littlewood again. While DC Grant and DC McKenzie can continue the interview his son. Now that we have more evidence, we know what to ask. Are you getting Frankie Hope and Jamie Thomson in for a line-up?"

"No sir, I was just going to get Tim to take a book of mugshots over to the showroom."

"That's probably better. And I've sent a couple of young uniforms over to the mortuary. And I want the forensics on that van."

"I hope that all goes well, sir." Hunter chuckled. It was the first time he had truly laughed in days.

***

Nadia and Colin walked into the interview room joking about who would play good cop or bad cop as they entered.

Les Littlewood was sitting waiting for them.

"I'm glad somebody finds that funny. Why have you got me back here? I've told you all I know.

"I don't think you have, Les. And I know we haven't told you all that we know." Colin sat down and switched on the recording equipment. He explained that Les was entitled to legal representation, but the man declined then, after all parties had been introduced for the benefit of the tape, he started the interview."

"What do you know about burying two bodies in one casket, Mr Littlewood?"

"It doesn't happen."

"Let's assume, just for a moment, that it has happened, and that DC Chan and I know it has happened in funerals where your business was employed. What would you be able to tell us about that, Mr Littlewood?"

"I know nothing about that at all."

"Wasn't there a political party in the USA in the nineteenth century called the Know Nothing Party, DC Chan? Are you a member of that historical, American political party, Mr Littlewood?"

"Have you gone mad? I don't know what you're talking about."

Nadia took over. "Mr Littlewood, we have found two murder cases where the corpse disappeared. In both cases, the victim came from the LGBTQ community. In the more recent case, the body of the victim was found discarded in the Mortonhall Crematorium garden of remembrance. It was put there by people who left the scene in your old white van. What will the forensics of that van tell us, I wonder?

"We have also found another two instances where the deceased persons, neither of whom was murdered but who both belonged to the LGBTQ community, was buried along with another corpse, in both cases, your undertaking firm was employed by the family of the other deceased person in the casket and you put notices in the deaths column of the local paper to make the burials of our missing persons look legitimate."

231

"So, Mr Littlewood, what do you know about two corpses being buried in the one casket?" Colin asked again.

Colin watched as Les hung his head and then looked up at them. "I wasn't involved in most of them. I was in jail. I was in jail for something I didn't do."

"Aren't they all, Les?"

"I only know about one almost thirty years ago, it must be, and the farce of one that happened recently. That's been all over the bloody papers. It became a complete nightmare."

"It all started when Inglis came across Jonesy, Hamish Jones, on the pathway by the water of Leith. He never got over the divorce. It wasn't planned or anything, but the red mist came down. He strangled him and stabbed him and then he was dead. It might have been ages before the body was found. It was the back end of the year, but two lads came by when the body was lying there and saw it. Inglis had to get rid of it, quick, and I owed him more than one favour, so he came to me. I thought up just getting rid of the body with a wee woman I was attending to the following day.

"It worked. Nobody found Jonesy. Not ever."

"Do you remember who Hamish Jones was buried with?" Nadia asked quietly.

"Not off the top of my head, but it'll be in my ledger, in code. I just make a wee mark at the side of the page in my record book, by way of respect."

Colin snorted and looked at Nadia in disbelief.

"What about the recent farce?" she asked.

"Inglis never got over Hamish's decision to change. To be honest, wee Gerry never got over Rowan either. It's hard for the families, you know."

"Not as hard as for the individual just trying to live their best life. You should know about that, Les, you understand what it is to feel different to what is expected of you."

"I do. But I'm not a tranny."

"Les, we only get one shot at this. We all have to do our best," Nadia said. She was becoming exasperated. "Tell us more about Inglis."

"He was on his way to work one morning when he saw

someone who reminded him of Ursula, Hamish whatever. It happened sometimes; he couldn't help it."

"The person chose the name Hamish," Colin said.

"Yes, so Inglis followed this person into the wilderness bit at Morningside, I can't remember what it's called."

"The Hermitage," Colin said.

"Aye, like the pub. Inglis followed him, He knew it wasn't Hamish, he'd been dead long since. But he must have got angry. He said he strangled him with an old tie and then stabbed him again and again. The fellow hit his head on a rock as he fell down into the wee river, the Braid Burn I think it's called."

"It is. Do you know we have taken fingerprints and DNA from the body found in the grounds of the crematorium and they have been identified as William Evans?" Colin asked.

"For clarity, which of the Inglis brothers are you talking about? Can you guess who is implicated from the DNA we found under the victim's fingernails?" Nadia asked.

Les didn't respond. He didn't seem to hear her as he went on. "He called the business because he needed the van and a shopping trolley to help move the body, but, from the Liberton end. That was closest. He phoned to say he'd had to hide because there were two big blokes, a black one and a white one, checking out the body. Luckily, they ran off and the body could get shifted. But getting it over the fields in a shopping trolley must have been hard work because the body would be a dead weight trying to get it into the van. Of course, Inglis isn't the only one who has a problem with some kinds of people, like me. Wee Gerry never got over Rowan's change either."

All of a sudden, Colin realised why the photofit picture by the teenagers he and Nadia spoke to was so different from the one Rachael's witness had helped prepare: they had seen different people. One had seen an Inglis brother, the other had seen a Littlewood.

Colin and Nadia drew the interview to an end and charged Les with attempting to pervert the course of justice. They knew there would be a lot more to come, but that allowed them to hold Les for the time being.

Mel and Angus led wee Gerry along the corridor to the interview room.

"I really don't see why me and my dad are here again. I don't know any more to tell you. I mean, there's nothing more to tell," he whined.

"We'll be the judge of that, Gerry, go into the room second on the left," Mel said. "Your other left, that way." She pointed out the room in question.

She closed the door when they were all inside and indicated the seat on the far side of the table to Gerry.

"What do you bolt the chairs and table to the floor for? Do you think I'm going to nick them or something?" he asked.

Mel ignored him as she ran through the necessary preliminaries to the interview and checked that Gerry did not want a lawyer present.

"Why would I need a brief? I haven't done anything."

"Okay, Gerry, we'll find out if that's true. Starting with the most recent body, perhaps you can help us with that case."

"We did that last time," Gerry moaned.

"But things have moved on from then," Angus said. "We found the body in the remembrance garden of the crematorium and the group of men you were with told us a funeral was cancelled, but we now know that was not true. Why did you allow us to believe you had intended to go to a funeral that was cancelled?"

"I didn't."

"Don't be boring, Gerry, yes you did," Mel said. "Do you even know whose funeral you were meant to be going to? The celebrant told us that as soon as some genuine family members turned up, your group all took off in the van your business owns. Did you leave in that with the group?"

"Yes, but I was only there as a make number for old Inglis."

"Why would he want to make numbers? He said it was just a former colleague. It's none of his business how many people go to the funeral. He claimed he didn't even remember the person's name. Do you?"

"I don't think I ever knew. We all just decided not to stay, and we went to the pub. Going to the pub isn't a crime. You both saw us there, I remember."

"Yes, but a body was dumped between the time the family members arrived for the real funeral and a witness finding the body in the garden of remembrance. The only people there were you and your mates and the only place the body could have been hidden was in your van. We will get forensics back on that, you know."

"Come on, you're changing the subject, Gerry. Was the intention to sneak the second body into the coffin of the deceased who had no mourners present?" Mel asked.

"Couldn't say."

"Was the corpse from the van dumped because that plan became impossible when members of the family turned up?"

"I didn't do it."

"But you were there," Angus growled.

"You can't fit me up just for being somewhere."

"We won't need to fit anyone up, Gerry. We have fingerprints and DNA that will tell us who was involved. Why didn't you report what you knew to us?"

"It was only one of them, really. And nothing to do with me." Gerry paused. Then he looked at Mel. "You have no idea what I had to put up with. My dad dressing like a dame, my mum going off to a hareem and my nephew becoming my niece. The teasing, the ribbing, the inuendo."

"Did you ever think it's not always you that matters, Gerry. Everyone has their own life to live."

"No, it's not all about me, DC Grant, but I always seem to get the flack. I'd do my best and then, even in the big house, dad couldn't stay straight. Oh, Inglis enjoyed that. I had to do a deal with him. I was young, but he demanded a high price to leave dad alone."

"Tell us about it."

***

"So, what do we know about the sister?" Hunter asked Bear as they marched along the corridor to interview room two.

"Pam Littlewood. Looks remarkably like her brother. If it wasn't for the grey hair and the height difference, they could be twins."

"Poor woman. Married?"

"Never married. She is Les's older sister. Looked after the funeral business with Gerry when Les went down."

"He was in a long time. She's put a lot of graft into that business," Hunter said. He opened the interview room door and smiled at the woman sitting in front of him.

"Miss Littlewood, thank you so much for coming in today. We need your help with a series of cases that goes back about thirty years, so I hope you have a good memory."

"No worse than most I suppose. How can I help?"

"Would you like a cup of tea? I'm sure DC Zewedu wouldn't mind getting us one."

"Coffee please. The real thing not instant. Black as you big man, and no sugar."

"Thank you, DC Zewedu," Hunter smiled. He knew Bear had heard it all before and bore such comments quietly. He also knew his own coffee pot would be raided for three large mugs of coffee when Bear had the chance.

"We'll just wait until DC Zewedu gets back before we begin the interview, Miss Littlewood. But I must say, you have an interesting family. You all keep busy, don't you? You, Les and wee Gerry with the funeral home and Rowan must work extremely hard with the horses."

"She wants to be a jockey, but it's not so easy for a girl. Not so many of them, you know."

"I don't know much about horse racing, but my guess is that would be true. Although I don't know why. You'd think a woman should be every bit as good as a man."

"Of course, Rowan is different," she said quietly.

They sat in silence for a few minutes until Bear kicked the door and Hunter rose to let him in.

"Well, done, you found the good coffee," Hunter grinned at him.

"It wasn't too difficult, boss, if you know where to look." Bear winked at Hunter and put the three mugs on the table.

"Maybe this will make this room smell better," the woman said.

"I think that would take a great deal more than coffee," Hunter replied.

He took a sip of the warm, dark liquid from his mug and then set up the interview formally. He introduced each person there for the benefit of the tape and explained that the interview would be recorded by the cameras as well as in audio. He looked at Miss Littlewood and saw her nod. He thought she looked sad. He noticed how much like her brother she looked.

"Miss Littlewood, can you tell us a bit about how you came to take over running Littlewoods Undertakers?" he asked.

"Yes, you lot fitted up poor Les and stuck him inside for God knows how long and I had to look after the kids and pay for their food and clothes somehow because his bloody wife had gone off."

"The kids would be wee Gerry and his sister?"

"Kate, yes, Gerry and Kate."

"Were they able to help you at all?"

"After a few years, they grew up and could help. But then Kate married a borders man and went to live in Peebles. Then it was just me and the wee man. But he's got broad shoulders that lad."

"Who was in charge of putting the bodies in the caskets?"

"Either of us would do that."

"Have you ever been aware of two bodies being buried in the one casket, Miss Littlewood?"

Hunter noticed the woman's eyes move up and to the right. He was aware of some psychological studies that talked about the direction of eyes during lies. These revealed that typically, when people look up and to the right, they are lying or tapping into their imagination. When they look up and to the left, they are remembering or recalling something, tapping into the memory part of the brain. He listened to her answer with this in mind.

"My goodness me, no. That would never happen."

"Think a little harder, Miss Littlewood. Would you be surprised if I told you that we know of at least three cases where your business did just that. And I believe the plans for this to happen a fourth time were hastily abandoned at the last minute."

"I am sorry, DI Wilson, you are mistaken. Now, if that is all, I will take my leave."

"That is not all, Miss Littlewood. You were running the business when three of these instances occurred. Let me refresh your memory."

Hunter told the woman about the first occasion that two bodies had been buried together, so many years ago when he himself was just a boy. "Your brother has told my colleagues all about this, Miss Littlewood."

"I had nothing to do with the business then. I was keeping house and looking after the children for my brother. Doing what his wife should have been doing, but she went off."

"I heard. I accept that you probably had nothing to do with that incident. But your brother established a way to make bodies disappear after his, and your, contacts had murdered them." Hunter glowered at her.

"This is nonsense."

"Miss Littlewood, do you mix with many people who have a fear or hatred of the members of the LGBTQ community?" Jane asked.

"It's against the law to discriminate now, isn't it?"

"That's not what I asked. Do you know many people who take a stance against people in that minority group of society?"

"One or two, maybe, but not Les. He's as daft as a brush, himself."

"What about Kate or Gerry?" Jane asked.

"Not Kate, she helps Rowan all she can, more than is good for her if you ask me."

"Really? I thought most parents do all they can for their children. And what about wee Gerry?" Hunter asked.

"Ah, well he's had his own problems. He was bullied because of his mum and his dad. Rowan almost broke him.

But he would never hurt her. I know he would never hurt her on purpose."

***

"I've never done an interview with you, boss. Do you want me just to sit quietly and let you ask all the questions?"

"No Angus, the lassie knows you. You ask the questions. I want to know how the different members of her family reacted to her decision to transition MTF."

"Aye, so when she decided to take the transfeminine hormone therapy and then the surgery, how did the family react?"

"That is exactly right, Angus. It's the hormone therapy and sex reassignment surgery that change the secondary sexual characteristics of transgender people from masculine to feminine."

"Should I ask about the big scar across her face?"

"You never said anything about that."

"Well, girls don't like you saying anything about marks or scars, do they? It's embarrassing for them."

"Then I'll ask about the scar because I've never met her before," Hunter said.

"Hello, again Miss Sprigg," Angus said as he and Hunter walked into the interview room. "This is my boss, DI Wilson."

Hunter shook hands with the girl and sat opposite her at the table.

"It's good of you to come in to talk to us today," Angus said. "We wondered if you might be able to help us with a problem case we are investigating."

Hunter sat and listened as Angus asked Rowan about the early life she led in Peebles, her love of horses and her decision to live her best life.

"How did your family take that decision?" he asked. "It's a huge change for them to take on board."

"My mum and dad took a while to get their heads around it, but my sister was cool. She's younger than me, but never bothered. Said it was my life."

"That's a good reaction. What about the extended family?"

"My grandmother was fine about it. She lives in the USA on a commune. So was Grandpa. But he's got his own way of enjoying life anyway."

"What about his sister?"

"The lovely Pamela? She has issues with me, and she believes that the reason she never married was because she had to look after Grandpa's family and business. She hates him for that. Never takes time to think that the reason she didn't get married is because she's a cantankerous old cow."

"No love lost there, then," Hunter said.

"None at all. She is always really horrible to me and my friends."

"Do you mind me asking how you got the scar on your cheek?" Hunter asked.

Rowan paused. She flicked her hair so that it covered the mark. "That was Gerry. Don't be fooled when they call him wee Gerry, it makes him sound all sweet and nice and cuddly, but he's a bastard."

"Gerry did that?" Hunter said. "It must have been a nasty wound when it happened."

"It was. The surgeon was lovely and sewed me up with lots of little tiny stitches to make the scar as light as possible, but it still shows. It's not so bad when I wear makeup, but I don't wear any at work. There's no point."

"I can imagine that would be true. What happened that Gerry did that?"

"I was trying to get money together for my operation. I didn't want to wait for the NHS, so I was saving up to go private. Gerry was down seeing my parents and they mentioned this and asked if the family business could contribute. When Gerry heard how much it was going to cost, he shouted at me. 'How many thousands does it take to make a fucking lesbian? No bloody way!' He smashed his beer bottle and whacked me across the face. My parents have hardly spoken to him since, but it has been a guilty family secret. Mum asked me not to report it to the police, because he would end up in jail and lose his job and everything, but I wish I had.

It still gives me nightmares."

"Bloody hell, that's shocking." Angus said angrily. "Who is he to judge anybody else?"

"I've never forgotten what he said. It was so hurtful. I just wanted to be me."

"Of course, Rowan. I know from personal experience that keeping a secret for so many years can be bad for the soul," Hunter said.

"When Grandpa heard about it from my mum, he instructed Pam and Gerry to give me the full amount of money that I needed from the business. He was in jail, of course, but he still pulled the strings."

"Did he? That's interesting," Hunter said.

"Pam and Gerry hate me and are not above taking that hatred out on other members of the LGBTQ community."

"Very interesting indeed."

Chapter Sixty-Four

Tim walked into Thomson's Top Cars with Rachael. He saw Jamie, Frankie and Donna all standing at the reception desk chatting.

"Hello, Blondie," Jamie called over. "To what do I owe this pleasure? The last visit we had from you lot Mel took away my best customer and half my staff."

"What a lot of nonsense, Jamie. I'm your best customer and wee Gerry would never be half your staff even if there were only the two of you."

"I saw your girlfriend at the beautician's the other day. I was there with Jamie's lassie, Linda. Your girl's a doctor?"

"Sort of, a doctor of languages, not medicine."

"Well anyway, she said if we knew anything about that murder, we should tell you."

"That's really why DC Anderson and I are here. Could you have a look at these photos and see if you recognise the man you saw in the store?"

"I wasn't there, just these two," Donna looked disappointed as she indicated Jamie and Frankie.

"Come on then, Blondie, show us the pin-ups. Frankie and me can help no problem."

"I need to do it with you one at a time. Can we go into the office, Jamie? Then when you're finished, Frankie can take a look."

Jamie led the way. He sat with Tim and looked at the book. Tim noticed that he looked serious and determined, two words Tim did not normally associate with him.

He paused over one picture. Then flicked back a couple of pages.

"Blondie, you've cocked up this time. You've got the same

one twice. Anyway, he's your man."

"Could you look really carefully, please Jamie? Is it possible you could choose between those two pictures?"

"What? But it's the same man. Oh, wait a minute, it's not. This one's even thinner faced than that one."

"Frankie thought he'd seen the man in the store at the jail. Is that possible?" Jamie grinned at Tim.

"Stop trying to trip me up, Jamie. Can you tell which man you saw in the supermarket?"

"I think it was this one. He pointed to the man with the thinner face, but I'll be honest, I can't be sure. Frankie is more observant than me."

"Thanks for that, anyway, Jamie. You have helped. Could you ask Frankie to join me now?"

Tim watched Jamie slouch away from the office and indicate to Frankie that it was his turn now. Frankie walked towards him slowly and looked as if he were trying to second guess the questions and the answers he should give.

"Hello, Frankie," Tim said.

"Hello, DC Myerscough. You know, Jamie and I don't want to be seen being too helpful to the boys in blue, it could ruin our reputation!"

"Ha, ha, very funny, Frankie. I just need you to take a look through this book of photos and tell me if you recognise the man you saw in the supermarket."

"Let's have a shifty then." Frankie frowned as he poured over the photos. He shook his head at the end of each page to indicate the person he had seen was not there. Then he paused. "Him," he said. "It was him."

"Are you sure? Could you look at the rest of the book, just in case you're mistaken."

"I'll look, but he's your guy. Wait a minute, have you put in the same fellow twice? No, this one has a fatter face. Let me think." Frankie swapped between the two photos, back and forwards, back and forwards. "It's this one. Definitely. This was the guy we saw following the lad in the supermarket."

"You're sure?"

"Yes. If Jamie said the other one, he's wrong." Frankie

smiled at Tim. "He never admits to being wrong, but that doesn't mean it doesn't happen."

***

Tim knocked on Hunter's door. He entered to find Mackay sitting opposite Hunter drinking a large mug of the fine coffee only available in this room.

"DC Myerscough," Mackay said. "I'm just leaving."

"No, sir, I think both you and the boss need to hear this."

"Sit down, Tim. Would you like a coffee?" Hunter asked.

"No thanks, boss. I'm wound up enough already." Tim sat down and explained to Hunter and Mackay the identifications that had been made by Jamie and Frankie. "My guess is that these and the admissions you already have will be confirmed by the forensics Nadia is waiting on."

"I'm not keen on guessing. I prefer good, hard evidence. I need to interview Bernard and Arthur. Want to join me?"

"I wouldn't miss it, boss."

***

The two men walked in step down the corridor to interview room one. It was slightly bigger than the others and therefore usually did not smell quite as bad. However, the tables and chairs were still metal and bolted to the floor. There was a recorder on the table that was firmly bolted on and high up on the wall was a camera to record the interview. The barred window was too high up to see out to the sky. In fact, it was so thick with grime and cobwebs it was difficult to see out at all. There was no mistaking this for anything but a police interview room.

Bernard Inglis was sitting facing the door looking singularly unimpressed with his surroundings.

"Mr Inglis, thank you for coming back so promptly," Hunter said.

"Can we make this quick? I am a busy man, you know."

"Of course, we will get down to business. Why do you have

244

such strong negative feelings towards the LGBTQ community?"

"I don't. I don't have any warm feelings towards my ex-wife, but I can take or leave the rest."

"That's not true, is it?" Tim asked. "You are known as a bully in HMP Edinburgh. You and your cronies would make life difficult for anybody who was different: my father and Les Littlewood have both mentioned it."

"Your dad isn't one of them."

"No, but he is different to the normal prisoner and you made life very difficult for him at the beginning of his sentence."

"Until he called on his big gun friends, perhaps I did."

"I'll take that as an admission. Now why did you stop bullying Les?" Hunter asked.

"That's a bit like asking when I stopped beating my wife, isn't it?"

"Did you kill your wife?"

"No! Fucking hell, I haven't seen Ursula, or whatever her name is now, I haven't seen her for over thirty years."

"That would be about right. Can you tell me who is in this drawing?" Hunter handed over a copy of the photofit picture he and Fraser had prepared with the police artist so many years ago.

"I don't know. It could be Ursula after her operations, I only saw her once after that. She came to my place to sign some papers. She said it would be the last time she ever had to sign that name."

"When would that have been?"

"As I say, about thirty years ago. I was living in Leith. Grim little place, I had rented because she fleeced me good and proper."

"How did she get to your place?" Tim asked.

"I don't remember, I doubt I ever asked. I know she didn't have a car then because she'd spent all my money on becoming a man, allegedly. She probably walked along the pathway at the Water of Leith. Who cares?"

"I do," Tim and Hunter said at the same time.

"When she left your home, did she go back the same way?" Hunter asked.

"I don't know. I didn't follow her. I phoned Arthur and he said he'd come over for a drink."

"Along the same pathway?"

"Fucksake, I don't know. I had other things on my mind. I doubt I asked, but be fair, this was thirty years ago. I honestly don't remember, exactly," Bernard said.

"Fair comment, but now tell us what really happened at the funeral you said was cancelled recently. Because it wasn't, was it?" Hunter asked.

"I was told it was."

"Who told you that?"

"My brother, I was standing in for him, a former colleague had popped his clogs, and he felt he should attend, so I went instead, just to represent the family. A few other lads came along to make numbers because he didn't think any family would be there."

"But with a former copper, there were sure to be old colleagues there," Hunter said.

"I thought you said before that it was a former colleague of yours, not your brother's," Tim said.

"Did I? Sorry about any confusion. Anyway, family did turn up, and we just buggered off."

"And dumped the body of poor William Evans in the garden of remembrance. That's where he was found. A witness saw a group of you getting rid of something heavy from the van before it drove off."

"No, no. I don't know anything about that."

"How strange," Hunter said. "The celebrant heard arguing and noise coming from outside the service and then the man came across the corpse in the remembrance garden when he was paying his respects to his aunt. The only people around at that time were you and your group of associates, but you know nothing about it?"

"You were giving it large and talking about the cancelled funeral and making disrespectful comments about the LGBTQ and minority communities in the pub." Tim frowned and looked at Bernard. "What you're claiming now, doesn't tie up at all."

"Perhaps you know about murder victims being buried in the same coffin as other bodies and can tell us about that?" Hunter asked.

"Two in a coffin? Does that happen?"

"The first person we know about that it happened to was your late wife, then Hamish Jones, the night you murdered him. You phoned Les Littlewood to call in a favour and he suggested the cheapest way to make the body disappear would be to place the body along with another person he was burying the following day."

"No! This doesn't make any sense. I never clapped eyes on Les until he was convicted and that was several years after you say Ursula died. I knew who he was, he had been collared a few times for drunk and disorderly and breach of the peace. Arthur told me that, we used to laugh about him, but I didn't know him. I did give Les a hard time when he finally ended up inside, mind you he asked for it, all that flouncing about. It meant I could get a favour off wee Gerry for Arthur to be able to stop in at the family funeral parlour if he needed something for a case."

"What could he possibly need?" Hunter asked.

"I don't know, extra photos of victims, maybe. But I admit, I did help dump the body at that funeral, but I wasn't involved in any murder. That's not my style at all. The smell on the van was barfing. It's why I got so drunk in the pub, to get rid of the thought and the pong. It was horrible. The skin felt all funny too and there were bugs in the eyes and stuff. I just drank and said anything to get it out of my head."

"But you say it was Arthur who knew Les before you and Arthur who needed the favour from wee Gerry?"

"Yes, but he never did anything wrong. He's a well-respected copper, Arthur is."

"I'll decide that, not you. Tim, book him. Perverting the course of justice."

"You can't do that; I'll lose my job."

"Not my problem," Hunter said.

"DCI Inglis, thank you for staying to speak to us," Hunter said.

He and Mackay were sitting in Mackay's room. Hunter had wanted to interview Arthur Inglis in a police interview room, like any other suspect, but Mackay sounded more cautious. He preferred a softer approach but agreed the interview should be recorded on Hunter's computer.

"Happy to help, DI Wilson. I understand you are close to resolving the murders that took place so many years apart."

"Yes, indeed, DCI Inglis. Just for the record, this interview will take place formally and be recorded."

"Are you mad, man? Do you want me to ruin your career? I'll destroy you."

"I don't think so," Mackay said quietly. "Please answer all our questions honestly. It will be much faster that way."

"Fast does not equate with just," Inglis said.

"Not always, that's true."

Hunter asked Inglis about his sister-in-law. He saw the man's face blanch. He asked about the favour he asked of Les Littlewood. The man hanged his head. He showed Arthur Inglis the drawing of his sister-in-law made to show her as she was the night she died. He began to weep.

"Bernard phoned me after she left his house. He was in bits. She had taken everything. I said I'd go and have a drink with him. I guessed she would take the quickest way home, so I walked along by the Water of Leith, I wanted to try to talk some sense into her. There she was, dressed like a fine little man, right down to the brightly coloured tie. I grabbed it. She stumbled and fell. I just saw red, so I struck her. I always carried a knife, self-defence, I still do but that night I knew I'd hit an artery. The way the blood came out. Then two daft laddies came along. She shouldn't have been found that fast."

"I was one of the daft laddies."

"I know, but it wasn't that difficult to put the investigation off course because I was part of the team working on it. Ursula lay hidden for all these years, just as she deserved. It was a nightmare when I heard you'd joined the force. I had nightmares that, one day, you would come back to haunt me. Looks like I was right."

"I've had nightmares about that night all my life. But you were on the scene. I remember you. You weren't covered in blood; how did you manage that?"

"Took my coat off and put my gloves on. In the dark, nobody noticed."

"Did you ever get to Bernard for that drink?" Tim asked.

"Yes, but a bit later than anticipated," Arthur said.

"You had Ursula, I mean Hamish buried along with someone else, so his body disappeared."

"Yes. I'd done lots of favours for Les and let him off with minor offences many times and kept him out of the jail. He owed me a big one."

"And after he was locked up, you arranged that Bernard got your favours from his son."

"It was the easiest way."

"Couldn't you just leave alone all the people living their own lives?" Tim asked angrily.

"Every time I saw a tranny or a gay, I just thought of Ursula and the hurt she caused Bernard. I couldn't help it."

"It's fucking murder. How many innocent people have you killed?" Tim shouted.

"None. They are not innocent. Each of them hurt someone."

"Not as much as you did. You killed people because they didn't accord with your way of life. We all hurt someone at times, we don't get murdered for it," Hunter said quietly.

Chapter Sixty-Five

David Murray sent the post-mortem reports to Hunter as his last job before the Christmas break. He was looking forward to spending the holiday period with his wife and five children. He did not yet know that a sixth little one was on its way.

He phoned Hunter. "Those results should be in your in box now, Hunter. Forensics tell me that the DNA of the skin under the fingernails is as you expected. It looks like there will be a vacancy in MIT, doesn't it?"

"I want to get this nailed before I think about that," Hunter said.

"Good luck Hunter. Call me or Aiden at home if you need anything."

"Merry Christmas, David and thank you."

***

Mackay called the meeting to order. He thanked the team for all their work on the multiple murder case and for clearing it up in record time. He brought out a case of beer from behind the table he was sitting on and passed the bottles around the team.

"Have we got a case that will hold together, Hunter?" he asked.

"Shouldn't you have asked him that before you handed round the beer, sir?" Bear joked.

"Probably, Bear, but yes, I think we do, sir," Hunter said.

"For my peace of mind, can we confirm the evidence we have?"

"The forensics from the van confirm William Evans had been in there," Hunter said.

"Sir, Les Littlewood has admitted to his part in the historic crime and most recent one, and it was his thumb print we found on the knife in the historic case," Nadia said.

"He killed Hamish Jones?" Mackay asked.

"No sir. At that time DCI Inglis had prevented him from being arrested therefore Les's fingerprints were not on file. He threw the knife away when he helped DCI Inglis move Hamish's body. That's how his prints got there."

"Has nobody checked them in thirty years?"

"Not that I could tell, sir."

"Goodness. We need to review our systems. What about wee Gerry?" Mackay looked at Mel.

"He became involved with DCI Inglis and his brother after trying to protect his father," she began. "We know he developed a hatred of those in the LGBTQ through their influence and didn't cope well with the transformation Rowan went through. He seemed to resent the family money that his father gave to Rowan to allow the therapy and surgery go through privately, but he hasn't admitted to much yet, apart from being at the 'cancelled' funeral and helping dump that body."

"Well, that's a start. We have too many other missing people to trace. Those who were reported missing and never found worry me. I am sure when we go through Littlewood's records we will find more double burials and I'm sure we'll prove he was involved while his father was in prison," Mackay said.

"I have traced the dates of the industrial actions against Littlewoods for the overly heavy coffins," Hunter said. "Those will give us approximate dates for the burials that we can cross reference in the business accounts."

"That sounds like a job for you and me, Nadia," Colin said.

"We also have wee Gerry for the attack on Rowan, of course," Angus said. "I have no doubt she will make an excellent witness because she is so credible."

"What about the sister? She seems to be a strange fish," Mackay said.

"She is." Hunter nodded. "She took over running the

funeral parlour after Les went down for murder. He has always denied that, which is why he didn't get parole, of course."

"It looks like we might have the evidence to prove he was telling the truth, about the murder, at least," Tim said.

"Yes, I think we might, Tim. The sister got roped into Bernard and Arthur's circle by the agreement wee Gerry made to keep his dad out of trouble in jail, but she hasn't admitted to anything criminal, yet," Hunter said. "I suggest we charge her with perverting the course of justice now and find the full extent of her involvement as we investigate the records."

"I agree, DI Wilson. That woman is in these murders and double burials up to her neck, but we just haven't proved it, yet," Mackay said. "I suspect the Inglis brothers will throw her under the bus as charges against them mount. All bullies are cowards, and those men are the most despicable bullies I have ever come across."

"And Rowan?" Angus asked. "The lassie hasn't done anything wrong."

"No, but she will be an important witness," Hunter said.

"Is it against the rules for one of us to date a witness, boss?"

"No, but it's not a good idea at this stage in a case. Are you keen, Angus?" Hunter watched the young policeman blush to the roots of his red hair. "If there's nothing else to add right now, shall we continue our celebrations in the pub? First pints are on me."

A loud cheer went up in the briefing room and the members of the team scrabbled to gather their coats. A drink at Hunter's expense was not to be sneezed at.

"Will you be joining us, sir?"

"No, Hunter, finding a crooked cop is not my idea of a moment to celebrate. Arthur has taken and ruined so many lives, for what? Because they were trying to be themselves."

"At least we will stop him from ruining any more lives, sir. That must be something to celebrate."

"Of course, it is."

"And there will be a DCI vacancy at MIT. Will you apply for that?"

"I'll consider it, only if I can be sure my post here will be in good hands."

"Well, we have the holiday season to think that over, sir."

"Take a few quid and get the next round on me, Hunter. I'm off home." Mackay smiled and pushed a wad of notes into Hunter's hand.

"That will buy a great deal more than one round, sir. Thank you. Merry Christmas."

Epilogue

Hunter's arrival in the pub was greeted by a loud cheer.

"We thought you were going to stand us up, boss," Bear said.

"When have I ever failed to stand my round, Bear? And I've brought the kitty courtesy of DCI Mackay. Tim, you get the order in, will you?" Hunter sat down and watched Tim and Bear head off towards the bar.

His phone vibrated in his pocket. He took it out to turn it off, but saw it was a call from Meera.

"Hello, pet, how are you coping? How is the family?"

"Sorry, Meera, I can't hear you. It's so noisy in here. Let me go outside."

Hunter stood up and walked towards the door. Then he heard her.

"Hunter, I have to go, they're calling my flight, I'll text you."

"Flight? What flight?"

"Dad needs to go to India to be with the family. Mum is not well enough to go, so I will accompany him. I'm sorry, Hunter. Merry Christmas, your present is in my underwear drawer."

"Meera! Meera when are you leaving? When will you be back? Meera!"

Hunter realised he was shouting into thin air. Meera's phone was off and Tim was standing behind him.

"Boss, what's wrong?"

"I have been learning Hindi for six months to ask Meera's father for her hand in marriage for no good reason, young Myerscough."

"It sounds good to me, boss. You'll make a great couple."

"Except for the fact that she and her father are leaving for

India as we speak to mourn her grandparent's death."

"Boss, is that why you've been spending time with that other beautiful woman?"

"Yes. Why?"

"With all the creeping around you've been doing, Bear was sure you were cheating on Meera. He'll be greatly relieved."

"Aye tell him I don't have a death wish," Hunter said. "What the hell, I'll tell him myself. Let's go back inside, it's Baltic out here."

"You are welcome to spend Christmas with us, boss. You can help me referee my girlfriend and my father," Tim said.

"You know, Tim, that is very kind, but I think I might see if I can get a flight to Patna and support Meera and her family at this difficult time. It might also give me a chance to practise my Hindi."

Tim led the way back into the pub and carried on talking as if their conversation had always been on the topic of Jamie and Frankie.

"Frankie is going to propose to his young lady on Christmas day, boss. He showed me the ring. It's very pretty. She's a nice girl, young Donna."

"And Jamie has a girlfriend, thank fuck!" Mel said. "It doesn't stop his cheek, but at least it diverts his attention from me."

"She's joining them for Christmas dinner, so it must be serious," Tim said.

"Excellent news all round. I plan to take a break over the holidays and will leave you in the tender care of DCI Mackay. Merry Christmas!" Hunter lifted his glass to toast the team.

Hunter's Rules follows soon

Fantastic Books
Great Authors

darkstroke is
an imprint of
Crooked Cat Books

- Gripping Thrillers
- Cosy Mysteries
- Romantic Chick-Lit
- Fascinating Historicals
- Exciting Fantasy
- Young Adult and Children's Adventures
- Non-Fiction

Discover us online
www.darkstroke.com

Find us on instagram:
www.instagram.com/darkstrokebooks

Printed in Great Britain
by Amazon

68012634R00156